SCUB.

SCUBA DANCING

NICOLA SLADE

ISIS

LARGE PRINT

Oxford

First published in Great Britain 2005
by
Transita

Published in Large Print 2006 by ISIS Publishing Ltd.,
7 Centremead, Osney Mead, Oxford OX2 0ES
by arrangement with
Transita

British Library Cataloguing in Publication Data
Slade, Nicola
   Scuba dancing. – Large print ed.
   1. Village communities – England – Hampshire –
   Fiction
   2. Large type books
   I. Title
   823.9'2 [F]

ISBN 0–7531–7680–7 (hb)
ISBN 978–0–7531–7681–8 (pb)

Printed and bound in Great Britain by
T. J. International Ltd., Padstow, Cornwall

CHAPTER
ONE

It was late summer when the angel first manifested himself to Ursula Buchanan in the village shop, beside the notice board and just along the aisle from the bacon slicing machine.

The only reason Ursula paused in that particular spot was so that she could hitch up her shopping bag into a more comfortable position; looking at the poster was incidental.

A club? The advert was vague and all-embracing, suggesting as it did a mix of socialising — all ages welcome — mutual sharing of skills, for example art lessons in exchange, say, for advice on car maintenance; a little cooking to be paid for by a spot of gardening; any other ideas welcome, so how about it?

I used to be rather good at drawing, Ursula thought, tilting her chin proudly at the memory of those school reports with the annual comment: "In spite of her difficulties Ursula tries hard. She is a quiet, unassuming girl whose art work shows promise."

I wouldn't mind some lessons but I don't think I could teach car maintenance, she mused. Wouldn't you need to be able to drive? She read on. Oh, I see, it's the two of them suggesting it. Julia Fitzgerald at Forge

Cottage. Isn't she the lovely, big Irish lady with a younger sister who works abroad? And the other one, Rosemary Clavering? Of course, the teacher, pleasant woman, dotty mother?

A hesitant smile transformed, for a moment, Ursula's pudgy, currant-bun face with its dusting of fluff, into a living, breathing individuality. Dotty? Who am I calling dotty, she grimaced. I who have difficulty carrying out Henrietta's simplest command, who have barely any idea what time of day it is? Or even what day it is, sometimes.

It was at that moment that the angel chose to make his first appearance to Ursula. In a radiant shimmer of light he materialised beside her, just downwind of a stack of home-cured Wiltshire streaky bacon.

"Go on," he urged, pointing a glowing golden finger at the notice. "*Join the group, Ursula, it'll change your life.*"

And then he was gone, leaving the aisle empty and Ursula staring and startled. But not afraid, she realised. Why shouldn't she see an angel after all? For he had to be an angel, no question. She had read somewhere or seen on television maybe, that angels were big business in America; along with little grey men with oval heads and big eyes boring into you and impregnating you, angels were prone to drop in now and then on the most unlikely people. And not just in present day America either, what about Joan of Arc and her voices?

I wonder where he went? She peeked shyly round the stack of tinned apricots, stood on tiptoe to look over the bread stand and ducked back down towards the post office counter. No, nothing; no sighting of anyone seven feet tall and glowing with a heavenly radiance, no voice like a golden trumpet, no touch of a gentle feather on the cheek. I hope he'll come back, she thought wistfully, nodding goodbye to the woman at the check-out, oblivious of eyebrows raised in commiseration with poor, daft, old Miss Buchanan.

I don't really think I'd like to be impregnated, pondered Ursula as she headed home to where Henrietta would be waiting impatiently for the chocolate digestives to go with her coffee. Or is that only aliens? Still, you don't have to be a saintly teenage virgin to have a heavenly visitation these days, you might just as easily be a seventy-four-year-old one.

"Julia, come and look! Are you there? There's a naked woman in the garden. Ju?"

Finn looked at her watch. Seven o'clock in the morning? Her sister was usually awake and reading, though not an early riser as such. She tapped quietly on Julia's door. "Ju? Are you all right?"

Odd, Julia's bed had been slept in but there was no sign of her, upstairs or downstairs. Surely she hadn't gone out already? It would be very unlike her if she had.

Finn drew back the curtains, yawning. What am I doing awake at this hour she groaned, looking blearily out at the back garden, mysterious and shadowed but for a shaft of light where the early sun broke through. At least she had slept for an hour or two last night, though

3

her eyes were still tired from where she had lain awake in the small hours going over and over her performance at the office. How did I have the nerve, she marvelled. Luc was right, I acted like a complete, hard-boiled bitch, no wonder he was amazed. I was amazed myself! But it worked, didn't it? The thought insinuated itself into her mind, coming from nowhere as she recalled yesterday morning's nasty little scene.

"You're asking me to make you redundant?" Her boss gave Finn a puzzled stare. "But why?"

"*My* mobile, *her* text message," Finn replied through gritted teeth. "Ring any bells? It obviously slipped your mind that I share a flat *and* an office with *her*!"

"Ah . . ." Luc pursed his lips and avoided her accusing stare, fiddling with some paperclips for a moment or so. "Yes, hmm. Well, I'm sorry about that, Finn, but that still doesn't explain this redundancy thing. And what's this?" His eyes flicked down the page and he looked up at her in astonishment. "You want a year's salary as a package? But that's preposterous, you've only been with this department for just over two years!"

He was quite right, Finn agreed now as she stared unseeing at her sister's garden. It *was* preposterous. But, as she'd pointed out to him, somehow managing to retain her cool and not collapse into the sodden misery that had kept her awake all the previous night, *he* had been in his post for nearly twenty years, and what with the strict "no-fraternising" rules his anticipated promotion might be in jeopardy.

4

"But that's *blackmail!*" His eyes were round with shock. As he took in her set, white face he shifted his stance. "Oh, come on, Finn. We had a good time, didn't we? I'm sorry it had to end like this, but hey! That's how it goes."

"I *know* it's blackmail," she hissed angrily, forgetting her resolution. "Do you think I *like* doing this? I'm going to have to leave my job and the flat, and I'll have to pay *her* my share of the rent till next month. No way am I going to be in her debt. I'll go back to England and crash at my sister's — if she'll have me — till I get a job and somewhere to live, and I won't get the same kind of money outside Brussels." Her voice cracked slightly. "How could you? I never made any fuss about your wife. I knew being your bit on the side wouldn't lead to anything, but I never expected you to have another bit on the side of *me!*"

"Oh, all right." He took another look at her carefully prepared paperwork and gave a martyred sigh. "I'll go along with you to the tune of six months' salary, even though it'll have to come out of my own bonus."

"My heart bleeds." Finn marched off to wipe her eyes and redo the page which he signed with a sulky ill grace. That was when he'd said it.

"I had no idea you could be such a tough bitch."

"No," she had replied with a tired travesty of a smile. "Neither had I. But I'm tired of fitting in with other people's idea of me — Finn won't mind, Finn's easy-going, Finn won't make a fuss — I'm forty-five, for God's sake. It's about time I took control of my own life."

A movement at the bottom of her sister's garden caught her attention. Fairies? Surely not. Julia would have mentioned them, wouldn't she, if not six months ago when she moved to her new house, then at least last night when Finn had tumbled exhausted out of the taxi from the station.

The bizarre figure moved towards the dazzle of sunlight and started dancing on the lawn.

Finn stared. Dipping a toe into the garden pond the woman glanced up, spotted Finn and waved.

"Come on down," she called. "The water's lovely."

Pulling on some clothes Finn ran downstairs twisting an elastic band round her long, thick blonde hair. She put the kettle on and unlocked the back door, grabbing an old raincoat from the hook as she did so. Already it was very warm this morning but still no time to be skinny dipping in the garden pond, at any age.

"Good morning," the naked woman greeted her with great social aplomb, waving Finn to a seat beside her on the garden bench and turning away to admire the dappled sunlight on the pond.

"Good morning," Finn began politely. "Would you like to come indoors and have a cup of tea?"

The naked woman swung round and broke into a delighted smile.

"How truly kind," she exclaimed, sounding exactly like the Queen on a walkabout. "I was just thinking there was something I'd forgotten."

Finn blinked at this statement of the obvious but they weren't thinking along the same lines.

The old lady beamed and continued. "Yes, I quite forgot to make myself a cup of tea this morning before I went out for my morning stroll."

"Oh." Finn was at a loss for words, then she pulled herself together. "Would you like to borrow this coat just for now?" she suggested.

"How very generous," her mystery visitor nodded. "So thoughtful. I seem to have mislaid my own clothes." She cast a casual eye down at her nakedness and grinned cheerfully as she shrugged into the old raincoat. "What a hoot!"

She frowned for a moment then extended her hand graciously. "Where are my manners? How do you do, my dear, I'm Margot Delaney, but do call me Margot. And you are . . . ?"

Feeling surreal Finn shook the proffered hand. "Finn Fitzgerald, how do you do?"

Social niceties attended to Margot Delaney suddenly nodded off and Finn sat wondering what to do next. She stared at her companion; she was really old, very old, Finn discovered. The extravagantly curly orange hair had the matte deadness of an amateur dyeing session, an inch of scanty white at the parting, pink skin showing through. The body, though slim verging on emaciated, had the indefinable softness of old age, the skin on the arms sagging and the breasts wrinkled flaps. Her face was a mass of fine wrinkles though her cheerful insouciance gave her a kind of liveliness now as she jerked awake and looked round, smiling, through the bright green Dame Edna glasses perched on her elegant bony nose.

7

"I put the kettle on when I came down," ventured Finn, wondering what to do. "Shall we have that cup of tea now?"

"That would be delightful," announced the old woman rising and gathering her raincoat round her. "Someone offered me some tea not long ago, did I drink it? I don't think I've had a drink this morning, Rosemary must have forgotten."

"Rosemary?" Finn ushered her towards the kitchen, installed her in a chair and made the tea.

"My daughter, Rosemary," was the answer. "She's a good enough girl but she can be rather forgetful. Of course, she never married."

Finn blinked at the non sequitur. She poured the tea, obediently adding milk and two sugars as her guest demanded.

"Should I ring Rosemary and tell her where you are?" she suggested, wondering if Rosemary would really want to know. Finn had a sudden glimmer of how she would feel herself if Julia were gallivanting about the place stark naked. I think I'd leave town, she told herself, grinning at the thought of her generously voluptuous sister in such a scenario. She felt a pang of sympathy for poor, forgetful, unmarried Rosemary. Although her naked visitor was charming at the moment an underlying granite toughness was apparent.

To her surprise the old woman, "call me Margot, dear," she said again, obviously forgetting her earlier introduction, meekly agreed and dictated the number with no argument.

The voice at the other end of the line was middle-aged, pleasant and tired.

"Oh Lord, how on earth did she get out? I thought I'd locked up last night and I certainly haven't opened up yet this morning. How wretched for you. Oh well, thank you for letting me know and thank you for looking after her. I'll be there in five minutes, just let me get dressed." She hesitated a moment before adding, "Um . . . look this may sound strange, but you don't . . . you don't have any men in the house do you?"

Bemused, Finn said no, she was alone.

"Oh that's all right then," the voice sounded heartfelt with relief. "I'll explain when I get there, it's just that she can't be trusted with men any more. See you in a minute."

Less than ten minutes later Finn thankfully opened the door. Rosemary Clavering was a little below medium height, attractive, middle-to-late fiftyish, gunmetal grey hair in a tousled but stylish bob. Her smile was friendly, her grey eyes tired. She glanced shrewdly at the younger woman who greeted her with relief.

"Being difficult is she? I'm so sorry she's caused you such a lot of trouble." She hefted a bag in her hand. "I've brought some clothes for her so as soon as she's decent I'll take her off your hands. I've brought the car though it's only across the green; Margot's legs give way as she's liable to run out of steam without warning."

Finn smiled and waved her into the sitting room where Margot sat in state mumbling incoherent obscenities. In the last ten minutes her unwanted guest had shed the initial charm and become petulant and imperious by turns, demanding vodka or champagne and insisting that she must have a full English breakfast at once.

"Do you like men, my dear?" she'd enquired; a cheerful moment shining through.

"Not a lot," Finn scowled. "At least, I'm off them just now."

"I used not to like men much," Margot was still aboard the same train of thought. "But something must have happened because, do you know, my dear? I really rather like them at the moment!"

Dr Jekyll was soon obscured again by Mrs Hyde and Margot's final demand had been for a taxi to take her to town, accompanied by a threat that left Finn gasping.

"What did she do?" asked Rosemary bleakly as she thrust her mother's suddenly obedient limbs into her clothes. "I can see you've had a shock. She's been pretty good lately," she added wearily.

"She was fine at first then, um . . . she threatened to . . . do something if I didn't get her a taxi," admitted Finn, watching in horrified sympathy as Rosemary tugged, tweaked, zipped and buttoned, all with firm kindness, but with detachment too as though she had long ago hit on this as the only way to struggle through it all.

10

"What? Oh no, you mean she threatened to pee on the furniture?" As Finn nodded awkwardly, Rosemary turned angrily on her mother. "You wretched old horror, apologise at once."

To Finn's surprise Margot turned to her obediently.

"I'm so sorry, my dear," she whispered in quiet distress. "I seem to have been embarrassing. Please forgive me."

Rosemary Clavering's face twisted suddenly and Finn felt an instant gush of sympathy. The contrast between the arrogant, rambling old miscreant and the suddenly contrite ancient child was heartbreaking even to a stranger. What must it be like for a daughter?

At the front gate Rosemary turned to Finn for another word of thanks. Margot was safely stowed away in the car and Finn saw that Rosemary was looking utterly exhausted.

"I can't tell you . . ." she began and smiled her gratitude as Finn shook her head wordlessly. "It was so good of you not to call the police, too. Sometimes I wish I could just let her get on with it; maybe if the police did pick her up they'd put her in a home and I could get some peace." She shrugged and grinned. "Still, you can't choose your family, can you? I certainly wouldn't have chosen this, but then, neither would she."

She changed the subject. "I imagine she was looking for your sister. Julia doesn't mind if I have to bring her along to our meetings sometimes, depends if I can get a sitter."

"Meetings?" Finn was intrigued. "I didn't think Ju was much of a joiner. What kind of meetings?"

Rosemary looked slightly shifty for a moment then shrugged. "I expect she'll tell you sometime. Are you staying long? I saw Julia yesterday and she didn't mention that you were coming down."

It was Finn's turn to look furtive. "Bit of a long story," she confessed. "I didn't know myself till yesterday, it was all a big mess. You know . . . man trouble, job, flat . . ."

Rosemary shot her a sympathetic smile but made no effort to pry. "You're going to stay for a while? So you'll be looking for a job down here now?"

Finn made a face. "Depends how Julia feels about it, but yes, that's the plan. I don't imagine you . . .?"

"Sorry," Rosemary smiled ruefully. "Not unless you fancy a spot of unpaid babysitting." Reminded, she turned back to the car. "Drop in sometime for a coffee? I promise to keep Margot under control. It's the bungalow opposite the church. Julia will tell you, come with or without her."

As Rosemary Clavering started to pull away from the kerb Finn waved her to a halt as a thought struck her.

"Um . . . I don't suppose you've any idea where my sister might be, have you? I know it sounds mad but she seems to have gone out already. She's always loved her bed in the mornings. Do you think I ought to worry?"

She was taken aback at the other woman's peal of laughter.

"Oh honestly, listen to yourself! How long have you known Julia? She'll be fine, your sister's a big girl after all. She's just on a healthy kick at the moment, I expect she's gone jogging. She was OK at the meeting last night, maybe she's dropped in on one of the others."

Meeting, there it was again, Finn was intrigued. And the others? What others? What was her sister up to? And what did Rosemary mean, jogging? Julia had always been vociferous on the topic of exercise, fine for other people but not, definitely not, for her.

After a belated shower and a bowl of cereal Finn was shoving some clothes into the washing machine when she heard a key in the front door. Straightening up, she wiped her hands on a towel and strolled into the hall.

"Well, young lady? What have you got to say for yourself?"

"Coming home at this hour, do you mean?" Julia grinned and gave her sister an enveloping hug. "Didn't you forget the bit about using the house as a hotel? Is the kettle not on? I'm gasping for a cup of tea."

"It's all very well," Finn said severely as she handed her a mug of tea. "But this hour of the morning? Suppose there'd been an emergency? I wouldn't have known where to — Oh!" she broke off and shot Julia a shamefaced grin. "Oh all right, I know what I sound like. But jogging? You?"

Julia gave an enigmatic smile and sipped her tea "Bully! Why shouldn't I take up jogging? You think I'm slim enough already?"

Finn surveyed her sister's ample curves and conceded defeat. "I had a visitor while you were out," she volunteered. "Two visitors, in fact."

She gave Julia a description of her early morning social activities and asked about Rosemary Clavering.

"She's a sweetie," Julia said warmly. "She moved here a week or two after I did and we've become really good friends. She taught art in a big school in the Midlands and bought the bungalow by the church when she retired. She had great plans for setting up as a freelance artist and making a bit on top of her pension, but she's not got it off the ground yet."

"Why not, if she's had six months?" Finn was intrigued, Rosemary Clavering hadn't struck her as idle or indecisive.

"That bloody mother of hers, of course," Julia said bitterly. "No, that's hardly fair, Margot can't help how she is. It's the early stages of dementia, of course, though there's been no official diagnosis yet. She and Rosemary's father retired to Spain years ago and she remarried out there a year or so after he died, around five years ago I think. About twelve months ago Margot's second husband died but she stayed where she was. She seemed settled, apparently, and Rosemary used to go out occasionally to see her."

Julia shrugged and fumbled in her bag for a cigarette. "Oh feck, I forgot I'd given up — again, this damned health kick! Anyway, about a month or two after Rosemary moved here Margot turned up on her doorstep in a terrible state. The second husband had put all his financial affairs in the hands of some so-called broker who operated on the Costa Whatsit and he, surprise, surprise, turned out to be a crook. He sold the villa without asking her, cashed in all the

14

securities and bunked off somewhere with no extradition treaty."

"Didn't Rosemary check him out?" asked Finn aghast.

"Didn't get a chance," was the reply. "Neither of them mentioned it to her. The stepfather apparently presented Margot with a fait accompli and as both her husbands had always dealt with the money side and she was the Little Woman, she didn't query his judgement. Well, what could Rosemary do? I gather Margot's eligible for some kind of pension, but not much, the husband had opted out of all sorts of schemes, so now Rosemary's left holding the baby."

She patted Finn's cheek affectionately. "It's not just the money, though that's a major nuisance of course, the main thing is the constant vigilance, and to make matters even more bleak Margot's changed from being rather mousey and prim into a man-eating exhibitionist so Rosemary's always having to haul her off some poor man or other. Rosemary says they were never close anyway and when Margot remarried things got worse, or at least more distant, happier when they were miles apart — bit like you and me!"

"Poor Rosemary," Finn ignored the provocation. "And poor Margot, too, being conned like that." She wrinkled her brow as a memory chimed. "Changing the subject, do I gather you've got a new boyfriend, Ju? That's usually the reason for your sporadic healthy fits."

"Sure, I'd hardly call him a boyfriend, Finn," remonstrated Julia. "He's just turned seventy." She laughed at Finn's expression, and went on. "He's charming, all he wants is to go out somewhere nice for dinner once a week, an occasional dance, the odd drive out and about to a stately home or something and for somebody to listen to him. He's a tad eccentric but very good company, been a widower for a couple of years and no nonsense about wanting another wife. He only moved here a few months back, thought he'd better not live completely alone after he had a fall and broke his hip, I believe. He's staying with his son over the other side of the village at the moment but they're in the throes of sorting out accommodation for him. Also in Bychurch, as it happens; the old Parsonage here has been turned into rather charming flats."

She looked at Finn under her lashes. "I know you've never really approved of all my men friends, but what do you expect me to do? Sit at home and knit? I'd wait a long time if I waited for you to keep me company, wouldn't I!"

Finn gave her a guilty grin. "Oh I don't know," she said. "I'm here now, aren't I? And when did I ever say anything about it? Besides, I haven't hated *all* your boyfriends, be fair, and they didn't *all* end in disaster, did they? I liked that one when I was eighteen, with the shop in Southampton, *and* the one with the dark glasses."

"Yes," Julia's tone was dry. "Ron Davis had a sweetshop, didn't he? And let you — allegedly an adult! — run loose in there every Saturday afternoon until he and I broke up. And as for Giannini, you only liked him because you thought he was a Mafia Don."

16

"Uh huh," agreed Finn reminiscently. "He was scary, and that boy who came to visit next door made me watch the video of *The Godfather* so we were convinced Giannini was going to start leaving horses' heads in the beds."

"Nonsense, he was a perfect darling and he was a partner in the Italian restaurant in town. We ate out a lot that summer I remember."

"Didn't you ever think about getting married again, Julia, instead of, you know . . .?" Finn asked tentatively. They were on good terms but some things you just don't ask.

"Not really. After Colin walked out I was too down, then Mum died and Dad gave up on life and I was landed with a miserable, stroppy fifteen-year old sister on my hands. Not," she threw a laughing look at Finn. "Not that I ever regretted that for a moment, having you to look after saved my sanity. I just went on working and having my morale-boosting flings now and then. Dumping Colin's name and going back to Fitzgerald helped, I never did cotton on to Watson."

Julia opened the kitchen window and leaned out, breathing in extravagant gusts of wood-smoke-scented air.

"Mmm, somebody's got a bonfire somewhere. As for my men-friends, well . . . I don't expect you to believe me but I didn't actually sleep with all of them, specially nowadays — particularly nowadays. Some of them just want company, like I said, someone to go out and about with, a dinner date, somebody next to them at the theatre. There's a surprising number of men around who aren't that bothered about sex, you know, once they get older. And when I was younger, well, it sometimes worked in our favour, didn't it? Remember when I took you home to Ireland, to look after that castle for the whole of one summer? I don't think the fellow's wife ever realised I wasn't just a housekeeper — and you'd a wonderful holiday after all."

She turned to look at her sister, a long, appraising stare, noting a little puffiness round the eyes but no other sign of misery. Hurt pride, that was the problem, rather than a hurt heart.

"Feeling better?" she asked gently. "Want to talk about it?"

"Not really," Finn shook her head. "But thanks anyway, Ju. I've had it with Brussels, I've been getting restless for a year or two. The most important thing to do is start looking for a job, then I need to find somewhere to live. If you really don't mind me crashing for a few days it'll be a great help. I'll get out of your hair as soon as possible."

She looked up as Julia didn't answer at once and saw a speculative look in her sister's eyes.

"Um well, I was wondering about that, Finn." Julia seemed uncharacteristically diffident. "I thought we might give it a go if you'd like." She held her hand up as Finn opened her mouth. "Hang on, let me finish. I know what you're going to say, we couldn't possibly live together and you're probably quite right, two women in a kitchen and all that and this is a small house. But when you rang from Heathrow yesterday I sat down and thought hard about it. We could turn the house

18

into two unofficial flats, if you liked; you upstairs, me down."

Finn shook her head.

"That's sweet of you," she said firmly. "But I'm *not* dumping myself on you permanently. Grabbing a bed for a few nights is one thing, but why on earth should you turn your life upside down, just because I've messed up?"

"I'm your big sister," Julia grinned. "That's what we're for. Are you sure you — What is it?" Finn was staring at her with a very thoughtful expression on her face.

"On the other hand," Finn said slowly. "You *do* have that old brick store-room built on to the back of the garage. Do you use it? Could it be turned into a tiny flat, do you think? Or is it completely uninhabitable?"

"But that's brilliant," Julia exclaimed. "Of course it could. Think about it," she warmed to her theme, ever the optimist. "There's electricity in there already, and water laid on. Come to think of it you might as well have the garage too; I'm sure something could be done."

Finn was looking doubtful again as she leaned forward to make her point. "I want to make a completely new start," she said, resolutely. "I've been a wimp for years and it's time I got off my backside and did something about it, took control of my life. It would certainly save me a lot of bother, if we *could* convert the garage, but it just strikes me as wimpy old Finn letting somebody else take the strain — as usual!"

"Oh, come *on*," Julia laughed at her, nodding as the tension began to seep away from Finn's face. "You're allowed to accept *some* help, surely? And to be honest, it *would* be a lot more satisfactory from my point of view. You're right, I'm happily settled and this is a small house, but the garage . . . When have you ever known me put my car away? Also, don't forget, there's another shed in the garden, plenty of room for lawnmowers and things. Think it over, there's no panic. Look on this as a short holiday. Now, why don't we go and check it out? I really think it might work, you know. The door opens into the hall, so we'd share the front door, but that's all. For the rest, we could be quite self-contained."

"That's right," Finn told the middle-aged woman interviewing her that afternoon. "It's spelled Fionnuala, pronounced Finola, my parents were Irish. I'm quite happy to do anything for a while, secretarial, work in a shop, whatever, I know I can't expect anything like what I've been earning. I've come back to England because my elder sister needs me nearer at hand. She's not an invalid," she added hastily, seeing the woman's frown. "It wouldn't make any difference to my work, but she . . . she's suffered a bereavement recently, so that's why . . ."

She tailed off as the woman nodded sympathetically. Well, it's true enough, she thought guiltily. Julia's ancient Labrador had died only last year and Julia had been devastated, only the bustle and interest of moving house had kept her going.

By the time she got to the interview with the third agency Finn had her story off pat and almost believed it herself, though the image of a frail and elderly Julia pulled her up short, compared to the vibrant reality of her sister.

It was gone half past five when she made her weary way back towards Julia's car, parked in Bridge Street. Mulling over the interviews with their constant of frowns, pursed lips and shaken heads — can't promise anything, dear, not this time of year, certainly not what you're used to, the power station's just laid off people — Finn started to feel depressed. Hang on a minute, she exhorted herself. Get a grip, you didn't burn your boats so comprehensively just to slip back into your wimpy ways. Don't be so pathetic, try and act your age for once.

She straightened her shoulders and grinned, suddenly in Scarlett O'Hara mood. "After all," she proclaimed aloud, to the surprise of a passing pedestrian. "Tomorrow *is* another day!"

CHAPTER
TWO

After an early night Finn and Julia took stock, more comprehensively, of the garage and brick-built store attached at the side of the house.

"I really think this could work, you know," Julia waved an expansive hand around. "The old store-room could be divided in two, a shower and a kitchen — it's close to the main plumbing in the house."

"Yes," agreed Finn thoughtfully. "I'm not sure I ever took a proper look in here when you moved."

"It's pretty poky by modern garage standards. It wouldn't take much to finish it, plasterboard, that sort of thing, turn it into a sort of studio room. What do you reckon?"

"I think it'll do just fine," Finn hugged her gratefully. "Even though I still think I'm copping out, it's going to save me *so* much hassle. But I think we should live completely separately," she warned. "And you must charge me a proper rent. I'm rolling at the moment, don't forget. So what shall we do about this conversion?"

"Let's shift these boxes up to the attic for a start." Julia was already humping one towards the door. After a couple of hours the garage was clear so Finn made them coffee and a sandwich.

"I'd better get on with the job-hunting," she decided when they'd finished eating. "Is it OK for me to borrow your car again? That's something else I need to check out, I'll have a look in town this afternoon."

"Good idea," agreed her sister. "In the meantime I'll see if I can rustle up a work force and get some estimates for this conversion job."

Yesterday's trip had concentrated on the employment agencies, where the only things on offer were low-paid clerical jobs. There was no joy in the jobs section of the local Gazette, so this afternoon Finn wandered round town looking at the shops, hoping to spot Help Wanted signs. Nothing offered but she enjoyed the window-shopping anyway. Round behind the town hall she discovered a new shop in Paradise Row.

"The Starlight Strand?" She stared at the window display, intrigued. "Wow, this is a bit advanced for Ramalley, isn't it? Crystals and tarot cards and things?"

After a moment's hesitation she pushed open the door to the sound of wind chimes as the door brushed against them. "I'm just looking, thank you," she nodded to the assistant behind the counter, a woolly-hatted thirtyish man with a pasty porridgey-looking face, who opened sleepy eyes when she entered.

Finn toured round the bookshelves and display cabinets. Maybe I ought to buy some cards and find out what my future's going to be, she thought. A little shamefaced, she was pocketing her change when the wind chimes tinkled and an elderly man entered the shop.

He smiled at the assistant and Finn and raised his hat to them politely, then went to look at the displays for a moment, fidgeting a bit.

"Excuse me," he turned to Porridge-Face as Finn picked up the carrier containing her tarot pack. "I believe you sometimes have a clairvoyant here? Might I enquire when she's in attendance?"

"Thaat's a pity," replied the shop-keeper, his voice, with its long Hampshire vowels slowed down to a crawl, contrasting with his shining, eager-to-please manner. "She's not in this week, she's on holiday, but I could give you a call, she's usually here on Tues . . . Oh f . . . whassa marrer?"

He broke off as the older man gave a sudden groan and swayed, his long, elegant hand clutching at the wooden counter top. At the door, Finn heard the commotion and looked back at them.

As the customer keeled over Finn dropped her bag and rushed to his side, manhandling him to a chair that was mercifully near at hand.

"Here," she gasped to the shop assistant. "Got him too? He's slipping and I can't manage him on my own."

Together they managed to sit him down gently. He hadn't quite lost consciousness, it looked like a simple faint, and he was trying to wave them aside.

"So kind, thank you so much, so kind. Quite all right now, please, please don't bother."

Finn kept her arm round him for a few moments more then, as his colour improved, she knelt down beside him.

"That was rather nasty," she said gently. "I think we ought to call an ambulance and get you looked at by a doctor."

"Oh no, no," he interrupted hastily. "I do assure you, my dear, I'm quite recovered. If I could sit here for a little longer, I shall be perfectly well."

Finn surveyed him sceptically but she could see he was determined.

"Perhaps a glass of water?" she suggested to Porridge Face, who was hovering anxiously.

"Oh yeah, no probs. Or tea, perhaps? I've just made some."

He brought Finn some tea as well and they watched the other man as he cast a startled look of distaste at the thick pottery mug and braced himself. However plebeian the vessel the contents seemed to revive him and he proffered profuse apologies for being such a nuisance.

"If I could perhaps telephone my son?" he suggested after a few minutes. "He can come and collect me in the car, I'm afraid the walk is rather beyond me at present."

Finn started to protest that she could call him a taxi, give him a lift even, but he waved an imperious hand at her and leaned back with his eyes closed after presenting her with a business card. "Perhaps you could call him for me, thank you."

A sudden rush of two customers took the assistant's attention so Finn picked up the phone and called Mr Charles E. Stuart, of Ramalley Software Solutions. A pleasant male voice eventually answered after the receptionist had told Finn to hang on.

"Is he all right? He's only just getting over a vicious dose of flu. I knew it was too soon for him to go out. I'll come straight away. It's very kind of you. Where is he?"

"He's at the Starlight Strand," admitted Finn with a self-conscious gulp. "Do you know it? It's a — a shop in Paradise Row, behind the Town Hall."

"Oh." There was a sudden icy edge to Mr Charles E. Stuart's voice. "Yes, I know where it is."

Finn was embarrassed, then furious with herself for minding. What did it matter what Charles E. Stuart thought of her? He was a complete stranger, so why should his change of tone make her cringe? It wasn't as if she was in the habit of frequenting magic shops. Almost without noticing what she was doing she arranged a wodge of tissues and her handbag into the carrier to hide the tarot card pack she'd bought.

The invalid was perking up by the minute. Around seventy, Finn judged, he was still astonishingly good-looking, the high nose dominating the face, the dark eyes hooded but still alert, the thick crop of silvery-grey hair scarcely thinning. Although he was a little stooped he was still very tall, well over six foot and he radiated an ageless charm that even worked on Porridge-Face who was now offering him some home-made, chunky muesli biscuits which were waved aside with a gracious smile. As the young man bobbed eagerly about him, fussing, the old man caught Finn's eye and gave her a flashing, wicked grin, alive with conspiratorial mischief, combined with a spark of

26

interest, even now, in the tall, curvy blonde twinkling back at him.

Before she could respond the door was flung open and a tall dark man of about forty stormed in. He was instantly recognisable, the same saturnine good looks as his father marred, in his case, by a furious scowl.

"Pa? Are you all right? What are you doing here?" He turned anxious dark eyes from his father to the two who were watching. "Oh come *on*, Pa," he said, a rueful grin lightening his long face. "I thought you were kidding when you said you wanted to see a clairvoyant. You'll get carted off one day. *Please* tell me you weren't trying to get in touch with you-know-who?"

"Be quiet, Charlie, you go too far. Excuse me," his father struggled to his feet. "I must apologise, my dear, let me introduce myself." Amused malice gleamed in his eyes as he shot his son a covert glance before proclaiming, "I am James Edward Stuart, Claimant to the Throne of England, Scotland, Ireland and Wales, and this is my son — and my heir — the Young Pretender as he is known to the uninitiated, but to the faithful he is The Young Chevalier, Charles Edward Stuart."

He made her a flourishing bow and sat down rather suddenly, the smile wiped from his face.

Finn stared for a second, then hastily closed her mouth. Claimant to the throne of England? But he seemed such a nice, normal sort of man, not a first class, certifiable fruit cake. A swift sidelong glance at Charlie, the Young Chevalier, revealed that he was mortified, scarlet with mingled rage and embarrassment.

"I've got a job!" Finn burst into the house bubbling with excitement and stopped short at the chaos and confusion in the hall. A short, black-browed, elderly man trying to move a sheet of plasterboard singlehanded, was barking orders, in a marked eastern European accent, at Julia and another man, who were ignoring him as they pored over a pile of glossy holiday brochures showing Caribbean scenes.

"Come, Julia," scolded the bossy man. "You can read those later, after all we have plenty of time before we can think of a holiday. The sooner this work is done the sooner we can begin the fund-raising."

"What a bully you are, Marek," she sighed. "But you're right, of course. Oh, there you are, Finn, darling, how did it go today?"

"Um . . . fine," faltered Finn. "Can I give you a hand? I didn't know you meant to get started today, Ju, I thought we were supposed to get some estimates. Why didn't you tell me? I would have stayed in to help, if you'd said."

"Didn't know myself, till I got the urge," came the casual reply. "Oof! That's budged it. Here, grab the corner, Finn, and help Marek at his end."

I've only been out of the house three hours, thought Finn, impressed, and she's organised all this. The erstwhile garage was transformed. Somebody, presumably one of the two men in attendance on Julia, had been busy. There were wooden battens fixed to the walls and another sheet of plasterboard leaned against it, while a second doorway had been opened up into the store at the back.

"It's looking good, isn't it?" Julia waved an airy hand. "Marek borrowed a van and we went off to the DIY place and bought timber, etc. The plan is to put up a stud-partition wall in the store and tuck in a loo and shower; there's already a sink the other side so that can be the kitchen area. Luckily the garage is really well insulated and there's even some storage space where the roof-space is boarded. Somebody obviously once spent a lot of time and money in here, so when this new wall is done, and the partition finished, all you'll have to do is decorate."

"It's going to be great," admired Finn. "I'm not even sure it was a serious suggestion when I made it, but I think it might really work, thank you *so* much."

"Well, here we are in Finn's new bedroom," Julia waved a hand around the front end of the garage. "Don't you think we should christen it, Marek and Jonathan?"

"Christen . . .?" For a second Finn, who had followed her, misunderstood and cast a startled look at her sister and the two old boys, one dark and fierce, the other pink and meek and panting.

"*Really*, Finn!" A grin twisted Julia's wickedly pretty face. "What *are* you thinking? Champagne. In the fridge?" She nudged her sister and Finn jerked back to sanity.

"Oh, right. Fridge. OK, I'll get it."

"Cheers, everyone," Julia raised her glass in a toast to sister and helpers. "Now I'd better introduce you. My sister Finn — my friends Marek Wiszinski and Jonathan Barlow."

The two men drank one glass each and departed, Marek with a formal bow to Finn, heels clicking, and a bow and kiss on the hand for Julia; Jonathan fussing about, his head poking out of his jacket like a mild-mannered tortoise.

"Here," Julia noticed him rootling in his pocket and disappeared into the kitchen and came back with a handful of green leaves. "Don't bother with peppermints. Parsley, Jonathan, chlorophyll, best thing for breath problems. Chew the leaves and she won't smell the alcohol."

Jonathan scuttled off chewing gratefully, Marek marching behind him in soldierly fashion, clutching a parts list and a wad of notes pressed on him by Julia.

"Pay me when it's finished," she said, when Finn protested. "Don't worry, I'm keeping a tally. Now, let's finish the bottle," she suggested. "I've done us a salad for supper, you can start doing your own housekeeping when we get things sorted out."

"Who are those two, Ju?" Finn was curious.

"Marek fought as a boy with the Free Poles in the war and stayed on afterwards. I think his family had all died, I'm not sure though, he never speaks about it. He lives in the sheltered flats round the corner and he can turn his hand to almost anything. Jonathan's got a bungalow over by the allotments, he used to work for May's, the men's clothes shop but he's knowledgeable about things, he's been looking at the electrics in here, and he'll fit a cooker and some more sockets."

"They'll let me pay them, won't they?"

"It won't cost anything, only materials, we're all members of the Gang."

"You mentioned the Gang yesterday," Finn remembered as they ate their supper, lingering over coffee.

"Ah yes, the Gang." Julia showed no inclination to explain so Finn prompted her.

"So? Who? What? Why? Tell me, Ju."

"Why so nosey? It's just a group of us from the village, a club if you like, that Rosemary and I started because we were lonely newcomers after we both arrived here. It began as a social thing but it's kind of escalated and last night . . ." Her voice tailed away as she recalled last night's discussion.

"Maybe we should form a coven?" Marek had suggested the previous night, his eyebrows black triangles against his pale skin as he laughed at his own idea. "That would bring us some excitement, yes?"

Rosemary sighed.

"I wanted serious suggestions," she frowned. "And please don't suggest outings or bingo." She looked round the group and sighed again. "The group works very well as a bartering exchange and a social club, but I know some of you think life's a bit dull. Look, I'll go and make some more coffee," she suggested. "Why don't you each try to think of three *realistic* things we could do to ginger this group up now we've got it."

The room was heavy with concentration as she headed for the kitchen.

It had seemed such a good idea, this group, she thought while waiting for the coffee to drip through, when she'd started it out of desperation on Margot's explosive arrival.

"A sort of social group," she had explained to Julia Fitzgerald when they met in the coffee shop in town.

"What, for old biddies?" asked Julia. "Not really my scene, darling. You mean Darby and Joan kind of thing? Coach trips and sing-songs?"

"Of course not!" Rosemary's answer was an explosive giggle. She sipped her coffee and calmed down. "No, not restricted to one age group, but like-minded people who would enjoy a bit of company now and then. We could meet in each other's houses one evening a week; go out to dinner or the theatre when we can afford it. What else? Oh, I know, we could share skills, a kind of swap-shop."

"What? I make you a cake and you do my income tax return?" Julia raised an eyebrow. "That sort of thing?"

"That's the idea," Rosemary beamed with enthusiasm. "Mind, you'd better not let me near your tax return, I'd rather paint you a picture. That could be a secondary aspect of the group, and perhaps we'd develop other ideas but the primary function would be social."

Rosemary had been busy and cheerful for the first few months of her retirement from the High School in the Midlands, selling her flat, buying the bungalow in Bychurch, the pretty village just outside the country town of Ramalley on the border of the New Forest, in Hampshire. It had all taken time and kept her happily occupied.

It had taken the arrival, six weeks after she moved in to Church View, of the distraught and demented Margot to make her feel isolated, in sore need of friends to help her take the strain. That was when she thought of the group.

Now back in the sitting room with the coffee, she handed mugs and sat down, expectant. "Any ideas?"

There was a heavy, self-conscious silence into which fell the fluting tones of Ursula Buchanan, the oldest woman in the group — and by far its most eccentric member.

"Well," she said shyly, looking round the room with her usual diffidence. "I did have one idea. It's something I've always wanted to try. The trouble is, I don't have any money."

Encouraged by the others, Ursula outlined her Brilliant Idea.

Finishing up her coffee now, Julia shook her head at Finn. "I'll tell you all about the Gang some other time. It's just a social club really, for people who live in the village, it's made quite a difference to me already, we're all good friends now. And we have this barter system going so don't worry about the plumbing etc. I've promised to make Marek some new curtains, though it's always hard to compensate Jonathan, that evil witch of a wife of his mustn't get wind of it."

"Evil witch?" Finn was intrigued.

"Hideous parasite who sits in front of the telly and treats Jonathan like a dog. No wonder he spends most of his time on his allotment. That's it, I can buy him some grow-bags or manure, plants or something, to even it out. She doesn't know about the group, thinks he's joined a club for pensioners from his company and that it's restricted to ex-employees only, or she'd be in there, making life hell for him.

"And what about you?" She turned back to stare at Finn's brightened face. "Did you say you'd got a job, or did I imagine it?"

"Yup, start tomorrow," Finn announced smugly. "*And* I've bought a car. Let's go and sit by the fire and I'll tell you all."

"The guy with the woolly hat is the owner," she explained as she toasted her toes in front of the coal-effect gas fire. "He had a win on the lottery, not millions but enough to buy the business. He told me all that later on, but before that the other guy announced who he was! Talk about eccentric, I felt really sorry for his son. I didn't know what to say, it was rather awkward, to say the least. Anyway, like I said, the owner is called Hedgehog and he opened the shop a month ago. It was the weirdest interview I've ever had. He's a bit podgy and pasty, and really local, you know? Long, slow, drawly country voice and kind of a slow mover too, though I suppose with Hedgehog it could be drugs."

"It sounds lovely, darling," Julia shot her an old-fashioned look. "What's all this about an eccentric father and a pitiable son? You've certainly managed to hit town with a bang in a very short while, haven't you?"

Finn explained. "But it was when he introduced himself as the Old Pretender and the son as the Young Chevalier, I nearly had hysterics. Like I said, I felt sorry for Charlie, the Chevalier, he was *so* embarrassed, you could have fried an egg on him."

She realised her sister had taken a deep breath and was looking extremely self-conscious.

"What? *What?* You don't know them, do you?"

"You could say that," Julia let her breath out slowly and looked even shiftier. "Actually your Old Pretender to the Throne is my gentleman friend, Jamie. You know? He's a member of the Gang. I've only met Charlie a couple of times, he's been abroad on business off and on for the last two months. Jamie's very fond of him, though I found him a bit glum, mind you. I believe there was some terrible scandal about his wife."

"Julia!" Disregarding the life history of the Young Chevalier, Finn was shocked. "You mean you're shagging a basket-case?"

"Really, Finn," Julia reproved her. "There's no need to be *quite* so coarse, I told you already, Jamie is a perfect gentleman, all he wants is company. Anyway, he's got documentary proof that his family is descended from Bonnie Prince Charlie or maybe it's King Henry the Ninth, the last Stuart king, brother to Prince Charlie. He just — gets a bit obsessed about it, that's all."

Finn drew a deep breath and stared at Julia who was looking uncomfortable, not without reason, her sister considered.

"Oh really?" she retorted. "That's very interesting, Ju. I might point out that I used to have a crush on Bonnie Prince Charlie and one of the very few bits of history that I can remember is that the last Stuart 'king' was a Catholic priest, a Cardinal, in fact. So exactly how did he go about starting a dynasty?"

"Oh, I don't know," Julia was exasperated. "Jamie's got all the documents and stuff, it might not have been the cardinal, could have been Prince Charlie for all I know — or care — but to tell the truth I don't pay any attention. It all sounds pretty harmless, a bit like The Sealed Knot society, that sort of thing. He's a lovely man, though and — well, maybe you might understand for once — he's not demanding, it's not sex he's after, just nice, warm friendship, so an obsession about some dodgy ancestors is a small price to pay."

"Understand? Why would I understand?"

"Because, unfortunately, Finn, you've turned out just like me," sighed Julia.

Finn started to splutter indignantly then caught Julia's eye and subsided with a laugh. "You mean falling in love with the wrong men? You could be right," she grinned reluctantly.

"I know I am," retorted Julia. "We both believe wholeheartedly in happy-ever-after. I know exactly what happens, you start off with a terrific crush on someone, fall into bed with him, convinced he's the love of your life, and bingo! He turns out to have a wife, or a fiancée, or he's phobic about commitment, or he keeps his socks on in bed. Or he's gay," she added as she cleared away their coffee cups.

36

"Gay?" Finn was intrigued.

"None of your business, I'm not going into that one," Julia spoke defiantly. "Look at us," she indicated the mirror. "You're a chip off the old block, you poor kid."

Finn stared at the two of them reflected in the mirror opposite. "Oh God, never had a chance, did I?"

Matching cynical grins lit up the mirrored faces, so much alike in features that there could be no doubt of their relationship.

"Look at us," Finn echoed her sister. "Big bouncy creatures, both tall and — what? I refuse to say fat, I think I'll say voluptuous. It's only the eyes and hair that are different."

Julia laughed aloud at her.

"And thirteen years difference in age, don't forget. Anyway, go on with you, you're not fat, you're curvaceous, size fourteen is fine when you're almost six foot. Now me," she preened theatrically. "*I'm* the voluptuous one, always have been and I was never a blonde like you, a real, green-eyed, red-haired Irish cliché, that was me, and a tomboy too, at least till my boobs developed. *And* I'm two inches shorter than you."

She sobered rapidly. "I'm right though, aren't I? We're alike when it comes to men, too."

Finn sighed. "You know you are," she shrugged. "I never thought about it from your point of view, as a mother-figure. It must have been awful watching me doing the self-same thing, flinging myself in and out of love all these years, like a superannuated teenager."

"Very galling," Julia spoke in her driest tone. "Oh I know I was married to Colin for seven years and I certainly didn't stray, but the shine wore off a long time before he took off into the wide blue yonder. I don't know if I'd have done anything about it, though, if he hadn't made the decision, for I'd the ghost of Sister Mary Margaret sitting on my shoulder telling me divorce was a sin! I must admit, though, it was pretty frustrating watching you louse up school and college because of a procession of wretched spotty boys."

"Spotty boys? Are you talking about the *lurves* of my life?" Finn reached out and hugged her sister. "Jeez, Ju, we're a pair, aren't we? At least you never messed up any jobs because of men. Ever since I dropped out of uni because of my tutor, I seem to last a couple of years or so in each relationship and I've never, ever managed to remember the golden rule — keep work and sex separate."

"If we start talking about *my* more spectacular mistakes we'll be here all night, so go to bed, darling." Julia shrugged. "Just take things as they come, use this as an opportunity to find out what you really want, and maybe by Christmas you'll have a clearer picture of what you want out of life."

"You're a pal," Finn hugged her affectionately. "Like I said, I still think it's a cop out, moving into your garage and as to finding out what I want from life . . . Who knows? But part of it is what I'm starting to do — taking control, making decisions by myself. Well, look at today — a job *and* a car — it's a Renault, by the way, I pick it up tomorrow. It's a start, at least."

CHAPTER
THREE

Ursula Buchanan sang as she put the kettle on, in a high, breathy soprano, frayed round the edges. She sang as she put out stale bread for the birds and when she put the slices of bread into the toaster for Henrietta's breakfast. As she set out Henrietta's tray the singing increased in volume for sheer happiness. She even sang when she scrubbed the downstairs lavatory, but that was later in the morning.

Such a small thing, she mused, as she sailed into Henrietta's bedroom, pushed and pulled the pillows straight, pushed and pulled Henrietta into place and flicked open the legs of the bed-table, ignoring, for once, Henrietta's evil eye. Such a tiny, infinitely minute occurrence in the history of mankind, that glance of mine at the notice-board in the post office a while back, and look where it's leading me now!

The angel had been back a couple of times since his first manifestation, dropping in unannounced and perfectly friendly. Once he had forced her to stand up to Henrietta.

"Go on," he'd urged. "Tell her you're not a slave; say it, I dare you."

So she had.

"I'm your housekeeper, Henrietta, and your sister-in-law," both doughy chins wobbling in her earnest terror. "I know I'm lucky to have found a home with you since Mother and Father left me penniless, but you're lucky too. Yes you are," she pressed on, ignoring the squawk of indignation and averting her eyes from the dark glare of Henrietta's angry hooded eyes. "If it wasn't for me you'd have to pay for nurses and cleaners and you'd probably have to go into a residential home which would cost you the earth."

Reaction set in when Ursula reached the kitchen and she shivered beside the Rayburn.

"*That went rather well, I thought,*" remarked the voice like a peal of bells, and the angel perched on the scrubbed pine kitchen table. "*Buck up, Ursula, you won that round, didn't you?*"

"I don't know how I dared!" Ursula was so short of breath that she had to sit down. "What will I do if she decides to throw me out? For it's true, you know, I *do* owe her a lot, she took me in when I had nowhere to go. I never had a job, they all said it would be too much for me . . ."

She turned on the angel, suddenly indignant. "You know all this, surely? If you're an angel, I mean. All about the War and being trapped in the cellar when that house was bombed, why am I bothering to tell you?"

She wiped an angry tear from the end of her nose.

"I know I'm not clever and I forget things, but I — I used to be clever, you know, it wasn't my fault."

Rosemary Clavering frowned at the untidy kitchen. A whole day to herself and all she could think about was washing-up.

"A whole day . . ."

It seemed unbelievable but here she was, the day stretching invitingly before her until five o'clock when Margot would be decanted from the Community Bus on its return trip from the Day Centre. Oh the Day Centre! Wonderful, wonderful place and wonderful, wonderful social worker for organising Margot's disappearance there for two whole days each week.

"Will I like it?" Margot had asked, furrowing her brow while she tried to imagine a day spent with other elderly people.

Do I care, Rosemary had commented silently, but aloud, she said, "Oh, I think so, you've always loved meeting other people, haven't you? Maybe we could go into town next week and buy you something nice, a new jumper perhaps? You'd want to keep looking nice, after all."

"What if she has an accident," Rosemary asked the social worker diffidently. "You know, wet knickers or something?"

"Not a problem," was the brisk answer. "Just pack a bag with spares, mark everything with her name — oh yes, put something in that she likes, something familiar, so she can connect with home."

Now, in the messy kitchen, Rosemary shuddered as she recalled the horrible, kindly words and the horrible, breezy tone. Just like packing a bag for playschool, or boarding school, she thought with a pang of unwilling commiseration. She may be a bloody nuisance, but she's a human being, an adult, not a toddler, for God's sake. And she *is* my mother, like it or not.

For a moment the responsibility weighed heavily then she shrugged and marched into the studio she had set up in the dining room. Five minutes later she was settled at the table, water pot filled, paper pinned to her board, a hastily-plucked spray of chrysanthemums posing in front of her.

"If Ursula's idea is to get off the ground," she announced to the blackbird on the lawn. "I'd better get off my backside and this is one way I can see ahead, I'm sure the art shop in town will sell them on commission for me."

The social and barter club she had proposed had grown from an idle comment to Julia Fitzgerald to a fully-fledged entity, in a very short time. After that discussion over coffee she and Julia had talked about it again and again until Rosemary took the plunge.

"I've put a poster in the village shop," she announced when Julia called in a few days afterwards. "Inviting anyone interested in forming a club — and I've outlined the aims — to meet in the Lounge Bar of the Bychurch Arms at eight o'clock on Tuesday night. You have to come and support me, then if nobody else comes I won't feel such an idiot."

Presiding over the inaugural meeting Rosemary managed a serene and welcoming smile that disguised the nervous knot in her stomach. Margot had been difficult all that day, the heels-dug-in phase, in obstinate mode, so much harder to deal with than the imperious dowager duchess or the increasingly recurring periods of disorientation and incoherent incontinence. It had been touch and go whether Rosemary was actually going to get away at all but at last the raddled prima donna turned into a tearful and weary elderly child and slid into a deep sleep.

"Do come and sit down," Rosemary summoned up a wary smile at the diffident huddle of strangers and Julia surged to the rescue, warm and generous and welcoming.

"Have you all got drinks? That's great now! Look, Rosemary, why don't we all go and sit in the garden, it's so lovely just now. I'm sure there'll be somebody who'll smoke and keep the midges off?"

And before they realised it even the shyest members were being bustled out to breathe in the scent of spring and admire the glorious deep blue of the evening sky.

"Oh you . . ." Rosemary breathed in a grateful aside to Julia as they shifted chairs and tables into a cosy group. "I honestly believe you'd organise a party in a morgue."

Julia raised an amused eyebrow.

"Why not? You'd need a couple of stiff drinks, though."

"Idiot! But thanks, anyway. I think they're beginning to thaw."

"I left the advert deliberately vague," Rosemary told them, after introducing herself and explaining her reason for wanting to start a social group. "I don't really know what sort of group it might be, I just suggested a couple of ideas for barter, but I also thought we might get together for theatre trips, going to the pictures, meals out, that kind of thing. I mentioned art classes because, as I said just now, that's what I know, but I'm sure we can muster quite a variety of skills that we could pool. Your input will be very welcome."

She nodded pointedly to Julia who grinned and responded obediently, having been primed to volunteer as an encouragement to the rest.

"OK, well, I'm Julia Fitzgerald, originally from near Wexford. I live in Forge Cottage, I've no family, only a younger sister who works abroad, and I moved here from Basingstoke a few months back when I took early retirement as a theatre sister. I don't really want to offer nursing as a skill, as such, but I wouldn't mind teaching a first aid course or something similar. I can also offer lifts, maybe for shopping trips, or hospital visits, whatever. Oh yes, I'm not a bad cook so if anyone wants a dinner party organised, I'm your woman."

Ursula Buchanan was trembling in her seat next to Julia. She put up her hand and waved it excitedly at Rosemary who blinked, then nodded with a smile.

"I live with my sister-in-law, Henrietta, who is older than I am and in poor health. Before she gave me a roof over my head I looked after my parents till they died so I'm afraid I've never had much chance to find out my skills. But I can bake very nicely, Mother always said, and if anybody has a cat I'd love to feed it if they have to go away any time. I used to have a cat at home but he died just before Mother and Henrietta won't let me have one at her house, she thinks cats are vermin, but they're not, I love them."

Her voice rose and she sat down defiantly, a mottled flush on her pudgy cheeks. Julia turned to smile reassuringly at her and Ursula relaxed, basking as so many before her, in the warmth of Julia's approval.

The old Pole announced himself next, as Marek Wiszinski, said he had been in the War with the Free Polish troops and was now a widower, his English wife was dead and his English son was now living in Australia.

"He paid for me to go out there once," the old man said stiffly. "But we don't get on so well, I don't like the heat and I can't afford to go again, paying my own way, and I won't let him do it again. I can do some things, a little carpentry, perhaps, fix a dripping tap, a leaking joint, that sort of thing. I would like to trade it for — oh, I don't know, I suppose it would be friendship." He glared fiercely round at them after this admission but softened a little under the sympathy he sensed all around him. "This is for all of us, isn't it? That we are a little lonely? The loved ones gone, the old way of life vanished, the family and friends far away?"

"Oh yes," Bobbie Boyle breathed a sigh of relief as she smiled timidly round the room. "I had to take early retirement at forty-five from Plummers in Ramalley, after I was involved in a car crash and couldn't stand for long hours. I used to be in Ladies' Fashions. I can do dress-making and alterations and I'm a dab hand at mending and darning too and I can amuse small girls quite successfully. I've no family left and I've had to give up being Brown Owl in town because I had a nervous breakdown after my accident and they were afraid the parents wouldn't like it, even though it was three years ago and I'm quite all right now. They tried to be nice about it, said I'd always be welcome to help out, but it's not the same, is it? I — I was beginning to despair when I saw your notice but you've given me new hope!"

Julia caught Rosemary's startled gaze, this was getting heavy, they hadn't envisaged anything quite this serious. Rosemary turned gratefully to another woman, in her thirties maybe, who had raised a nervous hand.

"Hello," she smiled. "Do tell us about yourself."

"Oh, thank you. Well, my name's Sue Merrill and I teach Geography. My — my husband and I, um, lead separate lives nowadays and we've no children. I suppose I'm lonely too."

She sat down abruptly and reached surreptitiously for a tissue to wipe her brimming eyes as the elegant man beside her rose to his feet with a courteous bow all round.

James Edward Stuart, Old Pretender and Claimant to the Throne, made his presence known, described his hobby of genealogy and smiled graciously at the startled group of his subjects as he sat down in a momentarily silent pub garden.

Again Julia and Rosemary gazed at each other in astonishment and something bordering on awe. Where on earth had these people *come* from?

A cackle of laughter came from the last occupant of the grouped garden chairs.

46

"Well, well, well! I had my doubts about this club idea," announced the Cruella de Ville figure in black as she raised her glass to them all. "But I think I'll fit in rather well after all. Now, of course you'll want my potted biography?"

She settled her elegantly thin elderly legs, one crossed on the other, drew heavily on her cigarette, took another swig of what appeared to be neat gin, and told them who she was.

"Name's Delia Muncaster," she announced in a high, diamond-cut drawl straight out of a 1940s film. "I spent more than forty years married to Guy Muncaster, the art historian, you might have heard of him? Made a television series in the seventies."

"Lady Delia?" breathed Bobbie. "She's an earl's daughter, you know," she added in a reverent whisper.

The murmur of respectful surprise was sufficient answer and she continued, "He died before Christmas and when things were settled I went house hunting. That's how I've ended up living here at the pub while Daisy Cottage is being done up for me. I'll be moving in, hopefully, in a couple of months and your club sounds just the thing to help me get my bearings."

The introductions wound up with a shy contribution from an apologetic Jonathan Barlow who had tiptoed up the gravel path and hovered on the fringe of the group until Julia noticed and rescued him.

"My wife won't . . . she's an invalid," he whispered as he faltered to a stop in his introduction. "But I'd like to . . . very much, I mean, if I may."

CHAPTER
FOUR

"What were you saying about your interview for this shop job, Finn?"

Julia and Finn were washing up after supper when Julia suddenly recalled her sister's remark.

"What? Oh God, yes," Finn's laughter bubbled up as she remembered. "It was so funny. I sort of hung around to help The young Chevalier get his father into the car and even though he hated me being there he couldn't have managed without me, your gentleman friend was absolutely knackered. He just kind of flopped there while poor Charlie was struggling to get him strapped in, and explained very sweetly that he'd been hoping to get the clairvoyant to contact the Stuart kings for him! Mind you," she frowned reminiscently. "He did give me a rather naughty wink when Charlie wasn't looking."

"Really?" Julia frowned too. "That doesn't sound like Jamie."

"Oh, not a come-on sort of wink, more as though he and I were sharing a joke at Charlie's expense.

"Anyway, I waved them off with a sweet smile to Charlie that made him cringe and I was just going to head for the car when I spotted the hippy in the bobble hat putting a card in the window, saying Shop Assistant Wanted. So I turned round and asked for the job."

"Goodness!" Julia's response was satisfyingly astonished. "What about experience? Have you ever worked in a shop, Finn? I don't recollect one being mentioned. Or didn't he care?"

"Not in the least," Finn was still giggling. "I told him the score and said I'd no retail experience but thought I could pick it up quite quickly. He nodded, which was a mistake as he was a bit dozy, but he perked himself up and started asking questions.

"Like I said, it was the most insane interview. First of all he agreed and said I wouldn't have any problems with the till and so on, then he looked a bit shifty and the interview went a bit wobbly."

"Do you have any views on drugs?" the shop owner had asked her in a rather stilted manner.

"Drugs?" She stalled a bit then shrugged, what the hell, might as well tell the truth. "Not really, tried when I was at university, nothing heavy. Went to sleep, if you want to know. Didn't really do anything for me so I didn't bother again, haven't thought about it since. Does it matter?"

"Not a bit," he said, grinning at her in a much more natural manner, until he glanced down at a crib sheet on the counter and asked another of those stilted questions.

"Do you have any views on clairvoyants?"

She was ready for him this time, though even more surprised at the direction this interview was taking.

"You mean am I religious? Am I an anti?"

He nodded, watching her eagerly.

"Well, I probably wouldn't have come in here, would I? Still less have bought a pack of tarot cards. No, I think it's all a bit of fun, like most things, unless you get too intense about it."

"And that was about it," she told Julia that night. "Except he asked if I'd mind standing in for the fortune teller who comes in twice a week. Seems she has a habit of letting them down and no, he didn't make any cracks about unforseen circumstances."

"Fortune telling?"

Julia shrieked with laughter and Finn, after a momentary sulk, joined in.

"Well, why not?" she demanded. "I told him I'd never done anything like it and I'd not the slightest scrap of talent but he didn't care. He said I was a nice, friendly sort of woman and that was the most important thing. The rest of it, he said, I could soon pick up and give the punters what they want. I said wasn't it fraud and he just looked at me, with this goofy, country-yokel oh-so-innocent stare and laid it out for me. The people who come into the shop, he said, either believe in the stuff he sells, or they're ready to be convinced. Same with the clairvoyant, what they're looking for is reassurance and a comforting vision of the future. They don't mind vagueness, he said the lady that's usually there has a degree in Vague. Of course there's always the odd one or two who expect details, you know, shoe size and birthday of the tall, dark stranger on the horizon, plus a month-by-month agenda they can compare with, but there aren't so many of them, he reckons, and they can usually be fobbed off."

She drew a deep breath and grinned at her big sister.

"I wanted a complete change of lifestyle, didn't I? I think it'll be fun and it's certainly a challenge. Didn't you always say I should meet challenges head on? There you are, I'm doing what I'm told for once."

Finn soon felt she had spent her whole life in the little bow-fronted shop round the corner from the main square in Ramalley.

"You were right," she remarked in surprise to her boss. "It's so easy to pick up and it's fun as well, I didn't expect that."

He gave his lazy, dozy grin as he squinted down at the joint he was smoking and nodded.

"Told you, di'n' I?"

Finn smiled, then had a thought. "Hadn't you better get rid of that?" She indicated his cigarette. "What if somebody comes in and tells the police?"

"What? A raid? In Ramalley? You seen their Drug Squad? One fat old bloke used to go round the schools when I was a kid, they give him this job to see him out to his pension and they called it Drugs just to get some funding. You gotta be joking, they're all too busy faffing about parking in the Square and bumps on the bypass."

His name was Hedgehog.

Why? Because, he said when she asked, and he took off the bobble hat and showed her. His hair stood up on end, brown and bristly with blond tips.

"Um, yes, I see what you mean."

She stared frankly at him, seeing also the small black eyes and undeniably tapering snouty nose.

"Actually," she pointed out. "I think you look more like Eddie Munster."

He was delighted with the comparison.

"Pity you di'n't turn up years ago," he mourned. "Coulda bin called Eddie instead of Hedgehog."

"It's going really well," she reported to Julia. "I thought I'd be bored out of my mind working in a shop after the stress of my last job, but it's fun. Lots of interesting people and I get to play with the goodies. We've just got in a consignment of CDs of West African chants, and Hedgehog and I sit and drone away for hours. Oh yes, and I've seen that guy every lunch time, you know? Bonnie Prince Charlie? I know he recognises me but he stalks past with his nose in the air and pretends he hasn't seen me."

Ten days later she turned up at work and immediately found herself embroiled in an episode of the on-going protest about the shop, organised by the congregation of the chapel back in the Square.

"Used to be the Primitive Methodist chapel," Hedgehog told her as they cleaned the graffiti off the shop window. "Now it's them Primitive Wimmen they got in there." He guffawed and shook his head in amused tolerance. "They're Bible thumpers and a load of daft old biddies, most of them, but that cow that's their leader, she gets right on my tits."

Scrubbing away at the words *God will get you where it hurts*, Finn could only agree and when she met the leader of the God's Glory Mission she saw exactly what Hedgehog meant.

Well-established in the shop now she was running errands all over town and after a trip to the stationers she turned the corner into Paradise Row to be met at the shop door by a stranger.

"You poor, poor creature," a voice oozing sympathy broke into Finn's murmured apology for trying to squeeze past her. "So now that fiend of Satan has got an innocent woman in his clutches, while I've been away on holiday, has he?"

Finn stared at the woman now confronting her across the counter. Small, neatly dressed, pretty and prim, the chapel leader was gazing at her with melting concern.

"Go now, my dear, while you have the chance," she urged but before Finn could reply Hedgehog surged into the shop from the store at the back.

"Out! Out now, you interfering old cow! If I have to call the police again you'll be for it!"

To Finn's surprise the woman went, pausing only for a hasty call on the Lord to witness her trials on His behalf and to intercede with Finn and show her the way of righteousness. "Ask him why he was arrested," was her final suggestion.

"Meddlesome old cow." Steam was coming out of Hedgehog's ears and Finn brought him a cup of tea to calm him down. "Ta. Oh, I know I shouldn't get so riled up but she drives me bonkers. Still, she knows I mean it about the police, she's had a warning, so I expect she'll lay off for a while."

"So?" Finn looked at him curiously. "Why *were* you arrested, Hedge?"

"Load of bollocks," he snorted contemptuously. "I was in this pub one night — this was in my drinking days when I was still married — and this tart says to me, I bet you gotta big todger, Hedgehog. And her and her friends kept on and on about it, so I ups and unzips me fly and plonks it on the table in front of her." He grinned reminiscently. "You shoulda heard the screeching and bugger me if the silly tart didn't go and complain to the cops. Never came to court, mind you, they got more sense, just told me not to do it again." He winked at her as he said, "One good thing come out of it, the wife up and left because of it, so I was safely divorced by the time I had that lottery win, or she'd have got her claws in it."

He drank his tea and began to look happier but his hand went to his pocket and he shot Finn a look of sly amusement. "Go on, girl, best light up the incense burners a bit, I gotta calm my nerves."

She raised her eyebrows but complied and the scent of bergamot filled the room while Hedgehog rolled his own.

"Oh don't worry, girl," he grinned as he lit up. "I told you t'other day I don't do nothing heavy, not nowadays, I just like a bit of wacky baccy, just the odd puff, y'know?"

54

"Fine," she shrugged and drank her own tea. "So I'll look after the shop for you when we *are* raided by the Ramalley drug squad and you get sent down, shall I?"

Back at the house Julia and her cohorts soon had Finn's new studio flat in shape. Jonathan Barlow slid out of his back door whenever he could get away from the voice that never stopped even in his sleep, and he soon had a small electric cooker installed and working, along with a fridge-freezer, both of which Finn had spotted advertised in the local paper. Delia Muncaster offered the redundant washing machine from her cottage, left behind by the previous owners, and a plumber was imported, at Finn's expense, to install a shower and loo.

Mellowed by dicing with danger, risking a raid by Ramalley's finest, Hedgehog decided to knock off early and leave Finn to lock up.

She was curled up in the peacock chair peacefully reading a book about auras when the shop bell rang and she looked up to see the chapel leader bearing purposefully down on her.

"I'm sorry, Mrs er um . . . Madam, you know you're not supposed to be in here," she stammered. Pity Hedgehog hadn't given her some idea of how to get rid of unwanted Christians, lions and gladiators having gone out of fashion.

"Nothing is allowed to stand in the way of the Lord's work," came the proud reply, followed by the more mundane, "Hurry up, I've got a bus to catch. Where is that employer of yours? Out buying more of his sinful rubbish, I suppose?"

"He's gone home, and that's where I shall be going in a few minutes. Can I help you at all?"

"You can go down on your knees and pray to the Lord for forgiveness for conniving with that devil creature in letting this sink of iniquity loose on the town."

"Sorry," Finn shrugged. "I'm only the shop assistant, you'll have to take it up with Hedgehog."

"Shop assistant? Shop assistant?" The other woman's face turned an alarming shade of crimson and her voice grew shrill with triumph. "You poor deluded sinner. Don't you know that assistant is only an anagram for *Satanists*? Please," the sudden descent from rant to reasoning was unnerving. "Please, come with me to the Chapel and let us pray for your soul."

"No." Finn was getting fed up now, it was no longer a joke, and there was never a lion around when you needed one. "I can't do that, it's against my religion."

"What? I don't believe it, what is your religion then?"

"I belong to the Church of the Quivering Brethren," declared Finn stoutly.

"There's no such thing," the chapel spokeswoman said flatly, obviously not a great reader.

"Oh yes there is," chimed in a new voice. "Several members of my family belong to it and I can vouch for Miss Fitzgerald, she's an upstanding member of the congregation, does the flowers, quivers in the choir, all that sort of thing. Now, do let me show you out."

56

Finn stared open-mouthed as Charlie Stuart politely but inexorably swept the unwelcome visitor to the door, locked it behind her and turned round the Closed sign.

"Whew! Thanks a lot, I didn't know how to get rid of her, short of physical violence. I'm surprised to see you here, though?" She shot him a sceptical look and wasn't surprised to see that he showed signs of embarrassment, mixing uneasily with his customary glower.

"Yeah, well, I'm not surprised you're surprised." His sudden grin was disarming, lightening his face dramatically. Finn felt a familiar ripple somewhere around her diaphragm and hastily forced herself to consider insanity. "I came in to apologise to you, for yelling and being rude."

"Apology accepted," she said graciously, noticing, in spite of being off men, the laughter lines in his face and the way his thick, dark hair flopped forward over his right eye. "What changed your mind?"

"Pa set me right," he admitted. "He told me who you were. Julia's sister, right? The Irish lady? She's always seemed the only sane one of that crew Pa hangs out with and I thought you were probably like her."

"That's big of you," she sniffed. Sane was probably a relative term, she considered, when used by a man whose father thought he was the rightful king of England, but she knew what he meant.

"Look," hesitant and even more embarrassed, he ignored her sarcasm. "How about coming out for a drink, you can shut the shop, can't you?"

"OK," she said. "We'll call it quits. Besides, Julia borrowed my car, hers needed a new exhaust, and I was going to get the bus tonight. So, what shall we do, to celebrate our freedom? Do you want to go clubbing or something?"

"In *Ramalley?*"

His mock horror made her giggle.

"If that's what you want you'll have to make do with the Reno which is the under-age drugs dive or the Working Men's Institute where they still have club comedians. What I actually had in mind was a drink at the White Horse, or is that not cosmopolitan enough for you?"

"It'll do for a start."

Over their drinks they compared career notes and Charlie raised his eyebrows at the number of false starts Finn confessed to.

"You obviously like variety," he commented mildly.

"No," she snapped. "I didn't want to settle down when I was in my twenties, so I travelled all over, and since then I just have a stupid habit of falling for men I work with. You know how most places are these days, no relationships with colleagues? It just always seems to be me who ends up leaving."

"OK, OK," he held up his hands in surrender. "Don't shoot. Did I say anything? Is that what happened this time?"

Recalling her bare-faced blackmail she had the grace to blush as she shrugged and refused to answer, looking sidelong at him. What was that about a scandal with his wife? Julia had said something or other, hadn't she?

"Enough about me," she said firmly. "What about you? You're married?"

"No!" The denial was explosive and she stared at him.

"Sorry, I thought my sister said something about a wife," she said mildly.

"No," he was less vehement but definitely upset. "No wife, no marriage. And I don't want to talk about it," he warned as an afterthought.

Finn raised her eyebrows but didn't pursue the question.

"When you say Julia's gang are weird," she changed the subject tactfully, "how did you mean? How weird exactly?"

He grinned sheepishly. "You mean as opposed to being completely sane and thinking you're the direct descendant of the Stuarts and heir to the throne? Weirder than that?"

"Uh-huh, I presume you don't want to go down that particular road, do you?"

He shook his head in rueful amusement.

"My father is — well, he's himself and there's nobody like him but no, I don't feel up to discussing that one, either. Mind you, sometimes I get the feeling that he just does it to wind me up, God knows why. Anyway," he leaned back, relaxed, with long legs stretched out in front of him. "Tell me about you and Julia. Is she really your sister? She must be a lot older?"

"Simple enough," she told him. "The family moved to England when Dad got a job in London and I was a surprise afterthought when Julia'd not long turned thirteen. When Mum and Dad died Julia took me over and mothered me. That's why she's got an Irish accent and I've no trace of one."

"I don't know," he gave her a considering look. "Just occasionally, there's something in your voice, rather like singing." He drained his glass and tilted his head. "What about dinner? I know it's a bit early but I'm hungry, how about you?"

"Why not? I'll just give Julia a ring. We're supposed to be independent but she was muttering something about fish when I left for work. I'd better let her know."

As she explained to Julia, Finn was aware that Charlie Stuart was trying to conceal a grin and when she rang off he stopped trying and laughed out loud at her.

"What?"

"You and me," he chuckled. "Tied to their apron strings. Hang on while I call Pa and remind him there's cold ham and salad in the fridge."

Over dinner in the only Chinese restaurant in Ramalley that served edible food they furthered their acquaintance, finding tastes in common. Travel was a theme in both their lives and Charlie, too, had spent years as an ex-pat, working for oil companies in the Middle East. They both loved the cinema but hated art house movies, sang along loudly to any tune going, adored animals and shared reminiscences of games at school.

"I liked sports," Charlie told her. "It was just the Games Master and his Sergeant Major tactics. Once I got to Oxford I enjoyed it. My mother used to tell everyone I was an Oxford rugby Blue but she lied. I played for the reserve team that backed up the reserve team."

She noticed, with interest, that Charlie seemed to be enjoying himself, his expression lightening and deep dimples appearing in his cheeks. She was gradually realising that the lowering dark scowl disguised a deep vein of shyness.

"We were talking about Julia's weird friends, earlier on," she said, shifting direction. *What am I thinking? None of my business if he loosens up or stays an anal retentive for the rest of his life.* "If we discount your father who, although seriously eccentric, is an absolute sweetie —" She stopped to allow his ironic bow of thanks. "Yes, well. So far I've met Rosemary who seems quite sensible, though lumbered with her mother who definitely qualifies as weird."

She described her first meeting with Margot Delaney and agreed with Charlie that whatever their own relatives might get up to, at least it was preferable to public nudity and incontinence.

"Have you met Miss Buchanan?" he asked, pouring her another glass of Merlot. "No, go on, somebody's got to drink this and I'm driving."

"Is she the little furry one?" Finn was aware that the wine was beginning to get to her. *Must be mixing with the fumes from Hedgehog's puff* she thought, mildly confused and increasingly conscious of an unwilling attraction to the man opposite her. *Remember Luc*, she told herself, *and your broken heart, you're not a teenager for God's sake.* But Luc's image was fading as fast as her orgy of grief over him had done.

"That's the one, she lives with her sister or something; an old dragon, apparently, who bullies Ursula. I think there's some story or other about Miss B, some kind of injury in the war. I know she's not — not quite right, but she's harmless. Anyway, according to Pa she announced recently that she's started getting visits from an angel."

"What? That's seriously weird! Anything else? Anybody think they're Napoleon? That old Polish guy would do for that, I should imagine, he was bossing Julia about when they shifted furniture."

She described the new living arrangements at Forge Cottage and Charlie was loud in his envy.

"You're so lucky! I can't wait for Pa to move over to the Old Parsonage. It's like being a kid, having to explain where you're going and making sure you aren't late or he'll start to worry. Not to mention worrying about him in case he has another fall or breaks his other hip or something."

"When's he likely to move?" Finn was sympathetic, grateful to Julia for the way she had so enthusiastically leapt on to the idea of converting the garage. Although she had laughed in fellow feeling with Charlie about ringing her sister, tonight had been a one-off, the arrangement was working well.

"Not more than four weeks tops," he said hopefully. "They exchanged contracts on the flat the day before yesterday so it's just a question of waiting. Anyway, about the Gang or whatever they call themselves, have you any idea what they're up to? I'm worried in case they might be getting up to something illegal, don't ask me what?"

"What?" she asked automatically and grinned as he laughed in response. "Notice I didn't immediately say you're imagining it, because Ju's been unaccountably shifty about the Gang herself. But illegal? What makes you think that?"

"It's hard to say," Charlie's screwed his face up in exasperation and she felt another flash of sympathy, then the dark face lightened in that rare, gleaming smile and she felt, yet again, a ripple of excitement that was only too familiar. Oh no, once more she spoke to herself firmly, not again, you've scarcely drawn breath since you found out about Luc. You are definitely not falling for this one, Fionnuala Fitzgerald, he's moody, screwed-up and probably believes all that Pretender stuff in spite of what he says, just what you don't need.

Oh come on, replied her inner self, the wimpy, eager-to-please one, the one who believed so strenuously in happy-ever-after, think what he's had to put up with by all accounts? Julia said his mother was ill for years and now he's worried about his dad, that's not much fun. And what's the story about a wife, hmm? Something very wrong there.

"Finn? *Finn?* Are you all right?" Charlie Stuart was trying to catch her attention, an increasingly irritable expression on his face. "You OK?" he repeated as she came to. "The wine hasn't gone to your head, has it?"

"Of course it hasn't," she snapped, then smiled sheepishly. "I'm fine, just thinking about something stupid. Look at the time, I think I'd better be getting home now."

They divided the bill scrupulously between them, exchanging suddenly shy smiles as they walked to the car. The car journey back to Bychurch was rather silent until Charlie drew up at Forge Cottage.

"Can we do this again?" he said, eagerness and diffidence mingled in his tone.

"I'd like that," she said, aware that she was blushing like a teenager.

"Good," he said. "I'll drop by the shop tomorrow."

Still awkward and diffident he reached out an arm and pulled her towards him.

As kisses went it was just what she might have expected from a man like Charlie Stuart; firm, warm and full of urgency. After her first startled gasp she found herself responding in kind, melting into his arms and kissing him right back, their bodies nestling together, fitting — oh God, not again! — fitting as though they were meant for each other.

CHAPTER
FIVE

Julia called an emergency meeting of the Gang to be convened at Forge Cottage, rather than their customary meeting place at Rosemary's bungalow, Church View. Today however was one of Margot's Day Centre visits and Rosemary was only too glad to get out of the house.

"It's getting worse," she confided to Julia as they set out cups and biscuits before the others turned up in their usual dribs and drabs. "She's started playing with matches."

"Oh Christ!" Julia's cry of sympathy was heartfelt.

"Uh-huh," the other woman's voice was dull with despair. "Luckily I caught her, but I'm bloody terrified, Julia! What if she tries that at night? We could be fried alive."

"You've *got* to tell that social worker woman," Julia urged firmly. "They need to know what you're up against, Margot's a menace to herself as well as you. In the meantime, coffee's not strong enough for this kind of thing, here, get a slug of scotch down you and I'll join you so you don't feel like a lush."

Just then the doorbell rang and the rest of the club began to arrive so Rosemary blew her nose, wiped her eyes and downed her drink with a nod of gratitude to her friend.

"Right," announced Julia when they were all settled. "I've got some brochures here and you can take a look at them in a minute. I'll just let you have the gist of it as a start and we can have a discussion when I've done."

She picked up one of the colourful, glossy brochures and smiled faintly as she noticed Ursula Buchanan gazing with wistful yearning at the photographs of brilliant blue sky, turquoise sea, white sand and glorious, technicolour flowers.

"Everybody with me?" Julia counted heads, all nodding, in Ursula's case involuntarily with her slight tremor. "OK, well, Rosemary and I have trawled through the holiday brochures and the internet — now, you *did* all say you wanted to go to the Caribbean, didn't you? — and Rosemary's found a low season special offer, two weeks for a smidgen under £1600 each.

"I know, I know," she held up her hand at the murmur of dismay that filled the room. "It's a hell of a lot of money for each of us to find, but that's the point, isn't it? That's what we said right from the first?"

It had been the night Finn descended on her, Julia recalled, that she and Rosemary had challenged the others to come up with something to enliven the Gang's existence. Ursula Buchanan had made the first, and only, suggestion, all other, unarticulated, ideas paling into insignificance at the daring and grandeur of her idea.

66

"There's something I've always wanted to do," Ursula had announced, in her fluffy, woolly voice, peering round anxiously at the rest when she realised she held the floor. Meeting nothing but encouragement and a measure of relief that someone, anyone, had something to say, she went on. "I'd like to do something completely self-indulgent. I've always longed for real heat, real sunshine, to feel like a castaway on a desert island, but a luxury one, all mod cons. I've always wanted to go scuba dancing."

There had been a moment of pure, silent astonishment, Julia recalled now.

"Oh, scuba diving!" Rosemary, trying desperately not to laugh, was gushing instead. "How marvellous, what a brilliant idea, Ursula."

"I couldn't afford to go *really*," Ursula warned, pleased with the success of her venture. "It's only a dream."

The babble of voices had assured her that it was a marvellous dream and one that most of them shared, now it was dangled in front of them, but again and again came the same comment, regretful but resigned, no, they couldn't afford to go to the Caribbean either, and yes please, would Julia and Rosemary look into it.

Now, Julia held up her hand again.

"Look, it doesn't *have* to be the West Indies. We could have a marvellous holiday in the Mediterranean somewhere, the Greek Islands maybe, Malta, or Majorca. It must be possible to find somewhere that does scuba diving."

"Well, some of us can afford it," Delia Muncaster's clear voice cut through the noise. "Let's see how many that is, then we can try to find ways of raising the money so the rest can come too."

"I don't know," Julia was still extremely doubtful. "We really ought to look for something cheaper, it's a ludicrous amount of money."

No. They were united in dismissing the idea and were already devouring the brochures. Surprisingly, it was Jonathan Barlow who voiced the group's feeling.

"It won't do, I'm afraid," he said stoutly, even as he shivered in his shoes at his own audacity. "You see, it's only a holiday to some of you, albeit an exciting one, but to the rest of us it's the fulfilment of a dream, an adventure we would never otherwise dare to imagine, still less actually achieve. If it's humanly possible, that's where we want to go." His sad spaniel eyes gazed at them all. "I haven't dared to dream for more than forty years," he said.

He sat down to loud cheers from the others and Julia yielded gracefully, holding up a hand to cut short the buzz of excitement.

"How can we argue with that?" She smiled at Jonathan and carried on. "Let's do a count, shall we? Remember, we're talking here about a *luxury* holiday and that's the price for July; naturally it's even more expensive in the winter when everyone wants to get away from the cold. How many of us think they can raise the cash? And how many know they can't? No false modesty now," she warned. "We're all in this together, don't forget. If we go ahead we must all agree to join in the fund-raising even if we have the fare ourselves, it's a group effort or it's nothing."

She counted hands. She herself, Delia, Jamie, Sue Merrill, pitifully few of them who could cough up the total amount. Rosemary stood up, slightly pink and apologetic.

"I can raise just on half of that amount," she said bravely. "If I hadn't spent so much on the bungalow it wouldn't be a problem but I'm having to draw my horns in for the next year, to make sure I don't get in a mess, and eight hundred is the absolute top I can manage."

She looked round the group and found only sympathy and in several cases relief at her frankness. "I expect some of the rest of you are in pretty much the same boat, aren't you?"

"I can contribute about five hundred pounds." Marek was very stiff, very formal, obviously hating any admission of weakness.

"Oh dear." Jonathan Barlow was wringing his hands in embarrassment. "I would so love to go, but I don't know what Pauline would . . . No," he straightened himself and spoke with obvious determination. "I'm sure I can put down three hundred, that's definite, and with a bit of jiggling about I could probably scrape up another two later on, but that's the limit, I'm afraid."

Julia smiled kindly at him and he sat down, comforted.

Bobbie took heart from the foregoing conversations and stood up eagerly, hands gripping the table in front of her, eyes wide with excitement.

"Me too," she whispered. "I mean, I know I can put down five hundred, and it might be more, it depends how long we have to save up. If you're talking about July and it's now early October, that means there's about nine months, doesn't it?"

Ursula Buchanan stood up, as usual scattering her belongings about her, a scarf here, handbag there.

"Oh dear," she twittered. "I seem to be the only one who can't pay anything at all. I only have my old age pension and there isn't much left after I pay Henrietta for my keep."

"*What?*"

"You're *kidding?*"

"Oh come *on*, you can't be serious?"

There was an outcry at her remark. Rosemary looked carefully at the older woman to make sure she wasn't fantasising. No, the doughy face looked just the same as usual, except that it sagged with disappointment.

"Let's get this straight, Ursula," she said gently, waving a peremptory hand at the rest. "Do you honestly mean you have to pay your board and lodging to your sister-in-law? But surely she ought to be paying *you*, as her housekeeper? That's monstrously unfair, you really mustn't do such a thing."

Ursula Buchanan's hand shot to her mouth in terror.

"Oh goodness, dear, I can't argue with Henrietta! She would be most distressed and the doctor says she must be treated with extreme delicacy lest any upset bring on a stroke or a heart attack. And it is most kind of her to give me a home, you know, most kind."

Seeing her obvious distress Julia motioned for quiet and changed the direction of the discussion.

"All right, settle down for now. We'll talk about that some other time. What it boils down to is that there are nine of us and we can only manage to pay something like half the amount needed, so we need to rustle up an additional five thousand, nine hundred pounds!"

She sat down rather quickly and drew her coffee mug towards her. You might as well say five million, she thought despondently. Then she looked up as Rosemary Clavering stood up, clutching a sheaf of notes.

"It's not *all* doom and gloom," she announced hopefully. "Sorry, Julia, I didn't have time to fill in all the details earlier. For a start, it's a resort hotel, that means it's all-inclusive, paid for up front so there are no other costs unless you want to go on outside excursions. Then, there are only nine of us and if we could find three other people to join in, particularly if they could pay their way — in fact they'd *have* to be able to pay their way. If we could get them we could call ourselves a group and this company here has a special offer for the later holidays, when the weather is likely to be unsettled, short bursts of torrential — but still hot — rain. It has to be before the school holidays start though, so we're looking at the very beginning of July. I know it's an awful lot of money but actually it's a very good price, you know; it's a new hotel and a new company and they're prepared to do special deals, offer last minute prices even this far in advance if we book now. They offer one free holiday for the group leader, but the group must consist of twelve people in total. More free holidays if there are more people, obviously, but that needn't concern us."

She was talking eagerly, trying to press the point home.

"Don't you see?" she urged. "If we get those three extra people, we can cut down the outstanding balance, then all we have to find is something under four thousand pounds and, as Bobbie says, we've got nine months. It isn't impossible."

Her voice faltered a little on that last wildly optimistic note and she sat down to the accompaniment of muted applause.

Jamie Stuart took the floor now, bowing with his customary grace towards his hostess, Julia, who considered, for the umpteenth time, how astonishing it was that a man of his age should still be so sexy. I don't know though, she sidetracked herself, look at Prince Philip, I bet the Queen knows how lucky she is. I wish he and I could . . . oh well.

"Delia, Ursula, and I have already put some thought into the matter," James Stuart explained. "We anticipated something of the sort, in fact it was obvious that we wouldn't raise the whole sum straight away. We've come up with a few ideas as a start."

"Yes," Ursula interrupted eagerly. "Jumble sales and Bring and Buy sales, then maybe a raffle? And with Christmas coming up we ought to do quite well."

She sat down smiling complacently and Julia's heart sank at the thought of disillusioning the poor creature.

72

"That's all very well," she began gently and Rosemary nodded too, reluctantly. "But, Ursula, we can't go around raising funds for West Indian holidays for ourselves! Think about it, nobody in their right minds would give us any money for something like that."

"I'm not stupid, my dear," Ursula responded with hurt dignity, looking round in appeal for support, which came at once in the form of an encouraging nod from Jamie. "I know that. What we thought was that we should announce our fund-raising as being for the Old Folks." She spoke in obvious capitals, and continued in the face of their stunned silence. "What we need to do is call ourselves something official-sounding, Evergreens or something similar, and say we're collecting to give older people some comforts. Apart from Sue and Bobbie we *are* Old Folks, and it's perfectly true," she added defensively. "It would certainly be a great comfort to *me*!"

To her surprise Julia and Rosemary, after a moment of total, shocked amazement at the audacity of the idea, burst into hysterical giggles and collapsed together on the fat settee under the front window. Sue Merrill, who usually wore an expression of extreme gloom, cast a scandalised eye at them as she exclaimed, "But that's immoral!" Then, as Julia agreed, saying, "Of course it is," she gave a wry grin, which was followed by a guffaw from Jamie. Bobbie let loose a timid tee-hee and Marek uttered a series of short barks, presumably denoting mirth. There was even an outbreak of her characteristic cackle from Delia Muncaster who was seated in the big armchair, snuggled up in close companionship beside the sherry bottle.

Only Jonathan and Ursula herself looked bewildered.

"It's *brilliant!*" Julia assured them. She and Rosemary had conducted a rapid whispered discussion on whether the plan was actually illegal, dishonest or just blatantly immoral and decided, in view of the general approval, to shelve their scruples for the time being. "Utterly and completely brilliant, though whether it would come off is another matter. But of course you're right, with Christmas on the horizon, nobody will be able to resist helping out the Poor Old Folks! What should we call ourselves? I'm not too struck on Evergreens, I must say."

"Me neither," agreed Rosemary, still chuckling in spite of her misgivings. "Any ideas, Gang?"

Ever happy to be distracted from the really serious matter in hand, namely the problem of finding a) three other like-minded and well-heeled holiday makers and b) the small matter of nearly four thousand pounds, which a jumble sale or two would hardly make a dent in, and c) the prospect of ending up in the Scrubs on a fraud charge, the Gang got down to business and the question was debated loud and long.

"I know." It was Delia Muncaster, tipping up the now almost empty bottle of Tio Pepe. "Let's call ourselves *Hope Springs.* You know the quotation?" She looked round at the rest of them and sighed as she registered several blank faces. "Hope springs eternal in the human breast."

They adopted it with enthusiasm and, in Julia's case, a certain amount of relief. She had been having difficulty in steering Bobbie away from her treasured suggestion: the Joy Luck Club, or her alternative, The Good Time Gang.

It was lunch time and the group was getting restive. Jonathan Barlow was fretting about giving Pauline her lunch and Ursula was twisting her hands as she worried about Henrietta, who could be more than usually unpleasant if her food was not on time.

"I'll have to go," Sue Merrill gathered up her bag and headed for the door. "I've a meeting in half an hour. Let me know what you decide, I can manage the first week in July, but not earlier," she warned. "I'll go along with anything you want, just hand me the rubber stamp. What about extra people though?"

At the sitting room door she nodded to Julia as a thought struck her.

"You could always ask your sister, of course," she suggested. "And isn't Jamie's son around too? Do they know each other? If they get on all right they might like the chance. At least they know our set-up, they might not mind tagging along in exchange for a cheap holiday."

Eventually Rosemary and Delia Muncaster were the only members of the group left at Forge Cottage. Julia raised her eyebrows at her friend and gave a tiny nod towards the predatory creature communing with Julia's own sherry bottle.

"How about a spot of lunch?" Rosemary rose to the occasion. "I could rustle us up a salad if you'd care to come across the green?"

Julia hastened to offer lunch on her own behalf too but both were waved aside by Delia who uncrossed her elegant, stick-thin legs with their amazingly long, bony feet encased in Manolo Blahnik pumps. She stood up, shrugging on her pink wool coat, very Jackie Kennedy, thought Julia in admiration, and arranging the matching pillbox hat on her glossy, blow-dried, improbably black chignon.

"Nonsense," Delia announced. "You two will come to the pub with me and we'll form a sub-committee of three, the sub-committee that actually gets things done instead of waffling about it all day."

They were greeted with smiles and nods all round at the pub, while Delia's reception was more in the nature of a royal one. News of the size of her final bar bill had flashed round the village like wildfire when she moved into her own house a fortnight ago after long delays: no wonder the landlord was almost on bended knee to her.

"Uh-oh," Rosemary backed precipitously out of the Lounge Bar. "Bandits at three o'clock! Let's go into the Public Bar, quick, before she sees us."

"But do you all get along OK?" Finn had asked Julia when she heard about the Gang. "It sounds a weird mix, don't they fight sometimes?"

"Not any more," Julia grinned. "But we did have to filter out a few oddballs."

The second meeting of the new social group had been held, like the first, in the garden of the pub, a week after the inauguration. This time their numbers were swelled by first two, then a third extra, all elderly women at sight of whom Julia sighed. It would be so nice to have more younger members, she'd never meant it to be a retirement club.

"I like knitting and bingo," one of the women said with a sweet smile, placing herself firmly beside Jamie Stuart and gazing up into his startled dark eyes. "My husband passed on five years ago and I like to keep myself busy. Mother, he told me just before he died, remember to keep yourself busy. Will you be having your meetings in the village hall from now on?"

"Er, no." Julia found herself deputed to answer this. "We thought we would move around a bit, use our own houses, those of us who can take a crowd, go out to dinner, the theatre, that sort of thing." Didn't you read the notice, she thought, it was set out pretty clearly.

"Oh dear, no I wouldn't want that." 'Mother' spoke with decision, wound up her wool and stashed it into her knitting bag. "I can't have people tracking dirt in. I'll bid you goodnight."

Julia caught Rosemary's eye and raised her eyebrows, but at that moment the third newcomer waddled out into the garden, stared round at the assembled company and plonked herself down on a folding chair that buckled under her weight. She cast a considering look at each member of the group then addressed herself to Delia.

"I'll have a Snowball," she announced. "Then I'll see if I want to join your club."

Apparently hypnotised by surprise Delia obediently trotted off to do her bidding, returning with a large gin of her own to help her over the shock. The stranger inspected the cherry on the cocktail stick, nodded approval and sipped at her drink.

In the meantime "Mother" had swollen up like a cat with its fur on end. She marched round the tables and hoicked out the remaining newcomer.

"This is no place for us," she said dramatically. "If you lot are going to be friends with *her*, you'll have to do without *us*."

"But what was the matter with her?" Finn was intrigued. "She's not still a member of your lot, is she?"

"No fear!" Julia shuddered with heartfelt gratitude. "But we had a hell of a job getting rid of her. We found out she'd been thrown out of the WI, the Mothers' Union, the Townswomen's Guild and everything else like that. She's got a poisonous tongue, you see. And *she* wanted bingo too, and expected us to organise outings, even though we'd laid it out, right from the start, that we weren't talking about that kind of club. We all tried, we really did, but it was clear all the time that she wasn't going to gel. For one thing, we all agreed that we'd use first names, but she told us her name was Mrs Parsons and she wouldn't budge. People who've lived in the village for years, you know, Jonathan and Ursula and Bobbie, were getting very nervous whenever she hove in sight, and Marek had a stand-up row with her — it ended in a draw! In the end Jamie came up with the solution. Somehow or other she let slip that she was eighty-four so he told her, very sweetly and kindly, that he was very sorry but we'd set an upper age limit of seventy-five. I think Delia actually shoved her hand over Marek's mouth to shut him up when he tried to protest — he's seventy-eight and he thought he was going to be chucked out."

Hoping they hadn't been spotted, the newly-formed subcommittee scuttled into the Public Bar and gave their order in a whisper. Under the astonished gaze of the other two, Delia knocked back what looked like a quadruple gin with a solitary bottle of tonic. "Now then, this special offer you've dug up, Rosemary. There must be *some* hidden costs? Excursions, you said, and food? Drinks?"

"There aren't any, honestly," Rosemary explained, tucking into her sandwich and mumbling rather thickly. "It's a fantastic deal, like I said. They're pushing a new hotel, it only opened last week, so they said they'd give us this reduced price if we booked now.

"It's ideal for a group like ours, with disparate incomes, I mean. It really *is* all-inclusive," she continued. "That means everything including drink. In fact the only thing you can't have is alcohol by the bottle. It's all right," she said hastily as Delia pursed her lips ominously "You can have as many glasses as you like, just not a bottle. You could always commandeer a bucket, Delia, and pour the drinks in it."

"Are you implying that I drink, my dear?" Delia flashed her wolfish grin. "Right-oh, that's the main worry off my mind. Now, what about this idea of booking the holiday? What kind of deposit are they after? Ten per cent?"

Rosemary nodded, gloomily.

"Cheer up, I'll divvy up," offered Delia casually. "No skin off my nose, that old blackguard left me extremely comfortable and I love the idea of spending his money on something he would have hated so bitterly."

The other two blinked at this but accepted the offer with gratitude.

"Another thing we need to do," said Julia, downing her own modest gin. "We must set up a building society account or something similar and pay into it all the available money as a start, then add to it as and when."

"We'll need somebody to keep tabs on the cash," suggested Rosemary anxiously. "Just don't let it be me, I'm not good at book-keeping."

"Bobbie might agree to do it," put in Julia thoughtfully. "I know she's very diffident about her abilities but I happen to know she ran the accounts for the whole Ramalley Division Guides and Brownies; did it for years. They're really fed up that she's given up but she insisted. If she couldn't be Brown Owl any more she wanted out completely. I think she'd be really chuffed to be asked."

The idea was voted a winner by the unofficial subcommittee and then Delia broached a very delicate subject with her usual sledgehammer brand of tact.

"We'd better write in some regulation to cover death," she said, waving an imperious hand to the barman who sped over with more iron rations. "Well," she stared at their astonishment. "We're knocking on, some of us, after all. What happens if somebody pops their clogs before the trip? The whole damn thing would be loused up, wouldn't it? You've been dealing

80

with the travel company, Rosemary, you'd better ask them about group insurance and things. And if it's a new hotel we don't want to find our cash going down the drain if the place goes belly-up."

Rosemary obediently made a note.

At that point they were interrupted by Mrs Parsons who pushed her face round the door.

"You got round to organising bingo yet?" she asked, mildly, then she answered herself. "Course you haven't, bunch of snobs. You just want to catch yourselves a man, that's all you started it for. Well, you'll be lucky, I tell you, daft old bags!"

Delia pursed her lips as the old woman made her exit, laughing loudly at her own wit.

"And what about these three like-minded, congenial people," Delia said, without further comment. "These people who will be happy to fork out more than a grand each for the privilege of spending two weeks in the Caribbean with an assorted bunch of eccentric pensioners — begging Sue and Bobbie's pardon?"

"You speak for yourself," grinned Julia. "I must say that until last night I wouldn't have thought about putting Finn together with Charlie Stuart, but guess what happened?"

The other two nodded sagely as she repeated Finn's guarded description of her dinner with Charlie.

"Hmm," Delia was sceptical. "One swallow does not a summer make — nor one dinner a romance. Julia, stop match-making!"

"Oh, I know," Julia shrugged defensively. "But she's had a rough time and so's Charlie. I know he can be moody and they got off to a bad start, but there — and he's so tall . . ."

"So?" Rosemary raised her eyebrows. "Does that matter so much?"

"Oh yes," Julia was definite. "You wouldn't know, you're only little, but believe me, when you're a really tall woman it's absolutely wonderful to be towered over by some man and don't bother telling me how sexist that is, I don't care. Oh, to be treated like a delicate little thing!"

"Is that what happened with you then, Julia?" Delia topped up her glass and leaned forward with interest.

"Sometimes," Julia sighed nostalgically. "The best lover I ever had was very, very tall, six foot five, in fact."

"You didn't feel any urge to make it a permanent relationship?" Rosemary asked with interest.

"Oh no," Julia shook her head. "I was forty and a twenty year age gap isn't ideal, is it? It was just a holiday fling, he was a lovely Swede I met in Majorca. But oh my, he had the most wonderful body I've ever seen in a man and believe me, I've seen plenty."

"Goodness." Delia was frankly envious. "Unfortunately I only ever slept with one man. It wasn't an inspirational experience and nobody's likely to want to have a fling with me now. But he must have been quite something, to have a body like that in his sixties?"

"Who said anything about sixties?" Julia's saucy grin should have alerted them.

"Well, come on, Julia," argued Rosemary. "You just told us you were forty so . . ." Her jaw dropped. "What? You mean he was only twenty?"

"Seventeen, actually," admitted Julia, preening. "But don't you dare let on to Finn, she doesn't need to know everything."

Amused at their scandalised expressions Julia gathered up her jacket and handbag ready to leave.

"Hold on a second," commanded Delia craning her elegantly long neck in the direction of the pub door. "I think I see a potential member of our merry band. See that chap just going up to the bar? Silver hair, smart cashmere overcoat?"

Ignoring Rosemary's dubious, "How do you know it's cashmere from this distance?" Delia hooted and waved until the stranger gave in and came towards them.

"Aha!" she announced, with a terrifying smile. "Just the person I wanted to see. Come and sit down with us for a minute or two. Girls, this is Hugh Taylor."

Introductions took place and the other two women took stock of Delia's captive.

Nice face, thought Rosemary, smiling shyly at him. Nice arse, Julia had noted as he put in his order at the bar.

"Hugh lives in the white house along the Ramalley road," explained Delia, patting his hand and making him look even more anxious. "Tell the girls about yourself, there's a good chap."

Hugh Taylor looked mutinous for a moment then caught Julia's eye and gave in with a good grace.

"How much detail do you want, Delia?" he demanded. "Size nine shoes? Collar size fifteen-and-a-half? No? Well then, I'm sixty-four, retired as managing director of the family firm near Swindon two years ago when my wife decided she wanted to move back to her roots in Hampshire."

There was an imperceptible sagging in his audience as Julia and Rosemary registered the presence of a wife, while Delia grinned maliciously.

"However, Joan died last year, I'm afraid, she had heart trouble, so I've been at a bit of a loose end since. I met Delia in the pub and we get together for a drink now and then."

"How have we never happened to bump into you?" asked Julia. "I know it sounds awful, but we're always in the pub! It's the village meeting place, after all."

"He didn't specify which pub," interrupted Delia. "I have a great many watering holes, though this is my particular favourite. No problem about driving here, you see. Now then, Hugh. I've mentioned our little group once or twice, how do you feel about coming along to a meeting to test the waters? Now, now," as he looked unconvinced. "Got to stop all this solitary drinking, you know. It's all very well for me, got a cast-iron liver, but you need taking out of yourself."

She looked around for her belongings.

"Right. You come with me, Julia, got something I want to discuss. You stay here, Rosemary, and entertain Hugh. Don't let him get pissed, he's like you, can't hold his drink. Come along, Julia."

"That's not fair!" remonstrated Julia as they emerged on to the sunny village green. "Why is Rosemary given a clear field? What about me? He's rather gorgeous, and available? It ought to be all's fair in love and war."

"Nonsense," Delia was firm. "Rosemary needs love and companionship and romance and that's exactly what Hugh needs. And it's right what I said, they're not drinkers, don't work hard enough at it. Now you, my girl, you don't want any of that mush, you've got Jamie and — don't interrupt, I know what you're going to say. All that's wrong with you and Jamie is that he needs Dutch courage and a good dose of Viagra. You don't want romance, whatever you think. What you need, my dear Julia, is sex and lots of it!"

CHAPTER
SIX

The next few days were action-packed. Rosemary found out about group insurance and had dinner with Hugh. Bobbie burst into floods of tears when the suggestion was put to her that she should become the bookkeeper for the group but she mopped herself up and accepted with becoming modesty, already murmuring about double-entry and checking out interest rates on savings accounts.

Finn and Charlie also went out to dinner again, at a pretty pub on the Salisbury road. And for a drink at lunch-time; to the cinema; another drink both lunch-time and evening; and for a brisk walk along the river into town where they shared a pizza before walking home, talking, talking, talking, laughing and squabbling as their friendship deepened. As he counted off the days to Jamie's removal to the Old Parsonage Charlie became increasingly cheerful and Finn kept catching glimpses of herself in the mirror, smiling. Without a word being spoken she knew that Charlie was looking forward to having an empty house, no inconvenient audience. The memory of Luc — Luc who? — was definitely no longer a problem. What she found interesting was this unusual reticence — unusual for her, at any rate.

I'm used to jumping into bed straight away with my latest grand passion, she mused over coffee one morning when the shop was bare of customers. I've no experience of this, I suppose it's what they used to call courtship; it's rather — nice.

A cautionary note was struck by Hedgehog, of all people.

"You're gettin' a bit serious, aren't you?" he commented one day as Finn danced into the shop after another blissful lunch with Charlie.

"So?" She was surprised at his interest, Hedgehog was the least interfering creature she'd ever come across.

"So," he inhaled lazily. "There was summat funny about him, wasn't there? Wife disappeared or summat like that. It was in the papers, I do know that, journalist came down from London, musta bin in the summer, not much proper news on, daft buggers."

"What do you mean, she disappeared?" Finn's voice was sharp and anxious.

"What I say. I don't remember the details, girl, it was in my bad old days."

Finn was unable to leave it alone. "You mean she — they thought she was *dead*?" Her voice rose in a squawk.

"I dunno," Hedgehog was clearly bored with the subject. "Probably did a runner, but it makes you think, dunnit? What kind of bloke is he, to have that happen?"

None of Finn's wheedling or nagging managed to elicit any further information so she shoved the problem to the back of her mind where it gnawed away. I can't ask Charlie, she fretted, and there's nobody else I can discuss it with. Julia doesn't know any details, though I suppose she *could* ask Jamie. No, I can't ask her to do that, and anyway, he might mention it to Charlie and I couldn't bear that. But I'll have to ask him as soon as it's feasible.

Asking Charlie anything soon became a remote possibility.

"Have you heard what those insane geriatrics are up to?" He burst into the shop — mercifully empty — the next afternoon.

"What?" She was almost frightened, his face was contorted with anger. "What do you mean? Are they all right? *Julia?*"

"All right?" He gave a bitter laugh and paced round the shop. "Of course they're all right, they're just fucking crazy. Didn't you know? I'll lay it out for you then: my father and your sister and the whole barking crew are raising funds to pay for a holiday for themselves — *themselves*, mind — in the West Indies! It's just a cover story, this business of collecting for the poor old folks."

"You're kidding?" Finn's immediate reaction was a disbelieving laugh which petered out as she saw his face. "But — I don't understand. How can they do that?"

"You might well ask." He ceased his pacing for a moment and shook his head. "Christ, if any word of this gets into the papers they'll be crucified."

"Oh, come *on*, Charlie," Finn's normal optimism reasserted itself. "Get this in proportion. Is what they're doing actually criminal? No, I don't believe it would be — they're not *that* stupid, or at least my sister isn't."

"And my father *is?* Thanks very much." He glared at her.

"Oh, for God's sake," she couldn't believe he could be so touchy. "Don't start on me, it's not my idea."

"I might have known you'd sympathise with them," he turned on his heel and stalked out of the shop, head down and shoulders hunched. "Charlie?" Finn shook herself out of her state of suspended animation and ran after him, but a knot of passers-by and a mini traffic jam concealed him from her view.

"Why is he taking it out on *me*, for God's sake? How can he blame *me*?" Anger began to bubble up at the injustice of Charlie's attitude and she spent the rest of the afternoon in a ferment and the evening alternating between anger and controlling her impulse to pick up the telephone and call him. "No, I won't," she announced to the walls of her flat. "*He's* the one who started this, *he* can get in touch to apologise."

Julia sulked for a day or so at Delia's high-handed interfering with regard to Hugh but her kind heart melted after only one glance at Rosemary's delicately balanced happiness, a welcome antidote to the grim determination radiating from her younger sister.

"Oh Julia!" Rosemary flitted in one morning, Margot safely despatched to the Day Centre. "It's wonderful, I can't believe it's happening to me." She shuddered. "I'm just waiting for something awful to happen."

"For goodness' sake." Julia sounded, and was, irritated. "Just enjoy yourself for once. How long is it since you had a relationship with a man? Ten years, didn't you say? Well then, lie back and enjoy it."

Rosemary had told her, soon after they became friends, about her long relationship with a married man. "He couldn't possibly get a divorce, he was a devout Catholic," she insisted.

She frowned when Julia, a lapsed Catholic herself, snorted, "Not that devout, if he had a mistress!"

It had gone on for fifteen years, from just after Rosemary's thirty-fifth birthday. "The usual thing," she said sadly. "You know, snatched meetings when his wife was away, a week once, wonderful but furtive, in Paris when he was there on business."

It had ended one morning as Rosemary called the register at school. His daughter, who was in Rosemary's class, was absent. "Anyone know if she's ill," Rosemary had asked casually. And then, in a babble of schoolgirl voices, she heard what had happened.

"A heart attack, Miss Clavering."

"Yes, her father, Miss Clavering, just dropped down dead yesterday on the golf course."

"And I had to go on taking the register," Rosemary told Julia. "I just said, Oh dear, how sad, and carried on."

Looking at her now Julia felt a moment's satisfaction in how far her friend had travelled in the last months.

90

"I *adored* him," Rosemary had told Julia. "He was the love of my life, I gave up the chance of having children to be with him and I've never, ever looked at another man and I know I *never* will."

Remembering the burning zeal of Rosemary's exasperating martyrdom Julia was too kind to remind her friend of this declaration. As for Delia's devastating analysis of Julia's own needs, she had to acknowledge the accuracy.

"Tell you what, Julia," Jamie told her that evening as they sat on Julia's sofa watching *Newsnight*. "Even though I have grave misgivings about Bobbie's impending initial fund-raiser — I mean, second childhood is one thing, but this is ridiculous! — I'll be damned glad to get out of Charlie's way. Roll on the Old Parsonage, he's like a bear with a sore head at the moment."

"I know, but Bobbie was so pleased with her plan and Delia — well, I reckon she's egging them on out of sheer mischief. Not to worry, it'll be fun. As for our dear young things, Finn's pretty difficult, too," Julia sympathised. "To do her justice she's a lot less puritanical about our little venture than your po-faced son but at the moment she's in such a temper with him, for blaming her, that she's impossible to deal with. The trouble is, of course, that they're not our dear *young* things. They've both been bruised over the years and they're just plain wary. I wish to goodness Charlie'd get his socks on and apologise to Finn, then we can all settle back down to peace and quiet."

"No chance of that happening at present," Jamie shrugged ruefully. "Charlie's right up there on his high horse, waving the flag of righteous indignation and anyone who's against him is taboo. My theory is much the same as yours, that he's protecting himself against any further hurt, but there's nothing much I can do, he won't listen."

He eased himself into a more comfortable position and smiled down at her. "Why are we worrying about them? They're supposed to be grown-up, after all. Let's talk about us instead. Do you realise that when I move into the Old Parsonage life will be a lot less restricting? No need to worry about Charlie upstairs, or Finn here at your place."

"But I thought . . ." Julia stammered to a halt. How, exactly, do you suggest to a man that you understood he had a problem with impotence, or erectile dysfunction as the adverts coyly put it?

"Ah!" He read her mind and grinned infuriatingly, giving her a hug. "That little problem will be sorted out by then. Not been able to bring myself to talk to the doc, but had a word with Finn's boss. You know? Hedgehog, they call him. Apparently he can get hold of all kinds of things."

Taking advantage of her astonishment he lunged at her, tackling her bra strap with a skill that also surprised her.

"Wow!" Julia was rosy and dishevelled, cuddled close in Jamie's arms after an extremely satisfying fifteen minutes. "If that's a sample of things to come, I'm all for it. What got into you, Jamie? I thought you were only interested in a platonic friendship? You've certainly never made a move on me before."

His satisfied smirk spoke volumes.

"I was playing hard to get," he boasted, idly stroking her breast. "Oh all right, I suppose I didn't want to risk not being able to function, and I didn't want to disappoint you, so I kept it strictly on a low level. But now — well, as I said, Hedgehog's going to help me out, though I'm not so sure I need it after all, and I think we can look forward to a new era."

Julia shrugged herself back into her clothes and fetched them both another drink, looking very thoughtful.

"What? What's the matter?" His face was crestfallen. "I thought you'd be pleased."

"Oh I *am*," she reassured him hastily. "You have no idea. Or at least, I suppose you have only too good an idea. It's not that, Jamie. It's just . . . Oh, Lord, I don't quite know how to put this."

She drew a breath and dived in. "You're right, I shall love it if we can get it together with some kind of sex life. Purely selfishly what we just did would be fine by me, but you need satisfaction too and if Viagra works, whoopee!"

"Well, then?"

"It's not that. Oh for heaven's sake, Jamie, it's this Old Pretender thing. If we're going to get involved to that extent I'm not putting up with you coming out with that rigmarole to every single soul you meet. I don't want to hurt your feelings and I know it's important to you, but it's a seriously insane complication I can do without."

To her immense surprise Jamie Stuart burst out laughing.

"I've been wondering how long it would take you to pluck up courage to give me a rocket about that!"

"You . . . you mean you don't mind my saying that? You're not upset?"

"Look, Julia," he spoke seriously. "As you rightly say, the belief in our descent from the Stuarts *is* very important to me and I don't intend to deny it at this late stage. But you're quite right, I really must stop boring on about it to all and sundry. I know how embarrassing I always used to find my own father and grandfather — and if you think I'm a fruit cake, you should have met Grandpa! It was only after Janet died that I really got into it; became a bit of an obsession, I suppose, something to fill up the emptiness."

She was touched, Jamie rarely mentioned his adored wife.

"I suppose, as well, I did it out of mischief to annoy Charlie and it rather got out of hand and I was stuck with a joke that rebounded on me. He's had such a rough ride of late that maybe I thought a counter-irritant might take his mind off his troubles."

Julia laughed as they said goodnight.

"I think you may have overdone it with Charlie," she murmured as they shared another of those surprising and passionate embraces. "I imagine there have been days when he's been inches away from summoning the men in white coats to cart you off."

94

Next day Charlie Stuart really *was* on the brink of calling for the straitjackets.

Finn and Hedgehog were in the middle of rearranging the shop window — dragons on stone, dragons on glass, dragons draped over a bronze indoor water feature — when the phone rang.

"Finn, it's me. I'm in the Square, you've got to get over here, right now."

"Really?" Finn's response was chilly. "I can't think of any reason why I should do anything just because you say so."

"Oh? How about if I tell you that your sister and my father and some of their friends have set up as buskers and are singing in the street, with a hat in front of them for the money?"

"Jesus! OK, yes, that'd do it. On my way!"

"What the hell do they think they're *doing?*" Charlie was almost howling with wrath when he spotted her running across the Square from Paradise Row. "Apart from anything else I could lose customers if they connect me with this." He bent his furious glare on her and added, "And don't you dare try and tell me I'm being crass and materialistic, it's a real risk and I've got a living to make."

"I wasn't going to say that," she retorted, panting. "This time I'm with you completely. They'll be a laughing stock."

People were laughing all right, but not in the way Finn imagined. When she finally reached the scene of the crime she had to stop running, partly to catch her breath but mostly to giggle, along with an increasing crowd of onlookers, the only dissenting voice coming from a shapeless old woman.

"Load of toffee-nosed snobs!" she declared before straightening her hat and stomping off to the bus station.

The Gang had chosen fancy dress for their first fundraiser. No whisper of their plans had leaked out as they had hugged the secret to their chests, and no wonder. Finn gazed in hysterical disbelief at the superannuated schoolgirls and boys who were valiantly singing songs from the forties, fifties and sixties. The women wore what, in some cases, looked like authentic gymslips with black tights and straw hats and the men were in grey flannel shorts, made from cut-off trousers, with jackets or, in Jamie's case, a striped blazer of venerable vintage. Jonathan was lurking at the back with a false moustache and dark glasses concealing his face lest any crony of Pauline's should pass by.

"Saint Trinian's!" Finn turned to Charlie and clutched at his arm. "Hang on a bit, Charlie. Don't rush in and make a scene, nobody's laughing *at* them, they're just joining in the fun. Oh my God," she started to giggle again. "Oh look, I've just spotted Delia Muncaster, look at her!"

Delia was singing lustily as part of a chorus consisting of Ursula, Marek and herself, accompanied on the guitar, with surprising skill and brio, by Bobbie, wearing what turned out to be her mother's nineteen-forties guide uniform. Somehow Delia managed to retain her customary elegance, even in a brief green

96

smock-like garment that hung like a sack above her thin, black-clad legs.

"Come on, Charlie," Finn coaxed, forgetting that she wasn't speaking to him. "Look at the money that's pouring in, that guy just dropped a five pound note into the hat. Give them a break, they're not doing any harm, after all."

Charlie was clearly beginning to retreat from his high moral ground, a process helped by the confiding hand tucked into his. He looked down at her and then at the ridiculous performance in front of him, and sighed.

"Oh, all right. Tell you what," he steered her towards the group, "if you can't beat 'em, join 'em. Any straw hats going spare, Pa?"

Jamie, who was doing lead vocals with Julia, grinned and pointed to the back of the group where their coats were heaped against the statue of the local bigwig which stood in the centre of the Square. Charlie jammed a hat on his own head and reached into his pocket for his Ray-Bans. He picked up another boater for Finn and turned to see her hastily plaiting her long blonde hair into two thick pigtails. Suitably clad they cast aside common sense and wriggled into place beside their irresponsible elders.

"Jolly hockey sticks!" hooted Delia, despite the fact that she was waving a battered lacrosse stick. "How do you like my jibbah, Finn? This highly flattering garment," she added, as Finn looked understandably confused. "We used to wear them for games and horribly unsuitable they were too. Unlike then, I'm wearing thermals underneath today."

"What's next on the programme?" Charlie grabbed the song sheet.

"Just starting on the songs from *Oklahoma*," Julia chuckled at his rolled up trousers and tie pulled askew. "*Can* you sing, Charlie?"

"Of *course* he can," Jamie chimed in proudly. "Charlie was a chorister at Exeter Cathedral choir school till his voice broke. He's a first-class baritone now."

Finn glanced at Charlie and caught his eye. He responded with a smirk of false modesty and held out an olive branch.

"I apologise, OK?"

"Oh, all right," she spoke grudgingly but was secretly delighted when, as the Gang broke into song, Charlie took her hand as they shared the song sheet.

"I knew you could sing," she told him later as they cemented their refound friendship in the White Horse. "I mean, you're like me, we both sing along in the car and so on, but I'd never heard you singing seriously. Your father's right, you *have* got a lovely voice."

"I've set things in train for our next fund-raising efforts." Delia Muncaster seemed to have elected herself Chairman of the group to nobody's dismay and to everybody's immense relief. "I think we'd better go for rather less high-profile affairs than our busking experience. I was hard put to find a suitable comment when that chap from the Gazette asked me which charity we were supporting. I had to take him off to the White Horse and pour whisky down his throat. Luckily he had no stamina and was also venal, so he took a bribe to drop the story." She gave a reminiscent, crocodile smile.

"There aren't enough of us to muster for a jumble sale and it's not something we'd make much money from anyhow. What I've done is book two tables at the Antiques Fair in the Town Hall in Ramalley on Sunday, so I need you all to start looking out for things to put on the stall. Settle down, settle down." She raised a hand to quell the mutterings of dismay that arose.

It's not as daunting as it sounds, we can just put any old stuff on, it's not a high-calibre do. Any old bits of china, glass, old table runners, prints, that sort of thing. Now, first of all we need a collecting point. Who's got an empty room we could use? No good trying to sort stuff in a garage, now the weather's broken. Bobbie? You volunteering? Good girl. Hear that, everyone? Start handing your odds and ends to Bobbie.

"We'll also need newspaper for wrapping and loads of plastic carrier bags to send the punters away happy. The rest of you can provide them, I never bother with bags, Threshers always send my deliveries by the box. Now don't whinge, we got off to a flying start with our impromptu busking. The fifty-eight quid we picked up there will pay for the tables at the antique fair, for a start, and kick off our savings account."

Inexorably Delia wore them down until everyone had sworn on his or her mother's grave — in Rosemary's case with a fervour that had them all laughing with her — that they would collect up bits and pieces and beg from neighbours and acquaintances.

"That's good," she graciously conceded at the end. "Rosemary and Julia, you two can man the stall, unless anyone else wants to take a turn. No? There you are then. Sue, you can drop in and relieve them or give them a hand, or just keep them company. Bobbie, you'd better sort them out a float from our account, and you might look in on them now and then just to make sure they're not making a pig's ear of the takings."

Even as she spoke Delia could hear Guy's voice in her head, those whining tones, almost as highly pitched as her own. Really, dear heart, cliché upon cliché! Who'd have thought you'd ever get involved with a collection of misfits and plebs. After all the years with me, surely you must have learned some refinement of taste. With *your* ancestry one would have expected a soupçon of elegance to be innate, would one not? However, even the most thoroughbred of lineages throws up the odd sport, I suppose.

It was easier to give in and do what Delia wanted than to stand up for one's rights so they all meekly agreed with her. That had been Monday night's meeting and all through the week the offerings began to cover the table in Bobbie's dining room.

They had an assortment of china, including some lovely pieces of Wedgwood from Hugh Taylor, who had been formally initiated into the club and professed all eagerness to join in with the holiday plans.

"It's nothing," he protested when Rosemary commented on the china. "The girls don't want it and I never really liked it that much, nor did Joan, it was her mother's. You know the kind of thing, too good to chuck out but not what we liked ourselves so it lived in a cupboard except when my mother-in-law came to stay. I'm happy for it to go to a good cause."

"Delia," Rosemary had protested after the meeting. "I can't go out all day Sunday, it simply isn't safe to leave Margot on her own."

"Do you good," came the crisp reply. "I'll babysit your mother and if I have any trouble, which I won't, I'll call in reinforcements in the shape of Marek and Jonathan. She'll be so perked up to see a couple of men that I'll have no nonsense at all from her. All you need to do is drop her over to me at Daisy Cottage on your way to the Town Hall. Pack a bag of spares for her if you like, though it won't bother me if she has an accident. I had Guy in nappies at the end, poor bugger."

Hugh was dragooned into providing transport.

"She simply informed me that I had that stonking great Mercedes and therefore I was the obvious candidate," he told Julia, Jamie and Rosemary over a drink in the pub the next day. "She's the worst slave-driver I've ever met, but you can't help admiring the old dragon, can you?"

He and Rosemary then put their heads together to discuss adding potted plants to the stall's complement.

"Are you sure, though, Hugh?" Rosemary was doubtful. "I could understand if we were selling aspidistras! But plants and antiques?"

"Checked it out," Hugh told her with a kindly patronising manner that made Julia wince but Rosemary glow with pleasure. "It's called an Antiques, Collectables and Fleamarket Fair and apparently pretty much anything goes. Not ordinary household junk, of course, but then again, if your household junk happens to date from before the War . . ."

"I can't believe I ever fancied Hugh Taylor," Julia confessed frankly to Finn as they met in Julia's sitting room for a drink that night.

"Why shouldn't you?" queried Finn idly. "He's quite good-looking, lots of hair, that quietly distinguished look. Mind you, I much prefer Jamie, specially as you reckon he's going to cut down on the Heir to the Throne stuff."

"Mmm," Julia smiled reminiscently. "Why not Hugh? Well, for a start he's only about five foot eight, and I know that's about as shallow a reason as you can get, so don't even bother telling me. Two reasons really, one is that his wife still occupies his whole life: after all, she's not been dead long, poor woman. But I don't think I'd feel comfortable getting close to someone who is still grieving. Sometimes you can almost see her sitting beside him. It doesn't seem to bother Rosemary, I think she's just happy to have a boyfriend."

"I think you're right," Finn agreed. "I'd hate it if Charlie's wife — or whatever — cropped up at every turn. Speaking of which, I still haven't found out what that's all about, you know. He says he isn't married and never has been, but the barricades go up if I get close to the subject. It's not that he's still in love with her, whoever she was, I'm sure of that. I just don't like to push it till he's ready to tell me, specially after his temper tantrum the other day. Besides, Hedgehog said something . . . oh never mind. Anyway, you said two reasons for not getting involved with Hugh. What's the second one?"

"It's two and three, actually. For one thing he's a passionate golfer and all sport leaves me cold, and then there's his garden." Julia drained her drink and poured them each another glass of Chardonnay. "He's obsessed with it. I mean, I like flowers as much as anyone, gardening too, when it's not cold or wet, but he's fanatical. Out there weeding, rain or shine, hail or snow, he's the kind that probably uses nail scissors to trim the edges. And he bores for England on the subject; fertilising, potash, mulching. Do I give a damn about mulching? Nope," she stretched luxuriously. "Give me Jamie any day, specially now he —"

She checked herself and attempted to change the subject.

"Oh no you don't, Ju," Finn was intrigued. "Specially now Jamie what?" Her eyes grew round with interest. "Julia? You mean he and you . . .? I thought you said that wasn't on?"

"Never you mind," Julia said with a smug grin. "You keep an eye on your own love life and keep your nose out of mine."

The Antiques Fair was causing Ursula Buchanan some anxiety. I simply can't be the only person in the group who doesn't contribute, she fretted, going through her scanty treasures, the ring from Mother, the Bible from Father, the pretty cup and saucer from her godmother, sadly chipped now. The problem continued to haunt her as she fumbled through her chores around the house, pottered to the village shop and eventually clambered aboard the bus into town.

Now what am I doing in here, she asked herself when, laden with shopping, she found herself in a china shop. Such pretty things, she thought sadly, gazing at some little silver boxes, decorated with enamel flowers.

Suddenly she was aware of a sharply spicy perfume, a hint of lemon, a suggestion of thyme.

"Oh," she greeted the angel with a soft murmuring of pleasure. "I wondered if you'd ever come back."

"*I'm around all the time,*" answered the angel in his ringing, golden tones, making her look round anxiously. But no, there was no commotion, no gasps of astonishment. Nobody around at all, in fact, it was tea-break time and the only assistant was brewing up in the little back kitchen.

"*Go on,*" the angel indicated the small silver boxes. "*Stick a couple in your bag, they won't notice. Go on,*" he urged at her shocked expression. "*You know you want to.*"

Obediently Ursula slid three of the charming little trifles into her pocket while the angel looked on.

"*Now you'd better get off home,*" he suggested. "*That old besom you slave for will be wanting her tea soon.*"

Ursula was half way home, head nodding a little as usual, and looking out of the bus window, before the shock hit her. Oh my Lord! I stole something from a shop! What would Mother say? Or Father? Oh heavens, what have I done! How Henrietta would crow if she saw me taken off to the police station and thrown into the cells.

She shook and shivered all the way home from the bus stop at the end of Bychurch until a thought struck her. But nobody saw me, she realised. If they had there would have been a hue and cry, but the shop assistant didn't notice, she certainly didn't come running after me.

Indoors she put the kettle on before taking off her hat and coat. She made the tea and daringly poured herself a cup, ignoring the querulous complaints from upstairs.

The tea did its work. Instantly refreshed Ursula managed to calm down. I must give those boxes to Bobbie straight away, she vowed, and I'm never, ever going to do that again, not even if he brings the whole Heavenly Host to persuade me. Oh my goodness, what an escape.

When she felt strong enough to tackle Henrietta she found her squatting in an armchair, like a malevolent toad.

"I managed to struggle to the window," announced Henrietta the martyr to rheumatism. Obesity and idleness as the doctor privately described it to Ursula — it was the patient herself who insisted she was delicate and at risk of a stroke if crossed. "It's a

105

disgrace out there. You're to get out there tomorrow and weed that end border. You needn't try to wriggle out of it," she warned as Ursula began to remonstrate. "I only have to lift the telephone and you'll be taken into care." Her eyes narrowed as she noted the sudden increase in writhings and twistings of her sister-in-law's hands, the stark terror in Ursula's china-blue eyes.

"What have you been up to?" she demanded. "You look positively terrified. And don't try my patience with that stuff about me needing you as much as you need me, it's not true. They'll just send in a nurse and a home help."

Ursula was too far gone in fright to dispute this claim and in the end she evaded Henrietta's piercing interrogation by the simple method of scuttling out of the room.

On Thursday afternoon Sue Merrill parked her VW Golf outside Bobbie's house. As she heaved a large cardboard box out of the boot she was hailed by Julia Fitzgerald who was crossing the Green.

"What's up? Why the panic phone calls?" Julia asked, hauling out another box from the car and walking up the path with it.

"Just a sec," puffed Sue as she rang the bell, greeted Bobbie gratefully and dumped the box on the dining room floor. "That's better, weighs a ton, that box, it's all books."

"Books?" Julia looked doubtful. "Antique books, do you mean?"

"Nope, just books. That's why I rang you," Sue explained. "I bumped into Bobbie at lunch time in town and she told me we'd got a lot of stuff that can't be called antique, by any stretch of the imagination, so when I then had a message from an old colleague that her church was having a Car Boot sale this Saturday I booked us a couple of pitches and started clearing out junk."

"What?" Julia was horrified. "A Boot Sale Saturday *and* an Antiques Fair Sunday? We'll be knackered."

"Wimp!" replied Sue, robustly. "We can take it in turns, nobody said it would be you on Saturday. I'll take a car and we'll get Hugh or somebody else."

"You won't get Hugh using his car for junk. Anyway, he's providing transport for the antiques, isn't he?" Ignoring Julia's sceptical laugh, Sue went back to the car to check the boot was empty.

Charlie Stuart's Honda drew up beside them, tailed by Finn's Renault, whereupon the pair parked and came to investigate.

"What are you two up to?"

At Finn's remark Julia and Sue exchanged evil glances and Sue smiled sweetly at the pair.

"We're looking for somebody with a car to help us out tomorrow morning," she said, her voice dripping with sincerity. "Nothing too complicated," she added as Charlie looked doubtful and Finn downright disobliging. "It's just to help out at a Car Boot we're taking stuff to on Saturday. It's not for long, ten till twelve, and it's in a good cause."

Charlie was the first to crumble, so Finn shrugged as she cast a speculative eye at her sister. Julia was being unnaturally silent, Finn considered, which always meant trouble, but she didn't want to make a fuss and look bad in front of Charlie.

"Oh all right," she gave in suddenly. "I suppose it might be fun, as long as it doesn't pour. There's a load of stuff I don't want from the boxes of stuff I had sent over from Brussels, clothes and so on that I'll never wear around Ramalley. I thought you said you were doing something with antiques though, Ju?"

As Julia and Sue explained Bobbie shyly invited them all in for a cup of tea and to inspect the offerings on her dining table.

"Wow, this is quite impressive." Finn was wandering round, fingering delicate china and glass. "Look at these cute little silver boxes."

"Oh that was Ursula." Bobbie was bringing in mugs of tea. "She was a bit odd about them, just dashed in yesterday evening after supper looking furtive and scuttled off again without stopping. I hope they weren't family treasures, she worshipped her parents and she's even devoted to that awful sister-in-law."

"That's odd." Julia was examining the boxes closely. "They can't be family pieces, they've still got the price tickets on. She must have bought them, but we know how hard up she is, she hasn't got two halfpennies to rub together." She was speaking to Finn who was standing beside her and they exchanged startled, dubious glances. "Hmmm," Julia bit her lip thoughtfully. "I think I'll just take the tickets off, we'll be pricing everything as we pack it ready for Sunday."

Meanwhile Ursula had spent much of the day obediently weeding the back garden and her back was beginning to ache cruelly. However, she almost welcomed the discomfort as expiation of her sinful behaviour of the day before. The worst section of the border covered a curious mound, and it was when she thrust the fork into the slope under a cluster of peony tubers which needed dividing that she felt the earth in front of her give way. There was a splintering noise as her fork jarred hideously and disappeared, leaving Ursula collapsed on her knees holding on to the handle, which was all that showed above the ground.

"Oh my goodness!" she quavered, tears of pain starting to her eyes as she tried to right herself. No, no bones broken, it seemed, thank the Lord, but oh, what an ache in her shoulders and back. She was still clinging onto the fork handle and, staying on her hands and knees, she cleared a bit more of the earth away and peered into the hole that was revealed.

"Oh no, oh God no!" It was a heartfelt cry of anguish. Ursula was looking into what seemed to be an underground room. The earth-covered mound in the flower bed was obviously the roof, the entrance covered by an old door whose rotten wood had been pierced by the garden fork. An air-raid shelter.

Memories, hideous memories crowded in upon Ursula as she knelt panting in the slight drizzle that had begun quite unnoticed. More than sixty years on she heard again the discordant shriek of the siren, the drone of the planes, the sound of falling bombs. And sixty years seemed like an instant as she felt again the terror of being trapped in the cellar at her friend's house.

"It was twelve hours before they cleared the entrance," she once told Henrietta in response to some snide remark. "My memory may be faulty but that's one thing I *do* remember clearly. The house was bombed and my friend's parents were killed. I think she was sent away to relatives afterwards, but I don't know, I wasn't very well for a while."

"No stamina," Henrietta had sneered. "I know what happened, Gerald told me, you had a nervous breakdown and were never any use again to anybody after that."

Henrietta! I must go indoors and get her tea, Ursula thought anxiously, it must be way past time, she's always nastier when she's hungry. She clambered painfully to her feet and tottered to the scullery, brushing off the worst of the mud outside the back door.

A wash in hot water made her feel a little better and she dragged a comb through her fluffy, bog-cotton white hair, looking in the slip of mirror on the shelf, pausing only to put the kettle on before plucking up courage to tackle Henrietta's customary round of complaints.

In the hall she was startled to see the Stannah lift open at the bottom of the stair, instead of folded flat in the closed position against the upstairs landing wall.

Why today, of all days, she groaned to herself. Why on earth should her monstrously idle sister-in-law take it into her head to come down today?

"Henrietta? Where are you? I've just put the kettle on for your tea, dear. And guess what I've just discovered in the garden, must have been hidden for fifty years or more. Such a surprise! Where are you, Henrietta?"

There was no answer. Henrietta Buchanan had fallen and lay slumped in an ungainly lifeless heap across a chair, feet dangling on the parquet floor of the dining room where she had been running her finger along the sideboard, testing for dust, when the second, fatal, stroke hit.

CHAPTER
SEVEN

Nine o'clock on Saturday found Charlie and Finn loading up Charlie's car with the boxes Bobbie and Sue indicated.

"You two go ahead," Sue instructed. "Bobbie and I will be along shortly, we just need to check there's nothing left in the antiques collection that belongs at the Boot Sale. Here you are," she handed Finn an ice cream tub that jingled. "That's your float in there, you've got fifteen quid in pound coins, fifty pence pieces, twenties and tens, you shouldn't need five pence pieces or coppers. The fiver is for your pitch. Don't let anyone bully you into *giving* stuff away but don't be too fussy, the object of the exercise is to make money, after all."

"They're not taking to religion, are they?" Charlie asked as he pulled carefully away from the kerb to the accompaniment of loud jingling and rattling from the awkward pile of boxes in the back. "Blast, I knew I should have packed all this junk in myself, the way she's done it we're likely to have a disaster unless I do twenty miles an hour all the way. There!" A particularly ominous crash made him smile with sour satisfaction and they waited, but there was no follow-up. "Oh well, if it's all smashed we can just drop it off at the town dump. What was I — ? Oh yeah, this do today is at some church, isn't it?"

"The church is only incidental," Finn told him. "Some friend of Sue Merrill's is organising the Boot Sale, that's why we're going there."

They turned into the car park of Saint Wilfrid's church and Charlie handed over the five pounds entry fee.

"You're Sue's friends?" The harassed woman on the gate pointed them to a pitch next to a makeshift hot dog stall, manned by church volunteers. "Stick a box or something on the space beside you to reserve it for Sue, then you can keep together."

Long before the ten o'clock kickoff they were plunged into activity. Sue had turned up with Bobbie in train and she tossed tips at them over her shoulder as she set up her own pasting table.

"Don't be too fancy, paperbacks in a cardboard box at fifty pence if they're good ones, ten or twenty if they're run of the mill. Here, hang clothes on this airer, I brought two along. I don't think we've anything worth charging more than a fiver for, the better stuff's going on the stall tomorrow."

The other stall-holders, plus early punters, descended like flies and Finn found herself wrapping china in newspaper and arguing with stroppy customers.

"I *know* that's not the latest Danielle Steel," she informed an aggressive woman. "But it's only ten pence, so what on earth do you expect?"

Beside her she heard Charlie remonstrating with another woman.

"It's Poole Pottery, very collectable."

"But it's chipped!"

"Madam, I'm only charging twenty-five pence!"

The customer sloped off in a huff and five minutes later Finn spotted Charlie talking up the same vase.

"Poole Pottery, madam, one of tomorrow's antiques, only two pounds fifty."

"I don't know," she peered at the chip. "Will you take a pound as it's chipped?"

"Certainly," he grinned, wrapping it for her. "See," he whispered to Finn. "You can't pitch the price too low or they get suspicious. This way they get to barter and think they've got a bargain."

It was exhausting. By twelve o'clock only stragglers were left walking round the car park and some of the other sellers had packed up and gone home. The organiser came over to Sue who was closeted with Bobbie, counting the takings.

"Thanks a lot for coming, Sue," she said. "Done all right?" Without waiting for an answer she brushed her straggling grey fringe out of her eyes and went on, "Look, one of our parishioners has volunteered to do a run to the town dump, so anything you don't want to take home with you, just bung it in his van. The white Transit over there by the gate, see?"

"What a relief." Sue turned to Bobbie and nodded. "We were wondering where on earth to jettison the rubbish. Come on you two, let's shove everything into these boxes and get them on to the van."

114

"Have you filled up on hot dogs or shall I buy us lunch?" Finn asked as they drove out between the wrought iron gates.

Charlie looked self-conscious, hesitating before he answered.

"Are you starving? Because, if you're OK, I promised Pa I'd get back and help them finish sorting the stuff for tomorrow. You know, pricing it and wrapping it."

She gave a resigned laugh.

"Why did I even bother to ask? You know I'll help." She turned her gaze away from the pretty stone bridge over the river and grinned at him. "I just can't believe myself, you know. If anyone had told me a few months ago that I'd be spending my spare time hanging out with my sister and her insane crew. Or that I'm best friends with a weird old biddy who knocks around with a delinquent angel —"

"What? Miss B's angel? How do you know he's a delinquent?"

"She told me." Finn giggled then quietened down. "I feel really sorry for her you know. Julia says she was trapped underground in the war, when a bomb demolished a house; she's not been quite right ever since. Look, stop at the newsagent's just here, I'll buy us an ice cream Mars bar each.

"Yes. Ursula," she returned to the topic as they sat in the parked car overlooking the village school playing field, reluctant to plunge back into their world of elderly society. "I saw her yesterday at lunch-time in Ramalley. I forgot I hadn't told you, she was hanging about outside the police station looking really weird, in a real state. She wouldn't tell me what was the matter but I managed to persuade her to come into the shop and have a cup of tea. That's when she told me about her angel."

At this point Charlie interrupted her.

"Tell me about the angel later on," he said firmly, finishing his Mars bar and reaching for her. "Just at the moment I'm bored stiff with other people, mad or sane, *and* with the kind of people who go to car boots. Where *did* they come from, under a stone? I'm fed up, in fact, with everyone except you and me . . ."

For five minutes they were far too pleasurably occupied to bother about anybody else's heavenly visitations. When at last they drew apart Finn sighed and stretched herself like a cat.

"Look, Charlie," she pointed out, laughing. "We've steamed the whole car up."

"That does it," Charlie announced firmly, kissing the tip of her nose. "I'm sick of this messing about like a couple of seventeen-year-olds; snogging in cars has never been my style. I know I'm foul-tempered and I don't deserve you but . . . stay with me tonight, Finn? Pa won't interfere."

"Oh!" She was suddenly seized by an unaccountable shyness. "I'd like — yes, Charlie, I'd like that."

His dark eyes lit up with anticipation, then, aware of her confusion, he gently stroked her scarlet cheek. "It'll be magic," he said happily, turning the key and driving into the village where he parked in his own drive.

116

"What were you saying about Ursula's angel?" he asked as they walked hand-in-hand across the green to Bobbie's narrow Edwardian semi. "You were telling me how come he's a delinquent. Isn't that an oxymoron, a delinquent angel?"

"Pedant," she thrust at him. "I *do* know what you're talking about and no, it's perfectly possible to have a bad angel, look at Satan. Not that Ursula's is *that* bad, anyway." She looked up at him and gave a tiny shrug. "What the hell are we doing, discussing degrees of wickedness in angels? No, Ursula reckons her angel keeps giving her rather suspect advice but she's so pleased to see him she just does as she's told. I think she's just a born doormat, bomb traumas or not."

Pushing at the open front door they went in and joined an excited throng in the kitchen. Bobbie, her sad, thin little face pink with happy importance, was bustling around with a tray full of glasses. She pressed one each on to Finn and Charlie.

"No, please," she insisted. "It's champagne, Delia brought it round. We've done *so* well, but I won't tell you, I'll leave it to Delia."

"Glasses charged?" Delia was in her element. "Righty-ho, chums. Raise your glasses to the first successful fundraising efforts of our gallant association, *Hope Springs!*"

They all drank the toast, Charlie raising his eyebrows across the room at his father who was also looking surprised at his first sip, but pleasantly so.

"What?" hissed Finn. "What's the matter?"

"It's Moët," Charlie muttered. "Lady D must have coughed up, unless they're frittering their profits on classy booze."

"But how much did you make?" Jonathan Barlow had slipped out when his wife wasn't looking.

"Didn't I say?" Delia Muncaster looked surprised. "Silly old bat. They took sixty-nine pounds seventy-three pence, all told. That's not bad for a load of junk."

"It's incredible!" Julia was all admiration. "How on earth did you manage it?"

"I don't know," Finn began, but Sue interrupted her.

"Well, Finn generously donated a lot of designer clothes which went like hot cakes with some of the ladies, as well as a load of make-up. And Charlie was brilliant at selling to middle-aged women. I actually saw him beat one up on the price of a coffee maker, the price was seven-fifty and she ended up paying nine for it! And Bobbie did a fantastic job with the books, I'd suggested ten pence but she bullied people into paying fifty for most of them."

"It was a great effort," said Delia heartily. "Especially on top of the money we made from our busking. Thank you, Sue, for suggesting it and for organising it so successfully. I only hope tomorrow's show does as well."

"Pity Rosemary couldn't help, she'd have enjoyed it," Sue said. "Margot was sulking because of this morning's performance."

Delia looked a question.

"Poor old thing," sighed Julia as she carefully wrapped a Stuart Crystal vase in newspaper. "You can't help feeling sorry for her, she's getting worse, though she still has moments of lucidity. But of course Rosemary's tied worse than ever. Margot actually got as far as the bus shelter today, stark naked, too! Thank God for the Day Centre, that's all I can say."

At five o'clock Delia called a temporary halt. "Time for a tea break, don't you think?" she asked brightly, rummaging in her big black leather handbag.

"Not your sort of tea break," Julia scolded. "You drink yourself to death if you like, the rest of us have some respect for our livers, even if you don't. Bobbie, can you bear to make another pot of tea? There's only us six now and I don't suppose Delia will drink tea. I'll nip home, I made a coffee and walnut cake this morning, just the thing."

Bobbie's face shone even more with sheer delight. Finn went to help her with the mugs and plates.

"Oh, it's such fun," she gleefully told Finn, who had followed her into the kitchen to help with mugs and plates. "I was so lonely and in despair when I joined the group and now look at me! Surrounded by friends, useful again, having fun and when we've saved all that money we're going to . . ."

She pulled herself up abruptly, shot a guilty look at Finn and busied herself with finding paper table napkins to set on the tray.

"Bobbie?" Finn hastened to reassure her. "It's all right, Julia told me."

"Oh, good. But of course we'll be giving *some* of the money to charity," Bobbie said defensively. "In fact, *all* the left-over cash will be donated, we all agreed on that." She counted plates as Julia turned up bearing a large cake, and accompanied by Ursula Buchanan.

Finn caught Charlie's eye on her return to the dining room and, remembering their plans for the evening, retired with him into a corner, blushing furiously as he reached down and surreptitiously took her hand in his.

Julia noticed the electricity between them and drew her own conclusions. She was about to murmur an invitation on her own account to Jamie Stuart when Delia drew attention to Ursula.

"Why don't you put those bags down, Ursula, they look very heavy. Are they for the fair tomorrow?"

"Yes." Ursula's answer was faint, then she gulped and spoke up. "I've had a look round for some family bits and pieces I could donate. I hope they'll be acceptable."

Jamie Stuart hurried forward to relieve her of her burden and Julia and Bobbie carefully unpacked her offerings.

"But, Ursula!" cried Julia. "This vase is Royal Worcester, and so's this dish, they're far too valuable to give." A murmur from Bobbie drew her attention. "Oh my goodness, what's this? The most beautiful embroidered linens. Ursula, you mustn't give away such lovely things."

"Oh but I must, my dear," Ursula stood her ground, pink with pleasure at this reception. "They belonged to

120

my father's mother and they've just been sitting there in the house all these years, doing nothing."

"But what about Henrietta?" Julia put it into words and the others all nodded anxiously.

"Henrietta didn't make any fuss at all when I packed up the bits," Ursula replied boldly, and with perfect truth, though her head started to dodder even worse than usual. "Besides, they're all Buchanan family items, not from her side of the family, so that's all right." She looked round at the group. "I want to pay my way," she said, her voice sounding much firmer now. "I don't have the cash but I can at least make a contribution in this way." She sat down shaky but determined. "There's lots more stuff in the house that we can sell if tomorrow's stall goes well."

Julia put an arm round the frail shoulders and hugged her.

"It's a magnificent gesture, Ursula," she said gently. "I gather they get quite a lot of dealers looking in at the local fair; you know, from Winchester and Reading, London even. I'm sure somebody could surf the Net and find out a rough idea of what price we should put on these things. Any volunteers?"

Hugh nodded rather importantly, and was rewarded by a feline grin from Delia Muncaster.

"Excellent," she announced, striking him a hearty blow on the shoulder and baring her teeth even more terrifyingly as he buckled at the knees. "Tell you what, when you've found some prices, why don't you drop in to Rosemary's? Don't ring her, you never know if the telephone will wake her mother, just call in and take her a bottle of fizz to cheer her up. Here, there seems to be a bottle left. Good God, how on earth did that happen? I must be slipping."

The party broke up then, Hugh stepping out with a spring in his step, obviously picturing his arrival on Rosemary's doorstep armed with a bottle of Moët.

Delia poured herself an encouraging tot of gin to give her strength to tackle the two hundred yards to her own house and Bobbie and Ursula found themselves left in the chock-full dining room.

"Oh, Ursula," Bobbie spoke in her usual diffident tones as Ursula fluffed and fussed at the door. "I wondered if you . . . I mean I was thinking about what you said at the first meeting. Do you remember? That you'd love to have a cat?"

"Oh, I *would*," Ursula was stopped in her tracks. "But oh dear, I don't think I . . ."

"That's what I mean." Bobbie's words tumbled into confusion. "Oh dear, I'm not explaining this very well. What I wondered was, why don't you and I *share* a cat? It could live here, at my house, but it would belong to both of us, and you could come over and spend time with it whenever you wanted. What do you think? I could never have a pet while I was working all day and out so much on guiding business in the evenings, but now I've plenty of time and it would be such fun, wouldn't it"

She looked anxiously at Ursula, who appeared to have gone into a trance.

"Are you all right, Ursula?"

122

"*Oh,*" Ursula breathed an ecstatic sigh. "What a wonderful, truly wonderful idea, Bobbie. How clever you are! Could we really do that?"

"Of course we could," Bobbie was delighted. "Look, I saw this ad on the notice-board in Waitrose in town. It's a lady who runs a little cat sanctuary, a completely one-woman venture. I wrote it down, here: *Cats and kittens always needing good homes, please help us to bring happiness to these little ones.*"

She gulped and gazed at Ursula with wet eyes.

"We could go and see her tomorrow, couldn't we? I'll ring now and make an appointment, what do you think?"

Sue Merrill opened the door to an empty house. On the kitchen table lay a note from her husband:. "*I can't bear not to be with her, I'm sorry. I'll see you tomorrow, I expect.*"

CHAPTER
EIGHT

Julia watched out of her landing window as Finn ran down the drive in answer to a hoot from Charlie's horn. While getting ready for her own evening's entertainment she had forced herself not to drop into Finn's flat to offer big-sisterly advice. Julia Fitzgerald, she told herself firmly, Finn's a big girl now, she's not your baby sister any more.

Left to her own devices Julia laid the dining table, checked that the soup was ready for reheating, the stroganoff ingredients ready for the off and the mini pavlovas looking luscious in the fridge, then she sauntered into her room to change.

My goodness, she thought, slipping into her tobacco-brown silk jersey top and skirt and fastening a string of amber beads round her neck. Talk about a teenager on a date, this actually *is* a first date, isn't it? The first proper one with Jamie, at least. Oh God, I hope it goes well, for both our sakes.

Alone in the house Ursula wondered, for the hundredth time, what to do about Henrietta. For two days she had managed, more or less successfully, to ignore the problem by dint of shutting the dining room door and keeping out of the house as much as possible.

I can't go on like this, she thought, forcing herself to look at the situation. I ought to call an ambulance or the doctor or something. But then they'll turn me out of the house and where will I go?

There was a faint scent of spice on the air and the familiar rustle of heavenly wings. The angel was lounging in the Windsor chair by the Rayburn, looking at her with a quizzical expression.

"Take a look at her Will, Ursula," he offered. *"That's the first step."*

"Oh yes, of course, why didn't I think of that?" She was relieved. "Henrietta always promised Mother and Father that she'd provide for me, now where did she . . .?"

After some ineffectual dithering she discovered the Will in Henrietta's bureau. As she drew the folded document out of the long envelope Ursula's hands were trembling violently. How much had Henrietta left her? So much hinged on it.

"But — but — I don't understand?" It was a wail of terror. "Perhaps I've read it wrong?"

But she hadn't. Henrietta Buchanan had left her house, the contents, her securities and all other assets to the restoration fund for Ramalley Priory. There was no mention of the sister-in-law she had kept enslaved for so many years.

The angel watched as Ursula sat in desolate silence, trying to digest this disastrous news.

125

"*I've got a suggestion,*" he remarked after a long, miserable wait. She looked up, her face dull, with only a glint of interest. "*Yup,*" he went on. "*You don't actually have to tell anyone about this, you know. You could pretend she's still tucked up in bed upstairs and carry on living here as usual. It'd be like before, but better, because you could please yourself.*"

Comprehension began to dawn.

"But what would I live on?" she asked, brightening up.

"*You've got your pension,*" he said bracingly. "*And you can go on drawing Henrietta's as well; you know she signed the back of the book, when she got so lazy, so you could do it for her. You ought to draw some money out of the bank, too, not to look suspicious. That's not hard, you just have to imitate her signature — you can go in to the branch and tell them she's very doddery these days, they won't suspect anything.*"

"Oh, but I couldn't, that would be dishonest!"

The angel gave her a very old-fashioned look indeed and she had the grace to look disconcerted.

"You mean I've already been dishonest, don't you?" she said humbly. "Giving those bits of Royal Worcester to the Antiques Fair. But they really were from my family." She thought hard and made a decision. "I suppose you're right and what could they do to me? Only put me in prison and how bad would that be, compared to all these years working for Henrietta?"

"*Atta girl*", the angel encouraged her. "*Now, even more pressing, is the problem of the body in the dining*

126

room — *sounds like a Miss Marple mystery, doesn't it? Got any ideas about that one?"*

Ursula was reluctant to tackle yet another crisis decision so soon after the first, but as the angel bullied her gently she made some more tea and thought hard.

"I know," she exclaimed in triumph. "How would it be if I could get her into the wheelchair and put her in the air-raid shelter? I could cover it over again and nobody would ever find her."

Egged on by the angel she kitted herself out in boots, jacket and gloves and managed to manouevre the heavy body into the electric wheelchair. So far so good.

Out of doors she almost quailed at the enormity of the task in front of her. Luckily the hole she had nearly fallen into was almost large enough so she bashed away with the coal hammer at the rotten wood. There was a low cloud cover and the threat of rain so she had to retreat indoors to find first a torch and then some batteries and then take care not to flash it about in case she could be seen from the house next door.

The angel flitted around the garden looking ornamental but offering no practical help as she struggled down the crazy-paved path, shooting terrified glances around, but there was no sign of movement at the next-door windows. When she finally reached the splintered opening she was exhausted, her heart banging in her skinny old chest, lungs almost defeated.

"Sit down for five minutes," urged the angel. *"Here, sit on the wheelbarrow, you don't want them to find two corpses at the bottom of the garden! And you don't want to miss out on that holiday of a lifetime, do you?"*

127

Thus encouraged Ursula took a breather and set about Henrietta's impromptu burial with renewed energy. She had a momentary pang when she tilted the wheelchair and the body tumbled out in an ungainly tangle of arms and legs, landing just inside the doorway of the shelter with a thud. It took an enormous effort for Ursula to peer down into the gloom: just being there was reminder enough of her sixty-year terror, but eventually she dragged a piece of an old wooden wardrobe door across the hole.

That'll have to do for now, she gasped to herself, leaning heavily on the wheelchair and wishing she could sit in it herself and be pushed. Tomorrow would be soon enough to shove the door into a better position and cover it with earth. What shall I plant over it, she wondered, as she trudged wearily back to the house. Something nice and hardy, she decided, perhaps that small-leaved periwinkle, that would be ideal, close-matted, evergreen ground cover, just the thing.

"Oh dear," a thought struck her as she clambered into bed. "I should have said a few words over Henrietta, a prayer, maybe."

"*Such as?*" The angel, perched on the end of the bed, laughed cynically at her. "*Thank you, God, for letting the old bitch die? Don't be daft, Ursula, you know she's gone straight to Hell, save your prayers for yourself, and this holiday scheme of yours. You'll need all the help you can get, divine or otherwise, if you're to rustle up all those thousands of pounds and not get had up for fraud.*"

* * *

Although it seemed like the middle of the night to Ursula Buchanan as she crept about her gruesome business it was really only just after eleven. When she struggled into her lonely, spinster bed, Charlie and Finn were up to something much more sociable in Charlie's king-size divan.

"You're lovely, lovely," he murmured, nuzzling contentedly into her ear while he stroked her breasts in a tantalising figure-of-eight. "I knew we'd be magic together."

Finn sighed and stretched luxuriously. Magic was the word, she thought complacently, doing some interesting stroking on her own account. They'd managed to enjoy their dinner at the Elizabethan manor a few miles down the main road, but the crackling tension between them made conversation very tricky and it was with a sigh of relief that Finn nodded when Charlie looked at her.

"Had enough? Let's go home now."

She'd been to Charlie's house several times, enough to feel relaxed there, though she had wondered, but not ventured to ask, who had chosen to mix seventies flock wallpaper in greens and browns with cream, matching leather sofas. Surely not Charlie, he had no interest in interior design: she'd asked him that when they were discussing her own flat. But his house showed distinct signs of another hand, someone who *was* interested in style, in furniture if not in decorating, and, given that Charlie, in spite of his vile temper, was exceedingly attractive, it was odds on that that somebody had to be a woman, presumably the wife who had so mysteriously disappeared. But the woman who had chosen the cream leather would never have sanctioned the dreary brown and pink flowered curtains that drooped at the window. Perhaps she had chosen the furniture but disappeared so mysteriously before tackling the decorating.

The kitchen, too, where Charlie brewed coffee when they reached home, that had also been thrown together, with its odd assortment of state-of-the-art stainless steel equipment everywhere alongside the beige formica units and brown flowered wall tiles. If she hadn't been so worked up in anticipation she might have wondered about the bedroom, but when Charlie put down his coffee mug and took her in his arms she was in no state to think coherently at all. And when they arrived in the bedroom she couldn't have cared less if half-a-dozen of his ex-wives and girlfriends had sat around cheering them on, she was so drowned in desire.

"I'm on the pill," she said shyly in answer to his breathless query and then they were on the bed and Charlie was kissing her all over and it was wonderful, more than she'd ever dreamed.

Across the village green Julia and Jamie were also entwined in each other's arms, both happily exhausted and in Jamie's case, looking insufferably smug.

"Not sure I need a pill," he'd exclaimed cheerfully when she opened the door to him. "Not when you look so delicious."

130

"You old smoothie," she smiled at him. "I'll leave the decision to you, Jamie, but let's have a drink for now, dinner's all ready whenever we are."

Their comfortable friendship came into its own now, when the stakes were raised, so that although there was a heightening of tension, they were able to tuck in quite happily to their dinner. As Julia placed a crisp and gooey pavlova, dripping with blackberries and cream, in front of him, Jamie delved in his inside pocket.

"I think we'll play safe," he grinned at her and popped the Viagra tablet into his mouth. "You have to take it about half an hour before you 'engage in sexual activity' it says on the packet. This is the lowest dose and I dropped in at the surgery yesterday and got the practice nurse to check out my blood pressure and heart-rate, just in case, particularly after that dizzy spell I had after flu. Passed with flying colours."

They took their drinks to the fireside and sat in companionable silence on the big chesterfield.

"What about alcohol?" Julia sat up in alarm. "Maybe you shouldn't mix it with the pill."

"Calm down, sweetie, I checked. A couple of glasses of Jacob's Creek isn't going to do me any harm, quite the reverse, I would have said. I know all the warning signs, what they call the contra-indications and believe me, I haven't got any. On the other hand, though . . ."

He put his glass down on the side table, his hand slightly unsteady and turned to meet her wide-eyed gaze.

"You really are the most delightful creature," he said simply as he put his arms round her and drew her

131

close. "Are you quite sure you want this? You could have any man you wanted, you know. Do you really want a seventy-year-old with an ancestor complex?"

"Oh, Jamie," she sighed as they kissed. "You really do talk a load of nonsense." After another warm, loving and increasingly passionate kiss, she looked at him almost shyly. "Do I take it that the Viagra, or at least, something, is working?" When he nodded with a grin of pure, red-blooded, masculine pride, she rose to her feet and held out her hand. "In that case, darling Jamie, I think we'd be better off in my bed, don't you?"

A little after midnight Finn woke up. For a moment she was disorientated but as comprehension dawned she lay there smiling in the darkness, listening to the unromantic sound of Charlie's gentle snoring. Charlie, oh, Charlie, she sighed inwardly. Their first coupling had been almost unbearably exciting, even savage, reflecting the pent-up passion and wrangling of the last few weeks, and Finn had an idea that it had been quite a long time since Charlie had slept with anyone.

The second time they made love — well, that was quite, quite different.

As she came down to earth afterwards she felt tears on her cheeks and when she could speak her voice was shaky.

"Oh that was . . . oh, I don't know; all the clichés, I think."

"What? Trumpets playing, shooting stars?"

His voice was warmly amused and she nestled closer. How satisfying that he didn't need to ask what she meant.

"Uh-huh, whole orchestra, entire galaxy, the full works. How about you?"

"Oh yes," he said simply. "Me too."

I've never felt like this, she thought, then laughed ruefully at herself. But I've said that every time, haven't I? But it *is* different, she insisted earnestly. There are layers and layers in this relationship that I've never experienced before. There's sex and friendship and liking and being in the same situation with my sister and his father and both of us lonely and — and hurt. I don't know what Charlie's problem is but I do know that he's been really badly hurt by some woman and all I want to do is claw her eyes out. The thing with Luc, that was nothing, nor with the others — a world away from this.

She slid carefully out from under Charlie's possessive arm and stumbled to the bathroom. After she sluiced water over her face she peered at her reflection in the mirror. A face she barely recognised stared back at her, a face transfigured, shining with happiness.

"Oh my God," she drew back in alarm. "Oh my God, I think I've gone and fallen in love with him!"

CHAPTER
NINE

Finn and Charlie stayed in bed all morning, making occasional forays downstairs to make tea and coffee, and once for bacon sandwiches, which they ate between bouts of ecstatic and energetic sex.

Julia and Jamie, on the other hand, decided that eight o'clock was as late as they could manage a lie-in.

"It's no use," Jamie groaned as he clambered out of bed. "I can't stay too long in bed these days, I start to seize up. Shall I go and start breakfast?"

Julia grinned lazily at his hopeful expression. "Breakfast? What breakfast? You just had it!"

"And without benefit of chemical assistance, too," he boasted. "Oh, all right, I'll go and put the kettle on."

It had been quite a night, Julia considered as she had a quick bath and got dressed. The little blue pill had obviously kick-started Jamie's confidence and he had proceeded to demonstrate more than once that he could do very well without it.

Over toast and tea they purred with satisfaction at each other.

"You really are the most adorable creature," he told her. "Can we make this a regular date? I haven't had so much fun in years."

At half past eleven they sauntered into the Antiques Fair at the Town Hall in Ramalley to check on progress and see if they were needed. Julia had another, secret, agenda, but as soon as she caught sight of Hugh Taylor's face she sighed. No sign of the radiantly smug self-satisfaction that characterised Jamie Stuart this morning. Rosemary was absent, too, her place taken by Delia Muncaster who was directing proceedings with her usual high hand.

"Certainly, my dear man," they heard her before they saw her. "This plate is, indeed, Royal Worcester and not a fake. Why is it so cheap? Because it was donated by a kind benefactor. However, if you'd prefer you may certainly pay me double the price. No? Very well, this lady will wrap it for you — here you are, Sue. I'll take the money, if you please."

Sue Merrill looked up at Julia's approach but carried on obediently with wrapping a large plate adorned with Highland cattle. She grinned as Julia raised an eyebrow towards their self-elected leader.

"She should have been a market trader, I've never seen anyone get so much blood from a stone."

"Ah, Julia! And Jamie too. My, my, what a pussy-cat grin, drop of the hard stuff work out all right?"

Sue looked puzzled but Jamie just grinned and Julia groaned.

"You shameless old besom," she scolded. "If you must make lewd comments at least make sure they're funny." She looked round the room. "Rosemary not here?"

Hugh's expression became even more po-faced as he turned towards them after selling a Caithness vase for ten pounds.

"Her mother is unwell," he said in a repressive tone. "A fainting spell I think it was. Rosemary had to call the doctor yesterday evening."

"She's not too bad today," thrust in Delia. "But Rosemary's going to have to make a decision soon rather than later, I'd say. Margot is definitely getting worse, markedly so in the last couple of weeks. I'd say it's only the Day Centre that keeps Rosemary sane. It won't be easy, poor girl."

Yes, poor Rosemary. Julia pursed her lips but there was nothing to say. Hugh hung around glowering until Charlie and Finn joined them on the stall when he mooched off to offer his services to Delia who was wrapping some china. Julia looked after him then caught Finn's eye.

"You had a lucky escape there, Ju," her sister murmured. "Hugh's not best pleased is he? Not a lot of support to Rosemary, just when she really needs him."

Julia nodded sadly.

"Be fair, though," she added. "He hasn't known Rosemary long and you have to admit that Margot is a lot to swallow. Besides, it's not that long since he nursed his wife in her final illness, it wouldn't be surprising if he felt a bit reluctant to get involved. Old wounds, you know. I'll check up on Rosemary after the Fair." She turned to look at Charlie who was enthusiastically taking up his selling career where he'd

136

left off after the Car Boot sale. "He looks pleased with himself?"

Finn nodded with a suddenly shy grin, then turned to Charlie who was insisting she admire him.

"Did you see that?" he crowed. "I sold a crystal vase for twenty-eight pounds, I could be good at this."

Finn was prowling around the other stalls looking for bargains when, just before lunch, Charlie's mobile rang. Seeing his sudden frown she sauntered back to the Gang's stall and eavesdropped.

"No problem," he lied, grimacing at her. "I'll be with you in about fifteen minutes, no better make that twenty. In the meantime, please don't touch anything else. *Please!*"

He reached out a long arm and pulled Finn close.

"Morons. Pressing buttons they've no business to." He kissed her hurriedly. "No idea how long I'll be, they may be idiots but they're also major client idiots. See ya."

She watched him as he left the room, his long, loping strides taking him quickly out of her sight, then she became aware that someone else was also looking after Charlie's retreating back view. A woman a few yards away was staring thoughtfully at the door, her eyes narrowed in a tiny frown.

Finn shrugged and turned her attention to an elderly lady who just wanted to chat about a glass jug and to confide that she had one at home, just like it.

"I'd like to look at that cup and saucer," a clear voice broke into the old lady's gentle maunderings, causing her to take off in fright.

The woman who had been watching Charlie was now staring at Finn, her eyes alight with curiosity and a definitely critical appraisal.

"This one?" Finn kept her voice neutral, allowing no sign of the irritation she felt. She handed over the delicate Derby cup and saucer and did a bit of covert assessment of her own. Slim, elegant, early thirties, maybe; *very* good-looking, *very* well-dressed, a perfect size eight in a five-foot-nothing body, with shiny dark hair and a perfect complexion. I hate you already, she sulked, then looked up as a man in his late fifties bustled up alongside the woman and put his arm round her.

"Found something you like, honey?" he smiled fatuously at her, then nodded to Finn. "How much?"

"It's seventy-five pounds," she told him sedately, disguising her surprise. "There's a tiny hairline crack just by the handle," she read off the accompanying card. "Otherwise the price would be much higher. It's a very sought-after pattern."

"Well, Amanda, darling? What about it? A nice little extra anniversary present, don't you think?"

"Oh, Neil," the woman fluttered her sickeningly long, thick eyelashes at him. "How sweet of you."

Julia had been watching the scene and brought over some bubble wrap as Finn silently counted out the change from his two fifties and Amanda stood by, still smiling that little-girl smile. Licensed prostitution, showing off her rich husband, Finn sniffed slanderously — why do I hate her so much? I don't even know her and please God, I'll never have to see her again.

"Do you have a shop?" Amanda was addressing her.

"A shop?" All Finn could think of was her workplace and she wondered wildly for a moment what Hedgehog's emporium had to do with anything.

"An antiques shop," Julia cut in smoothly. "No, nothing like that. We're just doing this for a good cause, treats for the elderly, you know the sort of thing."

"Oh," Amanda had lost interest. "How very — commendable." She cast another of those appraising glances at Finn, chewed on her lower lip and then, as her husband moved on to the next stall, she asked, with an air of speaking in spite of herself, "Will you be at next month's Fair here?"

"Who knows?" Finn spoke in an airy, but dismissive tone. She was getting seriously annoyed. Why was this woman so interested in her? For interested she certainly was and furthermore she was still darting surreptitious glances towards the door from which Charlie had made his exit.

For the next hour or two Finn brooded about the stranger. Did she know Charlie? Could she perhaps provide answers to Finn's increasingly urgent questions. Maybe she knew the mysteriously absent wife that Charlie insisted he'd never had, while others were so sure he *had*. I'll just mention her to Charlie, she decided, then a minute later changed her mind. Maybe not, not just yet.

Julia broke into her anxious musing. "Did you know that girl?" she asked curiously. "You know, the one who flashed her knickers at daddy so he'd buy her a pretty plaything?"

In spite of her forebodings Finn giggled. "He wasn't daddy," she argued. "He had to be her husband, the way he was doting on her. Though you might be right, sugar daddy perhaps. And no, I've never seen her before but I have a feeling she might know Charlie, I spotted her watching him as he left — with a very sneaky look on her face."

"Do you want me to have a word with Jamie, about Charlie I mean?" Julia was sympathetic.

"Oh God, no!" Finn was vehement. "That's the last thing I must do, he's got so many no-go areas, I daren't start prying. No, whatever it is, I think he'll tell me — eventually. I know he's been badly hurt, I'm certain of that, so it'll take time for him to trust me enough."

"Well done, people." Delia was jubilant at the end of the Fair as they packed up their remaining goods. "After subtracting the cost of hiring two tables, we've taken nearly eleven hundred pounds! It's absolutely magnificent."

The expressions on the faces of the regular stallholders bore this out, they were all pea-green with a seething envy, but Delia resolutely ignored them and gathered her troops about her as she continued.

"Although we've all been absolute slaves it's mostly down to one person." She smiled kindly at Ursula who had turned an unbecoming shade of brick. "Ursula's Royal Worcester vases kick-started us off well when Julia sold three of them to a London dealer for a hundred and fifty pounds each. What with them and with Hugh's pieces of Wedgwood I think the punters

140

were so impressed by the quality of our goods that they bought indiscriminately. Well done, again, folks."

She hadn't finished with them and just as the Gang tried to slope off home Delia struck again.

"Just one thing, chaps," she said in a wheedling tone. "I thought of another little fund-raiser. I'm proposing to hold a house-warming party at Daisy Cottage next Saturday evening and I thought, as so many people seem to remember my husband's extremely boring television series about historic homes, I could turn it to good use, so I'll lay out all his books and notes and stuff and we'll have a — what shall I call it — a salon? A *conversazione*? All you have to do is provide some food and invite at least two other people. I'll supply the drink and we'll charge ten pounds a head."

There was a chorus of groans, mingled with curiosity to see what Delia had done with her house. Most of them remembered Guy Muncaster's pontifications in his seventies television programmes. "*Absolute integrity and faithfulness to period is imperative,*" he had thundered at them, week after week. Had Delia been infused with the same ideals?

"I'll give you detailed instructions tomorrow," she announced briskly, taking no notice of their whinges. "In the meantime, you'd better get those invitations out. Seven-thirty for eight, Saturday night, drink, food and conversation, what more could anybody want?"

Glumly the group dispersed. Julia dropped Jamie off at home with a loving kiss and she and Finn repaired to her kitchen to share a frozen pizza. They were just clearing away the debris when Sue Merrill rang the front door bell.

"Sue?" Julia was warmly welcoming. "Come on in, Finn and I have just opened a bottle of Chilean Merlot, come and join us."

She poured another glass and the three women settled in Julia's comfortable, shabby old leather sofas. Finn was intrigued by Sue Merrill, barely seven years younger than herself but a generation older in manner and outlook. Julia had told her of Sue's introduction to the first meeting of the Group. Lonely? Yes, I can believe that, she thought idly, wondering how Charlie was getting on.

"I need your advice, Julia." Sue came to the point abruptly.

"Shall I go?" Finn half rose but Sue waved her back to her seat.

"No, of course not, you might have some ideas too." She sat in silence for a while as Julia and Finn exchanged raised eyebrows. At last she obviously came to a decision and looked up at them.

"I want to know if you think I ought to leave my husband," she said baldly. "Oh, I know it's not something anyone else can decide for me," she continued as they both murmured in surprise. "It's just ... I've never talked about it to anyone and it's festering away inside. I'll tell you the situation. When we first met, Julia, at that initial meeting, I said something like — my husband and I lead separate lives."

Julia nodded encouragingly and Sue carried on.

"It's true enough, but it's only recently. When I went to that first meeting I'd only just found out. I think if I hadn't come across you, all of you, I might have gone completely under, but you saved me, so much so that I think I might have enough strength to finish it properly."

She lapsed into that brooding silence again until Julia prompted her gently.

"What was it that you'd only just found out, Sue?" she asked quietly.

"That Philip had a mistress," came the answer. "He'd been carrying on with her for a year — she's his secretary — and he thought it would be nice and tidy if I got myself a lover and maybe we could all set up house together. That way he and I needn't separate, which would be a pity as he's still fond of me."

"You mean that way he could have his cake and eat it?" Finn's indignation was explosive. "Of course you should leave him, Sue, he's a complete shit!" She described her own experience with Luc and her handling of it.

"It's different for you," Sue argued, though she had brightened with interest at the story. "You're beautiful and confident, and you weren't married."

"Sue's got a point," Julia raised her hand to stem further arguments from Finn. "You weren't even living with Luc. It's more of a mess when there's property and legal things involved. But honestly, Sue," she turned her sympathetic smile on to the other woman. "Don't think about that. The main thing is how *you* feel about it. For a start, do you still love him?"

Sue looked startled.

"D'you know, I don't think I do," she seemed absurdly surprised. "I think I did, but when he came out with his confession I think it all started to fall away. What hurt me so much was that he told me he'd fallen in love with her and that it was vastly different from anything he'd ever felt for me. But now I think he was right, we just drifted into marriage because we'd been going out together for a year or two and it seemed the right thing to do, everyone expected it, even us. The other thing that really upset me —" She glowered resentfully at Julia and Finn who were listening to her, open-mouthed. "The really horrible thing is that he said she's fantastic in bed, in contrast to when he was with me. I should have retaliated and told him I never had much fun in bed with him either. Trouble is, I've no other experience to compare it with."

Finn and Julia exchanged glances again but Sue carried on unhappily.

"In fact, the last time I had an orgasm was . . ." She counted off on her fingers while her audience stared in even more fascinated sympathy. "Let me see, it was when we went to Italy for a holiday, that's two years and four months ago, almost to the day." She stuck out her bottom lip in sulky misery. "And *that* was self-inflicted," she said with a final surly flourish.

The two sisters gazed at her and then at each other, both struck at the same time by the bathos and absurdity of her final remark. Julia looked down hastily as she saw Finn's lips quiver in spite of herself, but it

144

was too late and they both burst into involuntary giggles.

"Don't be angry, Sue," Julia leapt up and flung her arms round her affronted friend. "We're not laughing at you, honestly, I know you're in a horrible situation. It's just that it sounds so bizarre."

Sue stopped bridling at their reception of her sorry tale and managed a wan smile.

"You're right," she admitted eventually, as she rose and shrugged into her coat. "I might as well laugh, crying doesn't work. Thanks, Julia and you too, Finn, it's been a help to talk it over though I still don't know what I'll do about it."

She picked up her bag and went to the front door looking resolute.

"I know what I'm going to do now, though," she told them as they said goodnight. "I'm going straight home and I'm going to knit myself an orgasm. You're quite right to laugh, *that*'s something I can do for myself, at least!"

CHAPTER
TEN

True to her word Delia was ready the next day with a draft of her master plan for what she insisted on calling her *Conversazione*, to be held on the following Saturday.

"Here we are." She dropped in on Julia just before lunch. "I've put in my order with Threshers but I suppose you lesser mortals will need to stuff your faces. I've done a rough list that shouldn't tax anyone's capabilities, see what you think. I mean, I know Jonathan won't dare to do much in case that vulture of a wife of his cottons on, but I should think he could rise to some packets of salted peanuts and crisps, wouldn't you? Marek, on the other hand, loves to cook so I've suggested he produce something interesting and Polish.

"I'm working on a rough estimate of about forty people. Yes," as Julia gasped, "I know it sounds a lot but if you count Finn and Charlie there are twelve of us, so if we all invite at least two other guests, and possibly more, there you are." She consulted her list. "I thought you could rustle up something wholesome and hearty like a couple of enormous shepherd's pies or lasagnes, just the thing for an autumn evening, don't you agree?

I know we're past Hallowe'en but maybe somebody could make a pumpkin pie?"

"Just give everyone a definite dish to make," suggested Julia. "And tell them how many it has to feed. You're making things too complicated by letting people choose. I agree about Jonathan, but equally, he can afford a catering box of crisps and ditto peanuts. And Marek's a superb cook, you're right about him too. He makes a fantastic goulash, I know it's not strictly speaking Polish, but it's his party piece. Just don't insult him by mentioning the cost or he'll go off into one of his Slav sulks. Tell him you're relying on him to help out and ask him to cook up enough for forty people, he'll be thrilled.

"Let's have a look at your plan. Hmm, can Ursula cook? Yes, of course she can, she said she can bake, so ask her to make you some apple pies, she's got apple trees and as long as Henrietta doesn't take it into her head to interfere. Mind you, she seems to be letting Ursula do as she pleases these days, maybe she's getting senile. Still, long may it last."

"I've put Rosemary down for a couple of bowls of green salad and french bread," Delia pointed to her list. "Whatever's going to happen with Margot, Rosemary won't want to think about food at present. Have you spoken to her yet?"

"I rang last night," Julia told her. "And this morning, twice, but I just got the machine. I thought I'd wander over in a minute and take some of this quiche as an excuse."

Delia approved this subterfuge and set off on her provisioning mission as Julia picked up her offering and crossed the green to Rosemary's bungalow.

"Oh, it's you," was her friend's ungracious greeting, then she pulled herself together. "Sorry, Julia, I must sound awful. It's just that I was expecting the doctor."

"Is Margot worse?" Julia deposited the quiche in the kitchen and looked quickly at Rosemary. "I tried to get hold of you last night but there were no lights in the house and you weren't taking calls so I thought you must have managed to get some sleep."

Rosemary shook her head dazedly. "You heard about Margot's funny five minutes, I suppose?"

"Uh-huh, Delia and Hugh told me. A fainting fit, wasn't it?"

"I think so, but she fainted again." Rosemary ran worried fingers through her hair and after another, thoughtful look at her, Julia delved into the cutlery drawer and handed her the plate of quiche and a knife and fork.

"Eat that," she ordered. "No, I've had my lunch already, I was hungry. I brought over enough for you and Margot but she can wait, you probably haven't eaten all day. Go on, eat up, you'll do better with something inside you."

Rosemary was too tired to argue but when she had finished up the last crumb she managed a faint smile.

"OK, you win, I *do* feel a bit better." Her face twisted and she resolutely banished her sombre

148

thoughts. "Tell me about the Antiques Fair and about you and Jamie. Did you . . .?"

"Certainly did," Julia grinned smugly. "In fact I'm wondering if the tabloids would buy my sordid story? That would bring us in some money, wouldn't it? I can see the headlines now — OAP Sex Romps in Sleepy Hampshire Market Town!"

"Absolutely not," Rosemary was roused from her own introspection. "And don't suggest we have an Anne Summers party to raise funds either, I can't cope with the image of Delia as a dominatrix in crotchless knickers!"

"Oh, I don't know," Julia began, but just then Rosemary's face crumpled and a dry sob escaped her. When Julia moved to comfort her she shook her head.

"No don't, please, I can't afford to get maudlin. But, oh God, Julia, it's been wretched."

"Tell me," invited Julia, confining herself to a friendly pat on the shoulder.

"Well, I'd told her she was going to Delia's for a couple of hours — that's what I'd agreed to though Delia actually offered to babysit for the whole day. She's one of the kindest people I know, under that hard-boiled exterior. Margot was quite pleased, she likes Delia and she was dying to see inside Daisy Cottage, as we all are, so she was feeling pretty complacent that she'd be the first person in the village to get a guided tour."

She sighed but carried on in a quiet, unemotional tone.

"She was really quite well, talking normally, taking an interest and then, of course, she insisted on having a dress rehearsal for the visit. I tried to talk her out of it but you know what she's like when she's with-it, a stickler for 'doing the right thing'? So I thought I might as well let her get on with it, the full works, the Barbara Cartland treatment, and she was *so* pleased with herself when she'd done. I sat her in the kitchen while I started on the meal for Hugh and me — I told you he came round with champagne Saturday afternoon, and I invited him for dinner? Well, I was wondering how soon I could get her to bed but I didn't want to rush her. Hugh wasn't due for an hour and anyway, we were getting on well, for once, having a reasonably rational conversation. Then all of a sudden she went quiet and kind of slid off her chair.

"I managed to catch her but she was all floppy so I got her into the sitting room and laid her on the settee, then I called the doctor. It was a locum and he wasn't interested, just said I'd better call an ambulance, when he heard her age. Of course, by the time the ambulance arrived, just as the same time as Hugh turned up, she'd come round and was as perky as ever, perkier than normal in fact, so I felt a complete idiot. I convinced them I could manage and they left, rather in a huff, so I went upstairs to get Margot's bed ready, leaving Hugh with a drink, keeping an eye on her. When I came downstairs again . . ."

Her voice tailed way and she looked at Julia with tragic eyes.

150

"Well, you can guess, can't you? That's right, she'd managed to strip down to her bra, which she'd put on over her vest in the first place, *and* back to front, and she was offering to give him a blow job!"

Julia let out a shocked peal of laughter.

"Oh, I'm sorry, Rosemary," she apologised. "You know me, no sense of decorum. So *that's* why Hugh was looking so upset yesterday when he turned up at the Antiques Fair. He just wouldn't be able to handle anything like that, and no wonder." Jamie would, though, she thought with secret pride. He'd be quite charming but firm and get her dressed again into the bargain. Oh, poor old Rosemary.

"So how is she today?" she asked as once again she took over her friend's kitchen, this time to make a pot of tea.

To her surprise Rosemary also began to giggle.

"She was a perfect lamb this morning, let me wash and dress her without a murmur, but then I couldn't for the life of me work out what she'd done with her teeth. They weren't on her bedside table and at first she wouldn't co-operate. Then she suddenly reached under her pillow and brandished them at me, snapping them like a crocodile and saying, 'Gottle o' gear, gottle o' gear!'"

She sighed and wiped away a tear before she continued.

"Once I managed to get the teeth in her mouth she was full of fun, really laughing at her own joke and remembering — as I did — that she'd always told me about her own grandmother playing the same trick

151

when Margot was a little girl. Just for a while we were back as we used to be — she was always a great one for jokes when I was young."

Her voice cracked and fortunately, just at that moment, the front door bell rang.

"I'll just take down some details," said the young woman doctor briskly. "Your friend? Oh, hi there, Julia, how are you? No, of course I don't mind, in fact I'm glad you've got someone to give you a hand. Now, what I don't understand, Miss Clavering, is why you've never got in touch with Social Services about your mother? I know my predecessor organised the Day Centre for her, but he doesn't seem to have done anything else. Was that the case or did you turn down any more offers of help? You could have been getting all kinds more assistance with your mother, you know."

Rosemary shrugged. "It didn't occur to me we would qualify," she said shortly, biting her tongue in an attempt not to cry out that the Claverings would never accept charity. The time for that kind of foolish pride was long past. "We had the attendance allowance and the Day Centre. All I want you to do today is check Margot out. I told your receptionist, *and* the locum, that she'd had a fainting spell but she's perfectly all right today." She rose to her feet. "Perhaps you'd like to come and see her, she's spending the day in bed because last night's events tired her out."

The doctor followed her meekly back into the dining hall, looking round with open curiosity.

152

"This is *so* nice," she said with approving envy. "I'm looking for a house just like this, I suppose you aren't thinking of selling?"

Rosemary shook her head wordlessly then knocked and opened Margot's door. She stood back to let the doctor go in and was surprised when the younger woman halted abruptly on the threshold with an exclamation of horror.

"What is it?" Rosemary peered round the doctor's shoulder and shuddered.

Margot, stark naked, was standing at her open window, waving to an astonished tractor driver in the field behind the house. There was an ominous smell coming from the huddle of bedclothes and a second, unconnected, smell emanating from the curtain.

The doctor was momentarily glued to the spot, appalled, as Rosemary sniffed the air, ignoring the smell from the bed, nothing new about that, it was the other that set off alarm bells in her head.

"Oh my God, Julia, come up here quickly, she's set fire to the curtains!"

Rosemary pushed her mother out of the way and tore down the smouldering curtain, stamping out the tiny flickering flames.

The doctor snapped out of her trance and grabbed a dressing gown from the hook behind the door and wrapped it round the old woman, while Rosemary stamped again on a tongue of flame snaking from the curtain towards her across the floor. She was vaguely aware that Julia and the doctor had managed to get Margot into a chair, where she flopped like a doll, all the fight gone out of her. The doctor was talking urgently into her mobile and Julia was briskly stripping the stinking bed and heading for the utility room.

The doctor flipped off her phone and turned to Rosemary.

"I've called an ambulance," she said crisply. "And this time she's getting into it. Your mother needs the kind of supervision you can't possibly provide, so please don't feel guilty. She can go to the geriatric ward of Ramalley Hospital for now while I look into long-term care."

Dazed, Rosemary obediently packed a bag for Margot, not forgetting the precious cosmetics. As they waited for the ambulance she sounded out the doctor about this ominous-sounding long-term care.

"I can't afford a decent private nursing home for her," she said abruptly. "I'm retired myself and Margot only has the basic pension. I can't bear the thought of her in one of those homes you read about . . ."

"Don't think about it just now," the doctor was coolly kind. "Anyway, Ramalley is pretty good about geriatric care, so don't worry. Ah, here's the ambulance, do you want to go in with her?"

"I'll take Rosemary in my car," Julia had set the washing machine going and rejoined them. "Here we are, Margot, all set for a ride with some nice young men, sweetheart?"

Rosemary caught her breath in a half sob but Julia shook her head and picked up Rosemary's handbag. Together they followed as the ambulance man wheeled Margot down the path and helped her into the back of

154

the vehicle. Margot nodded gaily to the driver who was helping and as he went to shut the door, they heard his patient speaking chattily to his colleague in that carrying, impeccably cut-glass voice.

"I think we've just got time for a quick fuck, haven't we, my dear? Come along, trousers down and let's take a look at your tackle."

Rigid with shock for a moment the driver caught Rosemary's eye and burst out laughing as he got the door closed at last. She bit her lip and pinched Julia's arm so that the inevitable gaggle of curious neighbours should be spared the sight of a sniggering daughter shipping her aged mother off to the workhouse.

"You OK?" Julia backed out on to the road and headed for the General Hospital.

Rosemary considered for a moment. "Surprisingly, yes I am," she answered. "I feel a bit of a zombie, but otherwise I'm fine."

Julia nodded sagely. "Relief, I guess, and sharing the load, it takes people that way. If nothing else comes of this at least you'll be getting some proper help with her. I'm all in favour of family pride and stiff upper lips — in their place — but you do tend to take it to extremes."

At the hospital they found Margot being tucked kindly and firmly into bed, looking subdued. She cocked an eye at her daughter but held her tongue, so Julia volunteered to sit with her while Rosemary allowed herself to be towed away for a spot of form-filling.

"Let's see, name, date of birth, etcetera, etcetera." The ward clerk worked rapidly down the form. "Anything we should know about Mrs Delaney? Likes, dislikes? Any little foibles?"

Rosemary gave her a blank stare.

"It all helps, dear," explained the woman kindly. "We do try to make the patients as comfortable as it's humanly possible."

"I'm sure you do," Rosemary pulled herself together. "It's just . . . let me think. Foibles? How much space is there on the form? Well, Margot likes to have her make-up handy; she'll want to tart herself up when there's a doctor around — a male doctor, that is. And I suppose I ought to warn you she likes to take all her clothes off."

She warmed to her theme.

"She's sex-mad and she's convinced she's absolutely irresistible to any man, so you should warn any male nurses not to get too close or she'll have a grope." She knitted her brow as she recalled a recent incident with a young assistant in Waitrose. "Oh yes, just lately, if I tell her to do something she doesn't want to, or if I tell her off, she'll just stand there and pee, and she can get quite vicious, too. I think that's about all."

To her surprise the other woman gave her a warm smile of sympathy.

"I can see you've been having quite a time of it," she commented kindly. "Don't worry about a thing, I'll warn any man who comes into her orbit to wear a cricket box and as for widdling out of spite, I think that must be universal at both ends of the spectrum, I know

156

my two-year-old grandson does it and so do half the old ladies in here. It's almost a pity this isn't a mixed ward, we get lots of sex-mad old men over the other side of the building, it'd cheer them up no end to find a willing volunteer."

She handed Rosemary a box of tissues and patted the suddenly heaving shoulders.

That's it," she soothed. "Let it all out and don't worry about her. There's nothing you can tell anybody on this ward about bloody-minded old biddies, we've seen it all before, and worse."

Back at Margot's bedside Rosemary summoned up a ghost of a smile as she nodded to Julia. Margot seemed, at first glance, to be dead, her skin greyish under the garish mask of make-up but as Julia rose to go and Rosemary bent towards her mother, a wary grey eye opened.

"Rosemary?"

The voice was a wisp of sound but all the marbles were firmly back in place.

"What is it, Margot?" Rosemary bent closer and Margot reached out a trembling finger to touch her wrist.

"The field, you promised."

Rosemary's face twisted. "I promise, Mother, I'll make sure it's just as you want."

As she drove out of the hospital gates Julia remembered this conversation.

"What did she mean about the field?"

To Julia's surprise, Rosemary smiled faintly.

"Didn't I tell you about that?" She waited as Julia negotiated the tricky corner in Bell Street then, as the car headed for the bridge out of town, she explained.

"Margot made me promise that: a) I won't let them resuscitate her if it comes to it — she put it in writing and got it witnessed at the Day Centre. And b) she doesn't want to be buried in the cemetery or cremated. She wants me to get Phil Owens to bury her in his field, the one behind our house, at the top end under the big oak tree."

"Oh, bless her, the daft old soul!" Julia joined in Rosemary's slightly wild laughter. "What did you say? You'll do as she wants?"

"Of course," said Rosemary simply. "I asked Phil and he says it's fine with him, that corner of the field is never put under the plough. He just insisted that I get the paperwork sorted out properly."

Instead of going straight home Julia drove into the pub car park.

"Come on, sweetheart, you need a stiff drink after that lot, I know I do." She led the faintly protesting Rosemary into the Lounge Bar, empty today even of Delia's custom. "Here, drink this down and let's toast your mum. Here's to Margot and may she go out when, and how, she would like best."

They raised their glasses in the ceremonious toast and eventually Rosemary began to relax.

"Well, it certainly put a stop to my romantic evening on Saturday," she said ruefully. "I sent Hugh home early on, it was plain Margot was going to take up all my attention and besides, he was pretty shocked at her offer." She looked curiously at Julia. "So . . . you and Jamie, eh? Charlie and Finn, too?" As Julia nodded Rosemary smiled and sighed. "Lucky old you," she said enviously.

To deflect her brooding attention Julia described the success of the Antiques Fair and informed her that Delia would be gunning for her pretty soon.

"I think she's got you down for enough green salad to feed forty," she explained. "And baguettes and butter to go with it. I wonder what she'll dish up in the way of entertainment? I've no idea who I'm going to invite or what will be on offer."

"Oh, I don't know." Rosemary roused herself to take an interest. "Guy Muncaster was pretty famous in his field, wasn't he? If she's planning to set out his books and so forth, I suppose she could also have his series running on the video, that might be interesting to some people."

"Good idea," Julia was just downing the last of her gin and tonic when a familiar voice rang in her ear.

"Julia, just the girl I wanted to see. I heard about Margot, Rosemary. You'll feel better for a little breathing space."

"What Machiavellian scheme do you have in mind for me now, Delia?" Julia asked with mild resignation. "Come and sit with us. Pull up a gin and unburden yourself."

"My little entertainment on Saturday," Delia said, finishing her first glass and turning to the second, waiting on the little tray in front of her. "Oh, by the way, before I forget — I had a visitation from Mrs Parsons just now. She told me she knows what we're up to." She let the outcry from the other two die down. "As far as I can make out she's been eavesdropping on Bobbie and Ursula, by the simple means of sitting behind them on the bus. She said she'd go to the police if I didn't give her what she wanted."

"What *does* she want?" Julia was round-eyed and Delia laughed scornfully.

"She wants to be invited to my little party. I said that was fine and she was quite welcome as long as she paid up ten pounds like all the rest. As for her threats, I told her the police would think she was gaga and put her in a home. She caved in surprisingly quickly, must be losing her touch. Now," She consulted her list. "I think you said part of Finn's duties at the shop is to tell fortunes? Well, there you are." She ignored Julia's exclamation. "Nonsense, of course she won't mind. We can put her in the study and charge people ten pounds for ten minutes — no, better make that five minutes, then we can rake in even more money."

She listened impassively as Julia railed at her, protesting that her sister was not to be exploited so ruthlessly and that, in any case, Finn would never agree.

"Nonsense," she said again. "I'll speak to her today. And while we're about it, don't you think it's time you got Finn and Charlie to confirm that they'll be tagging along on our holiday? I'm sure they'll enjoy it, but they ought to make up their minds."

160

CHAPTER
ELEVEN

Blissfully unaware that the iron fist of Delia Muncaster was about to descend on them Finn and Charlie ate a leisurely dinner and relaxed in front of the television that evening.

"Where's your father?" Finn asked idly as she cuddled close to Charlie on the comfortable cream leather chesterfield in his sitting room. "Isn't he moving to his new flat this week?"

"Uh-huh," Charlie was lazily playing with her hair. "He's over at Julia's this evening, I think they were going to take Rosemary Clavering out to dinner to take advantage of her freedom, but she cried off, said she was too knackered, so Julia volunteered to cook at home." He bent to kiss her neck, lingering over the pulse at the base of her throat. "Very kind woman, your sister."

"Mmm," Finn nodded, shivering slightly at his touch. "Runs in the family. Mmmm! Don't stop, that's lovely."

Eventually Charlie recalled the rest of her question.

"Pa's due to complete on the flat this Friday, at twelve noon, so he wants to move in the minute he gets the keys from the estate agents. I've promised to knock

161

off work when he picks them up and to give him a hand. There's not a lot to move over there from this house, he's had his furniture in store and that's on schedule to arrive about half past two on Friday. I hope nothing happens to delay the move, I might have to disappear off to Newcastle for a week or so. Might not happen," he said soothingly when she pouted in dismay. "But it's on the cards. Big project, loadsamoney, can't say no if they really do insist."

They sat in contented silence for a while then Finn roused herself as she recalled something funny.

"Who've you asked to Delia's housewarming, then?"

"I haven't," he groaned. "I suppose I could ask my current number one clients, the intelligent ones, at least, not the mad button pushers. Why, who are you asking?"

"Hedgehog," she giggled. "I just haven't got to know anybody else, apart from you and all Julia's mates, so I asked him. He was thrilled to bits." She smiled as she pictured her eccentric employer's excitement. "I said, could he bring somebody else with him so Delia doesn't bully me and he went a bit shy.

"Well, naturally I assumed he'd got a girl he wanted to bring, probably a Charlie Dimmock sort, bucolic and buxom, so I just mumbled some encouraging words and it all came tumbling out."

"What?" Charlie was curious enough to shift round so that he could see her face. "I don't see old Hedgehog as the confessional type, somehow."

"You'd be surprised," she teased, then relented and told him the whole story. "He's not really, he just

162

wasn't sure if anyone would mind if he brought along his ex-brother-in-law Bernard, known as Bunny for short, who's a farmer over Andover way. I said fine, of course, but he'd better warn Bunny it was likely to be excruciatingly boring, mostly retired people, and nothing much happening. But plenty of drink, knowing Delia."

She giggled reminiscently and went on.

"It turns out that not only is Bunny a friend of Hedge's, especially as he loathes his sister who was Hedgehog's wife, but he was a big fan of Guy Muncaster, loved his programmes and has all his books. Hedgehog was really chuffed at the thought of how pleased Bunny would be. 'Lady Delia's house,' he said. 'He'll be in heaven, a dream come true.' It was really rather sweet, apparently Bunny's been a great support to Hedge over the last few years. But why he was a bit iffy about how we'd take it, is that Bunny is gay and Hedge didn't want his feelings hurt."

"Well, blow me!" Charlie was mildly surprised. "I'd never have had Hedgehog down as the sensitive sort. Hey, you don't reckon he's gay too? No? I wouldn't either. If anyone asked me I'd have to say I reckon he's too stoned most of the time to know which end is which. Just goes to show, doesn't it? I hope you reassured him. Any other interesting news?"

Finn was tempted to reveal Sue Merrill's dilemma but decided against it, none of my business, she told herself. She was even more tempted to tell him about the mystery woman at the Antiques Fair, and even more certain she should hold her tongue.

***

On Saturday night as Finn was getting ready for Delia's party, she looked back to the previous Saturday. Only a week ago and she and Charlie were just friends; more than friends certainly — and reconciled friends at that — but not yet lovers, and look at them now. Julia and Jamie too, were now firmly established in everyone's eyes as an item and Julia had been much in evidence when Jamie took possession of his flat in the Old Parsonage.

Rosemary Clavering was gradually unwinding as she became used to Margot's absence, and the fraught look of strain had left her face. Finn, along with the members of the Gang, had looked in on Margot at the hospital. She had taken Margot a copy of *Vogue*, a pair of lacy knickers and a Dior lipstick in a shocking shade of scarlet.

Rosemary had thanked Finn with moist eyes.

"You're so thoughtful," she told her. "It's been just terribly kind of the others to go and see her, but apart from Delia who smuggled in some Drambuie, and Julia, who took her some Chanel No.5, the others have tended to give her grapes and hankies and lavender bath salts, that sort of thing. You can imagine what she thinks of it, but luckily she hasn't said anything untoward — I keep expecting an explosion of Feck! Arse! or Drink! But the knickers you gave her, she was absolutely thrilled and when I left she had them on and was hell-bent on showing them off to a nice young doctor who made the mistake of stopping and speaking to her."

164

Hugh Taylor seemed to be edging tentatively back into Rosemary's good graces but Julia confided to Finn that she thought he'd been badly shaken by Margot's generous offer and it would take time and patience to get him back in line. Julia was intensely irritated by Rosemary's reception of Hugh's stumbling renewed advances.

"She's a disgrace to the sisterhood," she proclaimed to Finn one evening. "She's just so pathetically grateful for a kind word from him, it doesn't seem to occur to her that she's a person in her own right. I tell her people chained themselves to railings just so she could smile meekly at a man when he nods his head to her."

"I'm sure she's very grateful to you," retorted Finn. "Calm down, Julia, you said yourself Rosemary's a born doormat. A doormat needs to be trampled on, let them get on with it."

At the other end of the village Ursula, another doormat, and Bobbie were taking very seriously their duties as new mothers.

"Do come and see them, Finn," Bobbie urged one evening when they met on the village green. "We only meant to get one cat between the two of us, but when we got to the cat lady's house and she showed them to us, we simply couldn't resist."

Ursula looked very much at home in Bobbie's mother's saggily comfortable arm chair, upholstered in faded Sanderson roses. On her face she wore an expression of complete bliss combined with pride: on her lap she held, with difficulty, a very, *very* large tabby cat with tufty ears and a long, bottle-brush tail.

"Oh, Finn," she exclaimed. "How nice, do forgive me, dear, but I can't get up. Sampson is inclined to fuss rather if he's disturbed." She beamed besottedly at the enormous creature and stroked him anxiously. Sampson raised his head and gave Finn a definite smirk.

"But didn't Bobbie say there were two cats?"

Finn looked round the room. Nope, no sign of a second feline newcomer, then a black fur wrap on the settee lifted its head and yawned in her direction, showing off a wide pink mouth and what looked like more than the ordinary complement of teeth.

"Wow! And who's this one, then?"

"Why that's Delilah, of course," Bobbie scuttled in, more brisk and purposeful than Finn had ever seen her. "Here we are, you'll join us in a little toast, won't you, Finn? Just to say hello to the precious moggies."

She handed Finn a glass of sherry and they toasted the cats heartily.

"But they aren't just moggies, surely?" Finn stroked Delilah's sooty velvet coat and looked at her curiously. "For a start, they're so huge. Are they some special breed?"

"Well spotted —"

"How clever you are —"

They both answered her at once but Ursula smiled and shook her head, so Bobbie explained.

"The cat lady said they're Maine Coon cats, you know? An American breed. She thinks Sampson is pure bred but Delilah probably has some ordinary pussy cat in her, that's why she's smaller and smoother. Aren't they gorgeous? They've settled in so wonderfully, they seem quite at home already."

"They sit at the window, waiting for me," Ursula boasted shyly. "And when I open the gate you should see the performance they put on, standing up and pawing at the glass and miaowing like mad."

As their adoptive offspring deigned to curl up together in front of the fire Ursula came to the front door with Bobbie to see Finn off.

"So sad," Ursula whispered, so the cats couldn't hear. "Their poor owner died a fortnight ago and her relatives couldn't, or wouldn't, take the darling pussy cats. But so fortunate for us, of course."

"Finn?" Julia knocked on Finn's door. "Charlie and Jamie are here to walk us over to Delia's house. Get a move on."

"Has anybody managed to get a look inside Daisy Cottage yet?" Finn was curious as she strolled along beside Charlie, her hand tucked in his. "I'm dying to see what she's done with it, all those years of living with an expert must have rubbed off on her."

"I'm not so sure," Julia was more cautious. "Delia's very pig-headed, to put it mildly, and I get the impression that she and the sainted Guy lived in a state of armed truce. I remember his TV programmes, very purist they were, everything had to be authentic and true to the period of the building. I don't somehow see our Delia living happily alongside historical accuracy. Very addicted to her creature comforts is Delia."

The exterior of Delia's house gave nothing away. It was very similar in design to Charlie's house, probably the same builder; four-square, early nineteenth century, built in a pinkish old brick, immaculately repointed in the recent renovations. The windows were newly double-glazed, certainly, but they had been done by a very expensive firm specialising in period houses. The drive was gravelled and weed-free and shrubs and heathers filled the flower beds under the windows.

"Come in, come in," rang out the voice of their hostess and Delia appeared at the door, gin, inevitably, in hand. "Who's this? Ah, Jamie and Charlie, how very smart you look. Thank you for coming in dinner jackets, adds a certain grandness to the proceedings, don't you think? And your lady-loves, too. Let's have a look at you, girls."

"We've played safe," Julia proclaimed, kissing Delia and doing an obliging twirl. "Finn's wearing the proverbial little black dress and I'm wearing a large one. Have our guests arrived yet? I asked the new doctor and her husband but she decided they'd come under their own steam as his shifts are difficult to predict — he's an anaesthetist at the hospital."

Stowing their coats in the small study to the right of the front door her visitors looked around with enormous curiosity when they emerged into the hall.

"Well?" Delia was looking at them with a more than usually inscrutable expression as she awaited their comments.

"Golly!" For once Julia was almost speechless then she rallied. "It looks ... um, it looks very ... comfortable."

"It looks very pink, you mean," countered Delia.

"Well, yes, that too."

"It *is* pink," Delia said, surveying the rose-patterned wallpaper and dark pink carpet with complacency. "Wait till you see the drawing room. Come on in, let's see if they've recovered the power of speech yet."

A mixed bag of people stood and sat in the large and undeniably pink drawing room, conversing in awkward whispers. Rosemary was standing beside Hugh Taylor and a couple of women Julia recognised as fellow daughters Rosemary had met visiting their equally incapacitated mothers at the hospital. Bobbie had dragooned a couple of her former Brownie parents into joining the throng and Ursula was there with the couple who owned the village shop. The latter two had been dying of curiosity and were highly gratified to be invited.

Equally thrilled were the pub landlord and his wife whom Jonathan had tentatively invited, knowing he could rely on them not to let slip anything to Pauline. They had also suffered from the rough edge of her tongue when they first took over the tenancy and Pauline had tried to whip up a campaign to stop them opening all day. Like everyone else in the village they liked and pitied Jonathan.

Jamie had brought along his new next-door neighbours, and Marek some fellow residents of the sheltered flats. They were all nervously sipping at their drinks and watching Delia like a flock of frightened sparrows in the presence of a hawk. Mrs Parsons had declined the invitation to pay for the privilege of mixing with "a load of snobs and losers."

"Everyone here?" Delia's voice dropped, bell-like, into the low murmur.

"I'm so sorry, Delia," Hugh Taylor's voice was apologetic and a little fretful. "My guests will be a little late, he's a member of the golf club, got some earlier function I think he said. He's bringing his wife."

"Not a problem." The answer was accompanied by a genial baring of teeth and Hugh sagged with relief. "They can catch up on the drinking when they get here. I'll just get the proceedings off to a start then we can get down to the serious part of the evening." She moved to centre stage.

"Thank you all, very much, for coming tonight. I'm very glad to welcome you, friends and new acquaintances, to Daisy Cottage. It's taken a long time to get things straight, much longer than I anticipated in fact, but here I am. And here I intend to stay, I don't fancy going through the experience another time. However, if anyone wants a good builder, come to me for a recommendation."

Waving a hand in the direction of her blushing builder and his preening wife, she paused to take a long swig from her tall tumbler. Revived, she continued her opening oration.

"Those of you who know of my late husband's reputation will probably be surprised now you've seen inside my own little shack. It is, as you can see only too

170

clearly, mostly decorated in a pleasing variety of shades of pink."

She sketched an all-embracing wave of her hand at the room. It was supremely comfortable with large classic sofas covered in hydrangea-spattered linen union chintz and plain silk brocade curtains in toning shades of pink with a cream velvet-pile carpet. Through the open door the dining room was visible, this time cream-walled with pink and cream upholstered seats on the chairs.

"Guess what colour my bedroom is?" Delia's terrifying leer showed as she fixed her gaze on first one, then another, of her petrified male guests. "It's all right, I won't make you go up there alone with me, a girl's got to protect her virtue! Got it yet? That's right, it's — pink."

Finn and Charlie watched the performance appreciatively and Jamie raised a glass to her in a silent toast as she glanced his way.

"Before I let you loose on Guy's notebooks and his programmes which are on a continuous loop on the video in the dining room, I suppose I should explain myself, and this orgy of pinkness."

There was an uncharacteristic bleakness about her which silenced them as she continued.

"Guy was forty when he decided he needed a wife," she said quietly to her captivated audience. "He was what, in those days, they called "a man's man" — these days we'd be less mealy-mouthed about it. I suited the bill perfectly. I was twenty-seven, unmarried and unlikely to be because I was too plain and too

171

sharp-tongued for most men. Even Guy found me a daunting prospect but I had one shining advantage over any competition."

She took another of those long, thoughtful draughts from her glass and absent-mindedly topped it up from the bottle of London Gin beside her.

"Guy was the most crashing snob and my father was an earl. Never mind that he was an earl with no money or that the tumble-down wreck of a castle we called home when I was a child had finally crashed down into a pile of rubble. I provided Guy with a noble father-in-law and he had a titled wife to introduce to his impressionable friends."

She lapsed into a brooding silence so Julia dashed to the rescue, her kind heart touched to the quick by the air of unhappiness so unusual in her hard-boiled friend.

"How interesting, Delia," she gushed. "Let's have a refill all round, shall we? Jamie? Charlie? How about acting as wine waiters?"

Delia nodded her thanks and waited till everyone was knocking back their generous refills, then she spoke up again.

"Won't keep you much longer," she said. "Good thinking, Julia. As I was saying, I had to spend more than forty years listening to my husband's only too-often expressed views on historic houses, interior design and the philistines who were let loose on such buildings, and I had to live in such houses, nasty draughty things they were too. I determined that when I was finally free of him, I'd find a small, comfortable house, no draughts, and paint it pink. Partly because I

172

like pink and chintz and roses and flowers, but equally because he would have hated it so."

She tossed off yet another of her enormous gins and stood up.

"Enough maudlin nostalgia," she announced. "Let's get on with the orgy. Only joking," she glanced round at the apprehensive guests. "Let the festivities commence. Anyone who wants to ask me anything about Guy and his career, just collar me and ask away."

"You poor old bat," Julia lifted her glass to Delia in a sympathetic toast. "He sounds a monster."

"He was," agreed Delia placidly. "However, one of my happiest thoughts, and one that I hug to myself in the small hours when I can't sleep, is the fact that he died of shock."

"Shock?"

"Yup, young whatsisname on the telly, you know — killed him!"

"Delia!" Julia was amused but half scandalised. "You can't go round saying a thing like that. What *do* you mean?"

"What I say," persisted Delia. "He always refused to watch what he called "the television set" but when he was bedridden I stuck a portable in front of him and made him watch things like *Coronation Street* and *East Enders*," "pleb stuff" he called it. He had a coronary when he was forced to watch what that man had done to somebody's regency bedroom. If I ever meet that young man I'm going to give him a *big* kiss!"

The evening progressed, if not by leaps and bounds, at least in staggers and lurches. Finn was installed, protesting all the way, in the small conservatory behind the dining room and told not to be a nuisance, just to get on with it.

Luckily her first client was the pub landlord's wife and Finn managed to acquit herself reasonably, predicting a longhaul holiday, news of a family wedding and a baby for a close relative, all of which were received with placid goodwill.

The first of the dutiful daughters from the geriatric ward was pleased to hear of a house sale in the near future and a trip across water to a mountainous country.

"You *are* clever," she said with admiration. "My hubby's just booked us a trip to Austria."

After a while Finn stopped feeling nervous and a fraud and threw herself into the spirit of the occasion, wondering whether she ought to have dressed in gypsy costume to add local colour and give further value for money.

"Hi, Finn."

It was Hedgehog, unfamiliar in a dark blue suit, and minus his bobble hat. The man beside him had to be Bunny, though at first sight he was an unlikely candidate as a best friend for a doped-up hippy. Bunny was made of tweed, apparently. Tweed-mix jumper, heather tweed suit, tweedy looking shirt, pepper-and-salt hair, ditto moustache, and shiny chestnut brogues that looked eminently suitable with all the tweed.

Finn greeted Hedgehog with an enthusiastic kiss which made him go brick-red and retreat into bashful mumbling.

"Want your fortune told, Hedge?" she asked. "I daren't do you a cut-rate, Delia would go ballistic."

"Nah, I get enough of that stuff at the shop, don't I? You could tell Bunny's fortune for him."

Finn ran through her spiel, surprised to find that Bunny was lapping up every word with an intent eagerness.

"I can see you, and Hedgehog too," she told him finally. "I don't quite know what to make of it, but you seem to be on some kind of holiday together, in fact on *two* holidays, one somewhere hot but the other's different. It's not abroad, it's somewhere like East Anglia way, that kind of thing. And there's a religious element to it too."

She broke off and slid her crib sheet out from under the tablecloth.

"Here, let me check it out. Let me see, yeah, later on a hot place, but first of all some kind of trip with a religious slant." She looked up at Bunny's expression of surprise. "What? *What?*"

"Hedgehog said you were clever," Bunny was regarding her with something like awe. "But that's brilliant. Had you mentioned anything to her, Hedge?"

Hedgehog shook his head and also gazed in admiration at Finn. Seeing her puzzled frown he explained.

"I don't know about a holiday somewhere hot," he told her. "You musta got that wrong, girl. But me and Bunny, we've just booked Christmas week, only this morning. We're going to Norfolk — see? East Anglia, like you said. It's a Christian singles holiday, based in

175

an old converted monastery. Bunny's a Born Again, and I'm tagging along to see if there's any crumpet on offer."

The evening was going with a surprising swing. Or maybe not so surprising, decided Finn, when you saw the enormous pile of empties by the back door. She took a break from her oracular activities to tuck into a plate loaded with Marek's savoury goulash and Rosemary's salad and she was just wiping the heel of her baguette round her plate when Delia commandeered her.

"Finn, just the girl I want to talk to. Come upstairs for a second."

For a nervous moment Finn wondered if Delia, like her unlamented spouse, might swing both ways but no, Delia just wanted to talk to her in private.

"I've been nagging Julia to see how you feel about our holiday plans," she began.

"I'm with Charlie on this one," Finn told her frankly. "I think you're insane and you could end up in jail for fraud."

"Don't talk nonsense," Delia spoke crisply. "Who's going to find out? Besides, we *are* going to give the old folks a treat. Not just ourselves, we'll do something for the local oldies later on. Now, what about it? Are you with us or do I have to go hunting for somebody else? I know it's a back-handed compliment, my dear," she was serious for a moment. "But we really would love to have you and Charlie. It isn't every couple who would spend so much time helping out with people a generation older than themselves. It'd be good for Sue

176

and Bobbie too, half the time I think they forget they're nearer your age than ours, you'd help them get young again, but you wouldn't be obliged to hang about with us, you know. You could spend the whole two weeks on your own."

"I don't know . . ." Finn was trying to fight off a picture of herself and Charlie together on a West Indian beach. The image was getting in the way of her more cautious self. "I suppose it all depends on Charlie," she shrugged helplessly. "Have you sounded him out yet? I haven't actually discussed it with him in any detail."

"Jamie promised to try and pin him down tonight or tomorrow," Delia explained. "He knows he'll get a rocket from me if he doesn't, we really do need to know; there are so many loose ends. How is Jonathan going to escape from Pauline, for example? And Ursula ditto, though I suppose the problem of how Rosemary can leave Margot is being resolved for her. What's this?" She turned towards a small commotion at the front door. "Aha, Hugh's golfing chum and spouse. And goodness me, what a decorative spouse she is."

Laughing, Finn turned to follow Delia's admiring gaze.

And froze.

Hugh bustled up to divest his guests of their coats and brought them to be introduced to their hostess. The woman from the Antiques Fair smiled and simpered, while her husband chucked in a Ladyship with almost every other word, clearly delighted to hobnob with the aristocracy. Leaving his wife to sparkle at the nobility the husband allowed Hugh to haul him

177

into the dining room and be plied with drink and golf gossip.

For a moment Finn stayed in a state of suspended animation, then, as she began to come to, the worst happened. Charlie sauntered into the hall from the kitchen, where he had been washing more glasses.

"All done, Delia," he began then, like Finn, he became rooted to the spot, staring in horror at the newcomers.

"Charlie!" The newcomer rushed across the room and flung her arms round him, squealing in her little girly voice. "Oh Charlie, how wonderful to see you! Are you pleased to see me? After all this time?"

Finn winced as Charlie almost audibly ground his teeth, his dark eyebrows meeting in a ferocious scowl. She could almost feel the effort he was making to stay calm, though she had no clear idea what was going on.

"Amanda," he said finally, in a flat monotone. Then he let fly with an angry snarl that Delia, Finn and Julia could hear but that nobody in the drawing room could make out.

"No," he said, with a furious, cold energy. "No, I'm not pleased to see you. Why would I be? And after all this time? What time would that be, Amanda? The time since you stood me up on our wedding day? That time?"

He towered over her, menacing and terrifying, his hurt almost palpable to Finn.

"I stood there for an hour, Amanda. Sixty minutes. I thought at first there was a problem with the car, a puncture maybe, or traffic. *Then* I started to worry,

178

maybe there'd been a crash. At no time — *at no time* — did I even begin to contemplate that you might be such a gutless, dishonourable bitch as to walk out without a word."

He drew back and looked down at her, the passionate fury abating.

"My mother, as you very well knew, was only there by sheer will-power; she'd fought all the doctors, everyone at the hospice, so that she could attend her only child's wedding."

A weary, blank misery flooded over his face as he turned away towards the front door.

"She died the next day," he said in a shaken whisper. "You killed her, you damned murdering bitch."

CHAPTER
TWELVE

The hammering in her head turned out to be twinned with the hammering on her door, so Finn crawled out of bed just as her sister lost patience and let herself in anyway.

"Go away, Ju," she said tiredly.

"No, I won't," Julia pushed past her carrying a tray with two mugs of tea on it, together with a plate plied high with buttered toast. "I need some breakfast and so do you. There's nothing you can do, Jamie called me. Charlie's gone to Newcastle and won't say when he'll be back."

"Oh," Finn squatted on the bed, her eyes lowered miserably, tears welling up. "No, damn it, I'm not going to start crying again." She looked down at her bare feet and noted, in surprise, that large tears were dropping faster and faster on to them. "Oh God, Julia, what can I do? I love him so much, I've never felt like this, never."

With a rustle of silk kimono Julia's arms were round her.

"There, there, sweetie, let it out. I don't see that you can do anything at all, to be honest." Then, as Finn shuddered in protest, she temporised. "Well, you could drop a note in at his office to be forwarded to him, just to let him know how you feel, that might help. And you could ask them to pass on a message. Otherwise I'm afraid you're going to have to sweat this one out, darling, until he's sorted out what he wants."

Finn wiped her eyes and Julia nodded in approval.

"That's right, honey, making yourself ill won't help him. Drink this tea and have a piece of toast. That's better. Now, do you feel up to telling me what happened when you ran out of Delia's after Charlie?"

They had all stared as Charlie barged out of Daisy Cottage, Finn recalled, then she, Julia and Delia had — as one woman — turned to glare at Amanda.

"Don't look at *me*," the outcast had shrugged. "It wasn't my fault, I just didn't want to have a scene and I knew Charlie would be furious. As for his mother, well, I'm sorry but I didn't know she was *that* ill. How *could* I have known?"

"Get after him, Finn," Julia urged and Finn, who had been frozen to the spot in shock, found she could move again, so she raced out into the murky drizzle and ran in the direction of Charlie's house.

She caught up with him at his front gate.

"Charlie! Wait for me, let me come with you."

He forged on without stopping to reply. As he thrust his key into the lock he snarled at her, still without turning round.

"Go away, Finn, leave me alone."

She reeled with shock and hurt but it only made her even more desperate to throw her arms round him, to kiss him and try and make it better.

181

"I mean it, Finn," he flung at her when she cried out in dismay. "For God's sake!" His voice cracked ominously and he pushed her roughly aside. "I can't handle this, Finn, just go away."

"I didn't know what to do," Finn mopped her eyes as she told Julia the story. "I mean, he was nearly crying and I wanted to hold him but he just shoved me out of the way and slammed the door. I hung around for a while and then I came home and rang him, but he'd put the ansaphone on and when I went over to his house a bit later his car wasn't there. He must have packed a bag and taken off straight away."

"Poor Charlie," sighed Julia. "And poor Finn. He'll have to work out how to handle it and you'll just have to sit tight and wait till he's ready for you, sweetheart. It's tough but you don't have a choice, not if you really want him."

In spite of her extremes of misery Finn felt slightly comforted and, feeling like a little girl again, allowed Julia to bully her into a bath and then into getting dressed and drinking another cup of tea.

"What happened at Delia's?" she asked eventually, after fruitlessly trying Charlie's home number and his mobile again. "It didn't spoil everything, did it?"

"Nobody else heard a thing," Julia assured her. "Delia swept that girl into the drawing room and charmed and smarmed at the husband until he stumped up a cheque for fifty pounds for one of Guy Muncaster's autographed books. She also introduced him to Rosemary and somehow got him to commission a watercolour from her — he wants a picture of his

182

house, apparently. I had to kick Rosemary hard to shut her up when Delia announced in her lordly manner that Rosemary's fee would be two hundred and fifty pounds, but as she said afterwards, he wouldn't have been happy with anything cheap and cheerful. As it is, she talked Rosemary up so much that he thinks she's a well-known water-colourist and he's promised to tell his friends to contact her. He's also under the impression that he's getting a privileged rate and that his pals will have to cough up a substantial lot more."

"That's nice." Finn was feeling better, enough to realise what a difference such a contact could make to Rosemary. "When you've stopped your fund-raising for this crazy holiday it means Rosemary can work up a profitable sideline. Good for her."

The weather was vile all day, reflecting Finn's mood. Hourly calls to Charlie's mobile brought no result, nor did Jamie have any further insights. Delia looked in to report that the evening had netted a satisfactory amount and that she had warned Hugh off Amanda and her husband.

"He was inclined to be a bit sticky at first," she admitted. "Thinks the sun shines out of the husband's arse, but I soon put the fear of God in him. How?" She sank the gin Julia automatically put into her hand on arrival. "Simple, I just told him that the girl has a reputation for seducing older men and causing horrendous scandal. I said I'd spotted her eyeing him up last night. Of course, I said, she only ever goes for the most attractive men, and I reckoned he was next on her list."

"You're evil." Julia laughed at her and topped up her glass as a reward. "I can imagine Hugh's expression of terror."

"Uh-huh, he scuttled back to hide under Rosemary's apron, poor sap. Still, he seems to be what she wants, can't think why. If I had a choice I'd go for something a damn sight sexier myself." She stood up and flung her aged, politically-incorrect fur wrap round her shoulders, her smile every bit as vulpine as the glassy-eyed fox on her shoulder. "Better get a move on. Now, what else did I want to say? Oh yes, meant to congratulate you, Finn, on your Gypsy's Warning stint. It pulled in a lot of money and you sent the punters away happy."

Finn smiled wanly then managed a small laugh as she remembered her efforts.

"Hedgehog and his friend were really pleased with my reading for Bunny," she told Julia and Delia. "I asked Hedge later on how Bunny squared Hedgehog owning an occult shop with Bunny's muscular sort of Christianity, but he said there was no conflict. Bunny does the praying, he said, and he does the rest. It's all smells and bells, after all, he reckoned."

She let out another tiny giggle, raising a fleeting smile of relief on her sister's face.

"I asked Bunny if he was into drugs like Hedgehog but he shook his head indignantly."

"I wouldn't touch a spliff if you paid me," he had told her. "I don't do drugs, my dear, I just drinks."

"And so he does," put in Delia with something like awe. "It's not often I'm impressed by anyone else's

184

intake but that tweedy fella really put it away last night *and* stayed upright too."

Finn spent the next few days in an unhappy daze. A visit to Charlie's office early on Monday morning produced no results.

"He's expecting to be in Newcastle all this week," said the lumpy woman who managed the office of Ramalley Software Solutions. "No, I can't give you his hotel number but I'll tell him you called in. What? Well, of course you can't get hold of him on his mobile, he's taken one from work, that's why."

Finn lost her cool and pleaded with the woman but she was adamant.

"I'll let him know you want to speak to him," was the best she would commit herself to. "Then he can get in touch with you — if he wants to," she added with a spark of malice.

All dignity in shreds Finn meekly nodded and asked if the woman would send on the brief note of love and longing she had scrawled during the night. When the woman grudgingly agreed Finn handed the envelope over and trailed back to the shop.

Never, in the last couple of months, had Finn felt so badly in need of a female friend to confide in. Julia tried her best and was, Finn admitted, a great comfort, but it wasn't the same; from the age of fifteen Finn had looked on Julia as a mother.

"I've got *nobody* to confide in," she bewailed to Hedgehog one day during the lull after lunch. "I'm not close enough to Rosemary and co, and Julia's too emotionally involved, she gets upset. I think I really need a proper heart-to-heart."

"You could try me," Hedgehog offered diffidently, plying her with home-made fudge sent by Bunny to try to mitigate her misery.

"Hedge, you're a sweetie," she gave him a pale smile. "But you're a bloke, in case you hadn't noticed."

"Don't be daft," he retorted robustly. "You can't go running to Mummy — even if she *is* your sister, all the time, at your age, so I'm all you've got. You can't rustle up that kinda friend just like that. Besides, just 'cos I'm off women just now don't mean I don't know nothin' about them. Try me."

She raised her head from where she had been resting it on her folded arms on the counter and stared at him. From the top of his spiky head to the bottom of his thick-soled clumpy boots Hedgehog was aquiver with the urge to be of assistance.

"You're a pet, Hedge," she reached out and patted his hand. "You're a really sensitive person, Bunny and I are very lucky to have you as a friend." She blew her nose and decided to give it a try. "I suppose I just feel so devastated, to realise Charlie's still in love with Amanda. I really thought he was happy with me. I knew I was falling in love with him and although we never talked about it, I was pretty sure he felt the same."

"Why should you think he's still in love with her, then?"

"Get real, Hedge. I told you what he was like, he was broken up, nearly crying. He wouldn't have reacted like that if he didn't still love her."

"Not necessarily," Hedgehog maintained sturdily in the face of her disbelief. "The way I see it, from what you told me, he sounds more as if it was his mum dyin' that did his head in. An' you can't blame him, can you? It musta bin hell for Charlie, seeing his mum so upset. And she woulda bin, wou'n't she? Stands to reason, her only child left stood at the altar, think how you'd feel yourself. And his dad, he's the strong silent type, in't he? Suffer in silence, stiff upper lip? He'd be no help, worse than Charlie."

In his agitation Hedgehog reached in his pocket and Finn sat in thoughtful silence, mulling over his words, till he was calmly blowing smoke rings.

"See what I mean? Your sister, now, think how she'd be if it was you. She'd be broke up that you was broke up, if you follow what I'm saying. Don't mean Charlie was still in love with whatserface, but he *did* love his mum, that's clear, and quite right too."

There was no word from Charlie. Finn struggled through the week in a state of unhappiness such as she had never known. It wasn't like this with Luc, she thought drearily on Friday evening as she trudged home by bus — the car was in for a new battery — the persistent murky drizzle suiting her mood. Nor any of the others. This time it's not just about me and my feelings, I suppose. I'm worried sick about Charlie, how he feels, what he's likely to do, I just want to hold him and keep him safe. Daily pleas to Charlie's battleaxe of a secretary brought no relief, except that at least she knew he was still working in Newcastle. I suppose that's

187

some comfort, she told herself as she turned the key in the lock at Forge Cottage, if he's able to work it must mean he's coping somehow and not standing on top of the Angel of the North, poised to jump.

"Come in and have a drink, darling?" Julia thrust her head round Finn's door, looking anxious.

Why not? Finn shrugged, hung up her coat and trailed disconsolately into the main house after her sister. Rosemary Clavering was huddled over the open fire and Delia Muncaster was totting up figures in a notebook.

"Oh, sorry?" Finn hunched her shoulders. "Are you having a meeting? Shall I go back to my place?"

"I invited you, darling," her sister reminded her. "Delia's been given a new brand of gin so she's using us as guinea pigs. Want some? Or there's beer in the fridge." She raised an eyebrow without comment as Finn wandered back from the kitchen with a bottle of beer. "OK? Well then, Delia, what were you saying?"

"We've got off to a terrific start with our fund-raising, I checked the figures with Bobbie this morning. We've already reduced the outstanding balance by well over a thousand pounds and while this means we still need over two thousand pounds, assuming . . ." She glanced briefly at Finn and changed track, Julia noticed thankfully. No need to remind Finn that final costs depended on her own *and* Charlie's participation.

"This gin tastes all right," Julia shifted the direction of the conversation. "Why were you iffy about it, Delia? Not Bulgarian or something, is it?"

"No, no, nothing like that," maintained Delia, draining her glass with a practised wrist movement and pouring a refill. "Just an old chum of Guy's who sends me a bottle now and then. This one's from Texas, so I thought it might be made from cattle by-products but it's not bad, is it?"

Finn roused herself to ask about Margot.

"As well as can be expected is about it." Rosemary was looking increasingly thin and strained. "Poor old Margot, she's still occasionally aware of what's going on and she gets terribly distressed. But she's much weaker. I feel so wretched when that happens because there's nothing I can do, or anyone else, for that matter. The consultant was quite kind about it, he says it's just a matter of all the systems quietly closing down."

A ring at the front door saved Rosemary from disintegrating into exhausted tears and she mopped herself up as Julia brought Sue Merrill into the room, handing out the inevitable glass of gin as Sue sat down.

"We've got some good news," Julia began, then she stopped short, eyeing her latest visitor with interest when Sue made an extraordinary sound, a cross between a gulp and a snort. "What? What's happened, Sue?"

For a few moments Sue struggled, a weird mix of emotions flitting across her heavy, pleasantly plain face. At last she made up her mind.

"I had sex with another man last night," she blurted out. "And it was fantastic!"

To the accompaniment of a chorus of Ooohs and Aaahs from the other women, even Finn who was struggling with disbelief and some embarrassment at the thought of discussing sex in front of someone like Delia, Sue told her tale.

It had been after seven the night before when she locked up her office, she said, and headed for the staff car park. As she walked past one of the other entrances to the main college building she heard a muffled but desperate sobbing.

"I couldn't just walk by," she told Julia and the others. They nodded in agreement and she continued. "I was nervous but I looked into the doorway and there was a young man hunched up on the step, with his head on his knees, obviously breaking his heart. He didn't look like an ordinary drunk or addict so I went a bit closer and spoke to him."

"Can I help you?" she had said hesitantly.

He looked up and she recognised him at once as Richard Fennel, a lecturer in the Maths Department. Last time she had seen him had been at a charity day organised by the students. In his late twenties, he had looked happy and contented, walking with his pretty wife and pushing a double buggy with two little girls side-by-side in it.

"Richard? What on earth is the matter?"

He shook his head, unable to speak, but he moved up so that she could squat down on the step beside him and he let her put a tentative arm round him. After a bit more coaxing she got the story out of him.

"His wife's twenty-eight," she told the other women. "She's not been well for a couple of months and last

190

month she was diagnosed with cancer of the pancreas. Yes." She nodded when they cried out in protest. "He said she's gone downhill so rapidly since then that she's only got days to live, poor girl. He'd been to the hospice when I found him."

"She sent me home to get some sleep," he told her, clinging to the comforting hand. "Mum and Dad have taken the children, she said goodbye to them yesterday. The doctors don't think she'll be strong enough much longer and she didn't want them to be frightened, they're only two and three." He looked round, puzzled. "I don't know why I came here."

Sue held him for a little longer till the shuddering sobs began to quieten down.

"Look, Richard," she urged. "I don't think you ought to be driving. Let me take you home. Will there be anyone there to keep you company tonight?"

He said no, he'd be alone and that was how he wanted it, but he accepted the offer of a lift so she led him to her car and settled him in like a child, reaching across to do up his safety belt for him when he fumbled helplessly with it.

"I live in Stockbridge," he said worriedly. "Isn't that miles out of the way? I can always get a taxi, I don't want to be a bother."

"No problem," she reassured him and headed towards the bypass, glad of something outside her own narrow arena of anxiety. They drove in silence until they reached the outskirts of the little town, when he roused enough to give her directions.

"Come in and have a drink, er — um, Sue," he stumbled over her name. "I've got some whisky. Come and help me get drunk enough to get to sleep for once."

The despair in his pinched young face gripped at her heart. Her own desolation seemed so minor in the face of his immediate tragedy. How did you set a dead or dying marriage against the impending death of a girl like Helen Fennel?

She parked in the neat drive and followed Richard into the pretty modern brick semi. I hope the neighbours won't talk, she thought, then grimaced at her own vanity. Why would they? I look twenty years older than he is. They'll think I'm an aunt or a social worker or something, poor devil.

Helen Fennel had furnished and decorated her little house with love and care, everything spotlessly clean, dazzlingly pretty. A little too pink and frilly for Sue's taste — how Delia would love it — but an expression of love well suited to the pretty girl in the photograph on the mantelpiece. Sue looked at the round-faced bride in the picture and thought of the frail wraith Richard had described. A lump in her throat threatened to choke her and she turned in grateful silence to take the glass he handed her.

The television was on as background noise and they sat in near-silence, exchanging only an occasional word except when Richard, drinking steadily, sobbed now and then. Once, when he looked at the screen he nodded bitterly towards the sexy scene being played out.

"D'you know what the worst thing about this is?" he demanded harshly. "I'm sorry for myself, *myself* mind you, because we haven't had sex for so long. She's been so brave and all I can think about is sex." He slumped in an orgy of self-disgust for a moment then picked up the remote and changed channels. Sue remembered she was driving, time to watch her alcohol intake, she thought wryly. I don't need a drink-driving ticket.

The little house was warm and she undid her cardigan, kicked off her shoes and curled up on the settee, to doze off peacefully.

"Sue? Sue?" Richard was shaking her gently. She blinked awake and looked up at him from under sleepy lashes. He smiled uncertainly at her and knelt down beside her. He was extremely drunk. "Sue?" he said again, leaning forward to kiss her, hesitantly at first, then fiercely.

"I can't tell you," she said now to her audience who were hanging on her every word, desperate for the rest of the story. "I can't tell you how I felt!"

Desire had surged ferociously through her blood, rocking her off balance, a rush of lust such as she'd never felt before. Richard's hands were feverishly trying to unbutton her blouse as she scrabbled frantically at his zip.

"Upstairs," he mumbled, kissing her on and on as they lurched and stumbled up the narrow pine staircase and fell together on the pink-flowered bedspread.

"I don't know if I can," she wailed softly against the dark hair on his chest. It's been so long, I'm all dried

193

up inside, she fretted. He silenced her protest with his lips, then kissed her cheeks, her brow, her nose, all the time mumbling into her skin: "Oh please, oh please, please . . ."

Overcome by her own need as much as by compassion for his, Sue tore off her blouse and dragged off her navy slacks, thanking her stars for elasticated waists. She cowered there, prim and self-conscious, in her white scaffolding bra and sensible knickers, as he kicked off his shoes, yanked off his tee shirt and slipped out of his jeans. Even as he fell on her and she felt his hot fingers pulling at her bra she noticed how fit his body was, how firmly muscled compared to the last time she had seen Philip naked.

"Oh, lovely, lovely," he groaned, taking her full, heavy breasts in both hands and burying his face in them. "Oh, lovely, lovely, lovely!"

She arched her back in an agony of pleasure as her skin tingled at the unaccustomed touch. She felt his tears and heard him whimpering, whether from passion or grief she neither knew nor cared as she managed to wriggle out of her knickers. Somewhere in the back of her mind, real-life, mundane Sue was watching fantasy Sue with utter astonishment as she rubbed and writhed her body against his.

She reached down and found his penis, hugely erect, much thicker and longer than Philip's. Aha, she triumphed, so much for the demon lover of his own reports. Then she was beyond gloating, beyond thought, as Richard cried out at her touch and

194

frantically began to kiss her breasts and belly. Down, down he went, ignoring her tiny squeaks of protests.

"Oh, it was marvellous," she sighed reminiscently, accepting a top up from Delia, who urged her to go on. "Can you believe I've never had oral sex before? Philip's a strict missionary position man, so it was unbelievable, the whole thing."

As Richard's body clenched at the moment of climax he had cried out: "Helen! *Helen!*"

Then he realised what he had said, what he had done, and the tears ran freely, gushing down his anguished cheeks. Sue, who was high as a kite, came down to earth in a rush and held him tightly, crying with him.

"Oh don't, Richard, *don't*. This hasn't hurt Helen, don't ever think that. This was just for you, to help you get through the night and the days and the weeks to come. And it was for me to give me hope, to make me come alive."

As she finished speaking Julia, Finn and Rosemary all sighed, nodding with fellow-feeling, and Sue wound up.

"I tucked him up and left a note downstairs, just my name and number and a bland scribble of thanks for the drink and to let me know if I could be of help. Just in case anybody else read it, his parents perhaps. Then I went home and had a long, long bath and decided to throw Philip out."

She grinned at their outcry.

"Well . . ." she temporised. "I haven't told him yet, but I will. I think I'd better check it out with a solicitor first." She calmed down as she finished her drink. "I'd better go. I just *had* to tell somebody and Julia and Finn already knew the score. Do you realise," she was serious now. "If you hadn't started this club I don't think I'd ever have plucked up enough courage to make this decision? And as for having a fling with a man I barely know, well . . ."

At the door Sue hesitated then spoke urgently to Julia.

"I mean it, Julia," she insisted. "I think you saved my life. I told you I hadn't had an orgasm for years and it was true. But last night was *so* different. For the first time in my life I actually found out what everyone's been talking about all these years. I've rejoined the human race."

CHAPTER
THIRTEEN

Saturday morning dawned, dank, drear and disgusting. Julia had spent the night at Jamie's flat — after anxiously making sure that Finn would be all right on her own.

"Just go, Ju," she had said tiredly. "I'm not going to do anything stupid, why would I? I just want to be home in case he rings here, or turns up, whatever. You making yourself miserable won't make it any better."

She heard the clang of the letter box as she sat morosely over her first mug of tea. It was a postcard of the Angel of the North, with just a few words on it: "Sorry. Back soon, C."

Such a short message but such a beacon of hope. She caught sight of her reflection in the mirror and stopped to stare at the transfigured face it presented. All this week she had been confronted by a face to sink a thousand ships whenever she cleaned her teeth or brushed her hair. Now, in less than a minute, she was utterly transformed, eyes shining, skin glowing, hair — aaagh! Her hair was a lank, dirty bundle of dull straw.

She whirled into the shower where she shampooed, conditioned, scrubbed, exfoliated, rinsed and moisturised herself until she was pink, smooth and slippery.

"Back soon." She quoted his words aloud, over and over. Whenever he came she planned to be ready and in ace condition. It was the enigmatic "Sorry" that intrigued her most and set her pulse racing.

"If he's sorry," she considered aloud. "What's he sorry about? For running out? Not getting in touch? Does it mean he's sorry he never told me about Amanda?" A hideous thought struck and her stomach lurched. "Or does he mean: Sorry, it was all a mistake with you and we're through?"

I won't think about that, she decided and looked around for something to take her mind off it. The flat was in a disgusting mess where she had been wallowing in piggish misery all week, so, with Julia's adage echoing in her ears — work takes your mind off your troubles — she set to and cleaned up, still wearing only her bathrobe. Into the washing machine went the dirty bed-linen — he might stay at her place. Into the sink went a week's worth of dirty dishes and she caught herself singing as she washed them up. Out came the iron, vacuum cleaner, duster, and she even cleaned the windows for good measure.

Clean house, clean body, she thought complacently, then realised that her body, though squeaky clean, was now clamouring for food. While the kettle was boiling for more tea and the bread was in the toaster she sorted out what she should wear. CK jeans and a Gap top? Or should she glam up in case he was on his way?

Informal would be best, she decided, I don't want to look desperate, so she prepared for the usual struggle to get into her best and most flattering jeans. To her surprise they slipped on without a fight — she'd lost weight. Dragging the jeans off she ran to the bathroom scales and jumped on. Way-hey! Half a stone gone, just vanished into thin air without even trying.

After breakfast she left a note to reassure Julia and walked into town, keen to capitalise on the weight loss by further exercise. Even the weather had cheered up, and for November the day was crisp and beautiful, the autumn colours glowing against the silver traces of an early-morning frost. Finn mostly worked on weekdays but occasionally Hedgehog asked her to stand in for him on a Saturday. Today, however, was different.

"Word's got round about you bein' a fortune-teller," he had informed her a day or so previously. "Musta bin them people at old Delia's party, you know how pleased they were. I got four bookings for Saturday morning for you and I told 'em we had to charge a lot more in the shop. Lady D's party, I said, was a private do, but the shop rate is double."

"Hedge!" she was horrified. "That's scandalous, you can't charge the earth for me to make up stuff. We'll get had up for fraud."

"Don't be daft," he defended himself stoutly. "What d'you suppose so-called *real* clairvoyants do? They can't all have natural psychic ability, whatever that might be when it's at home, course they makes it up. Anyway," as she looked less than convinced. "You *don't* make it up, do you? You just go by the book. I listened in, don't forget, when you done Bunny's cards, you never told him nothing you hadn't read first. So go on with you."

Tucked away in the little cubby hole beside the shop's kitchen Finn resigned herself and summoned up a smile to greet the first customer Hedgehog had lined up for her.

"You told my friend's fortune," the woman told her with eager anxiety. "She went to Lady Delia Muncaster's party and she said you were really good. Well," she gave Finn a wide-eyed stare. "It stands to reason, doesn't it? Somebody posh like Lady Delia, she wouldn't have anything to do with anyone who wasn't high-class, would she?"

Finn had a moment's wild hysteria which she managed to shove under a mental rock for the time being. Why on earth had she let Delia and Hedgehog get away with it? How could she possibly live up to a claim of being high-class when all she did was furtively consult the crib sheet she had concocted from Hedge's books?

"Let's have a look, shall we?" She launched into the spiel she had prepared and set about giving the woman as honest and worthwhile a reading as she could manage, within the parameters she set herself, from the meanings as laid out by the books she had read. Saints can't do more, she consoled herself.

At the end of the morning she felt better. She had acquitted herself fairly honourably, and the punters had gone away apparently satisfied with what she had predicted for them. Hedgehog was ecstatic.

"See? I told you it weren't a problem."

"Look here, Hedge." She was determined to get things straight with him. "I don't mind doing this

200

occasionally but I was only hired to stand in for your regular woman. What's happened to her? I don't want her turning up and putting a hex on me for taking over her job."

"She won't worry you," he replied comfortably. "Her husband's been transferred to Chichester and they're moving house. It'd be too far for her to travel, she says, so she won't be back in. Good job too, you're much prettier and you tell better stuff."

"Well, I'm not doing it very often," she warned him. "I was taken on as a shop assistant not a resident witch. I'm not doing more than two a day and that's it. You can tell anyone who complains that I'm guided by the spirits and they insist that I mustn't overtax my gift. That ought to shut them up. OK?"

Another memory surfaced.

"What about that woman from the Chapel who made a fuss? I haven't seen her for weeks. You haven't got her sent to jail, have you?"

"Nah, she's gone off on another tack, they've started up some group on the side where they shares their pain, that's what one of 'em told me."

She bought steak in Waitrose and flowers in the market, along with fruit and vegetables, bread, and luscious meringues from the French patisserie round the corner, plus a bottle of Moët from the off-licence, where the manager recognised her as a friend of his favourite customer and gave her not only a discount but also a lift home as he was just off to deliver Delia's weekend supplies. As a black cloud threatened rain she put her fitness kick on hold and accepted his offer.

★ ★ ★

"Nothing more from Charlie?" Julia greeted her when she arrived home.

"Nope," she shook her head. "Still waiting but I feel tons better now."

"You look it," agreed her sister, frankly, and when Finn tried out her worst-case scenario, Julia shot it down at once. "What nonsense, Charlie's not the sort to dump you by a postcard. Give him *some* credit, if he wanted to end things with you he's got plenty of guts, of course he'd tell you face to face."

In the afternoon they volunteered to visit Margot to give Rosemary a break.

"Take Rosemary out to tea," Julia suggested in a call to Hugh Taylor. "Why don't you find a really nice country house hotel and treat her to a cream tea with all the trimmings? She's desperately in need of a respite."

"Have Rosemary and Hugh got it together yet?" Finn asked idly on the way to the hospital. "God! You have no idea how weird that sounds, asking about people who are old enough to be my parents having sex. Coming back home to live with you has turned my whole world upside down, all my perspectives have completely altered and I'm not sure if I like it."

"Do you good to realise life isn't just for the young, or the not-quite young," said her sister unsympathetically. "As for Rosemary and Hugh, I don't think so. As far as I can gather Rosemary's too unsettled even to contemplate sex, while Hugh's not brave enough to

202

fling her over his shoulder and carry her off to his cave."

"Ooh, you old-fashioned thing, you!" mocked Finn. "You think that's what she really wants?"

"No question." Julia parked the car and they headed towards the geriatric wing. "Rosemary's old-fashioned. She believes the man should make all the moves and it would be unfeminine of her to push herself forward. I suppose it's to be expected, from what I can gather that's how Margot was with both her husbands. Well, I told you so, didn't I? Till she started going doo-lally, that is."

Finn raised an eyebrow in disbelief but Julia stood her ground.

"That's what it was *like*," she insisted. "It's one of the great successes of feminism that a woman of your age can hear such a thing and not believe it possible. I was a bit like that with Colin, you know, though nothing like so wimpy — of course."

"Of course." Finn smiled at her sister. "You'd better give Rosemary some lessons in seduction then, or maybe give Hugh a big shove up the backside."

Margot was much, much frailer. In the week since Finn had looked in on the old woman she had changed drastically. Never a big woman Margot was now a tiny skeletal doll barely making a dent in the bed, and the jaunty, orange crest of hair now lay scanty and white at the roots. But it was in her personality that Margot was most altered. Even last week she had responded with delight at Finn's gifts, leafing eagerly through Vogue and smearing on the red lipstick with cheerful vanity.

"She's just — just lying there," Finn said in a horrified whisper. "She looks dead."

Julia looked at Margot with professional compassion and agreed as she set their freesias in a vase on the bedside locker.

"Yes," she said. "Not much longer now, poor soul." She bent to take Margot's hand and spoke gently but clearly. "Margot?"

There was a tremor on the little lined face that might have been some kind of acknowledgement and they hovered there, waiting to see if she would respond. Nothing.

The staff-nurse appeared and looked an enquiry at them.

"Miss Clavering will be in about six," Julia explained.

"Good," came the response. "The registrar will be around then and I know he wants to talk to her."

Promising to pass on the message to Rosemary they kissed the lonely little creature and made their way back to the car, both struggling with tears.

"She was such a mad old thing," Finn said angrily. "Dancing about with nothing on, when I first saw her, but at least she enjoyed herself some of the time."

Evening came and still no word from Charlie.

"He only said soon," Julia pointed out when Finn showed her the postcard. "Could mean anything, so snap out of it. Are you planning to mope around at home on your own tonight or do you want an exciting evening over at the pub with us?"

"Oooh, tough choice!" Finn made a face at her, then gave in. "Oh, why not? I can always come home if the conversation turns to trusses and varicose veins, I suppose."

Later she regretted her decision but what was the alternative? Charlie had her mobile number and if he turned up unexpectedly he knew her haunts, such as they were. She might as well make the best of it. She listened vaguely to her neighbours extolling the virtues of their cats.

"Such adorable little things," gushed Bobbie. "The little boy has taken to going over to Ursula's house to visit her, bless him. I only hope Henrietta doesn't see him and make life difficult."

"She isn't causing any trouble these days," said Ursula, who was feeling incredibly laid-back now there was no fear of being harried from dawn till dusk. She had planted periwinkles and an evergreen honeysuckle over the air-raid shelter and the plants were thriving. She preferred not to think of the moral aspect, nor what lay under the flourishing greenery, though the angel referred to it on his occasional visits.

"*Your old dragon must be turning into good fertiliser,*" he remarked one day, drifting into the kitchen unannounced except for the now-familiar waft of spices, and a luminescent radiance from his golden feathers. "*It just goes to show that even something evil can be transmuted into good in the right circumstances, being dead, in Henrietta's case.*"

"Where do you come from?" Ursula blurted out the question she had been pining to ask for weeks. "Are you just a figment of my imagination? I mean, the things you tell me to do seem so much to be what I want to do, are you my subconscious?"

The angel gave her a considering glance.

"You'll have to work that one out, Ursula," he said finally. *"What is an angel, after all? An incorporeal entity, that's me, or maybe anthropomorphic is the word I want? Something to talk to like you talk to that cat now, and project your replies on to?"*

"I don't know." She was astonished at her own daring, arguing with an angel. "Everything you've encouraged me to do has turned out to be downright dishonest, stealing those boxes from the shop, not reporting Henrietta's death, selling the china." She gave a sudden shudder of dismay. "Maybe you're not an angel after all! Maybe you should be wearing horns and a tail."

"Ursula, Ursula, Ursula!" The angel assumed an expression of hurt amazement. *"What a thing to say to a friend, when all I've ever tried to do is give you a helping hand. Still, if that's what you think of me . . ."*

"Oh please," Ursula cried out as the radiance dimmed. The angel hesitated and looked at her guardedly. "Please don't go, I don't care *where* you come from or *what* you are, as long as you still visit me sometimes. After all, you're the only person I can talk to about Henrietta, I can't tell anyone else, they'd lock me up."

The cat lovers' gentle eulogies about their pets were soporific and their voices sank to a pleasant buzzing in Finn's ears as she sipped her drink and dreamed of Charlie, while her sister and Delia discussed possible new fund-raisers and the others chatted generally.

"Had a good afternoon, Rosemary?"

Julia broke off from her discussion about carol singing to welcome Rosemary who came in with Hugh.

"Bliss," Rosemary nodded with a smile. "I feel so much more relaxed. Mind you," the smile faded away. "Hugh took me in to the hospital on the way here and I saw the doctor. He says it's only a matter of a week or so at most."

Julia nodded sympathetically.

"But could you honestly wish her back?" she asked seriously. "The way she is, I mean? This is much better — for Margot's own sake — than hanging on in that state, never knowing if she was going to come to, doing something embarrassing."

Bobbie intervened after craning her neck to look round the bar.

"Anyone seen Marek lately? I left him a message about this meeting, but I haven't seen him around for days."

"You're right, you know," Rosemary broke off from her low-voiced conversation with Hugh. "Last time I spoke to him he was being very mysterious. I know he's been worrying that he hasn't contributed much to the fund-raising, even though we've all told him not to be so silly. I suppose he comes from a macho culture so he can't help it." She looked across to the Saloon door. "Talk of the devil!"

"Lady Delia." Marek stood to attention, very trim, in front of the group's self-appointed leader. He looked big with news. "Here I have some money for you."

Taken aback, Delia held out a limp hand as Marek, very importantly, began to count fifty-pound notes into it.

"There you are," he barked in triumph. "Eighteen hundred pounds, I think you will find it is all correct and present. Thank you!" He bowed all round the group, with a very smug smile on his dark features, then sat down beside Jonathan Barlow, without offering an explanation.

Surely he hadn't gone on the game? Julia remembered one of Marek's original jokey ideas for a fund-raiser, as a Viagra stud, but no — he looked pleased with himself, certainly, but not *that* pleased.

"Oh, very well." Marek listened with obvious delight to the outcry his actions had precipitated. "I tell you, OK? But you keep it under your hat, nobody got to know."

Finn jerked out of her daydream as she realised something was going on. In an excited whisper Bobbie filled her in, so she sat up and listened as Marek explained.

"I have been bad about not putting much in," he said stiffly, waving aside the protests that greeted this remark. "No, no, is true. You all gave to the antiques sale, but me, I had nothing left. After my wife died I gave things to my son, then to a charity shop, so when I took my new flat I started clean. Yes, you say, so I helped at the fair — so I should, it is my duty same as you, we're all in this together. Then I saw a thing on television about illegal immigrants and I spoke to some fellow countrymen I know of in London. From then on, is easy."

"What was easy? What did you do, Marek?" Delia asked the question for the rest of them. "You haven't taken to smuggling asylum seekers through the Chunnel, have you?"

"You think I'm scum?" his voice rose in indignation. "What I do is not bad, not quite legal, maybe, that's why we keep it quiet, but not so naughty." Delia was looking at him with a glint in her eye so he hurriedly went on with his tale. "I found out about a money-making scam, I think you call it. So I married a young Polish woman for money so she can get British nationality. Very easy, very quick, say I do, sign here, take your money in brown envelope, goodbye!"

There was a moment's stunned silence as the rest of the group stared in shocked condemnation at their fellow member then, as Marek's initial jaunty triumph began to dissipate under their barely disguised disapproval, Delia barged in to bridge the gap.

"Good heavens, Marek," she cried heartily, clapping him on the shoulder so that he buckled slightly. "What an astonishing story! And what a *huge* contribution to the fighting fund." She glared menacingly at the others. "What a variety of ways we've all uncovered in our fund-raising, to be sure."

Hastily-donned smiles served to reassure Marek as the others clamoured round him, postponing their moralising until he was out of earshot, realising perhaps that the moral high ground was pretty shaky in their own situation.

"A thought occurs," Jamie Stuart put in with his customary easy smile. "Won't this young lady have a claim on your estate, Marek? If something happens to you, I mean. Do you want that? I imagine your son, from what you've told us of him, would be less than pleased?"

"Ha! So you would think," Marek's eyes were bright with surprising malice. "So, this young Polish lady, if she tries to get hold of my money, she finds she is not really my wife. No," he shrugged in the face of their bewilderment. "When my Ivy died I did a foolish thing. I was lonely and I married against my family's wishes, what they call these days, a bombo." Confronted by blank stares he frowned until he came up with the right word. "No, a bimbo, that's it, a gold-digger. That's why me and my son fell out."

He sighed and shrugged again.

"He was right and I don't like to admit it. But she found out I wasn't rich after all and she went off soon and married somebody else. Only she didn't bother to get a divorce from me, or me from her, so now we're both bigamists — do I care?" He turned to Jamie and reached out to tap him on the shoulder. "You are right, my friend, nice thinking. I should remember this, so tomorrow I must go to a solicitor and make moves to divorce my bimbo. But it will be too late for my Polish one, she won't get my money, such as it is, either."

The finance committee had been doing some frenzied arithmetic while Marek spoke, and Delia now called the group to order.

"This is fantastic," she announced with a nod to the barman. "We're now less than a thousand pounds short of the total, and we have getting on for eight months to raise that in. Ah, here we are, let's have a toast; it's on me, chums!"

As they raised their glasses Julia's mobile rang.

"Yes? Yes, she's here. Rosemary . . ." she held out the telephone. "It's the hospital, remember you gave them this number as an extra precaution."

They all watched in silence as Rosemary took the call. They all knew, from her expression, what had happened.

"Oh, Rosemary!"

Julia was about to reach out and enfold her friend in loving sympathy when Hugh Taylor surprised them all by taking Rosemary in his arms and providing her with his immaculate, snowy white handkerchief.

"There, there, old girl," he soothed, and although Finn caught Julia's eye, neither of them felt like smiling at this English stereotype. "I'll take you straight to the hospital, then you'll come home with me."

The party atmosphere fell rather flat after that and Finn was wondering if she could sneak home, when she saw Jamie Stuart's face light up.

"Finn?"

Charlie stood awkwardly in front of her, brown eyes contrite, a flop of dark hair falling over his right eye.

"You need a haircut," she said stupidly and her heart sank. "And a shave," she added, compounding the insanity, when all the past week she'd rehearsed over and over again her opening gambit when — if — he should turn up.

"Uh-huh," his sudden grin made her heart leap up again. "I probably do."

He reached across Ursula Buchanan and hauled Finn to her feet.

"I'm a prick," he said, as he pulled her towards him. "A total, utter wanker."

To the enthralled delight of the assembled members of the Gang he sank on one knee and took her hand. By now the entire pub was aware of something unusual going on and the crowd of onlookers formed a circle round them.

Finn was aware that they were there, knew that both Jamie and her sister were watching with bated breath and that Julia's eyes were bright with tears, but she stood still, waiting for Charlie's next move, not wanting to upset the delicate balance.

"Marry me, Finn," he said simply, stroking her fingers with his thumb.

She looked down and met his gaze. He was wide-eyed with anticipation and small beads of sweat had formed on his forehead. The hand holding hers was shaking slightly and his bottom lip was tucked under his top teeth with the effort all this emotion was costing him.

She stared at him and thought about all the other men she'd imagined herself in love with, right up to the faithless Luc. She thought about Julia and her dull husband and she pictured all the married couples she had ever met, none of them particularly shining role models. Even here, in the village, there was Jonathan with the wife Finn had still never met, nor wanted to from the reports she'd heard, and now Marek with his gold-digging bombo.

But then there was Hugh, his much-loved wife recently dead, desperate to recreate that closeness with Rosemary, and there was Charlie's own father too. Jamie had adored his wife, Charlie had told her, and had been worshipped right back. Yes, that was a better comparison, the likeness between father and son was particularly marked. She looked at his saturnine features, tough and vulnerable at the same time, and she remembered the fun and friendship and passion they shared in bed.

All these thoughts swirled and scurried round her brain in a nano-second as she looked into Charlie's eyes.

"Outside," she said, biting her lip and rising. She ran out to the car park, sudden rage threatening to choke her.

"You just walked out!" she berated him as he followed her anxiously. "You just walked out and left me standing. I was out of my mind with worry till I got your postcard and since then I've been off my head with rage. How could you just dump me like that? You should have phoned, I'd have understood."

"I'm sorry," he said, taken aback by the storm of fury. "I just wasn't thinking straight. Like I said, I'm a total prick."

"You think that's it? That's enough? That all you need to do is snap your fingers and I'll come running? Give me some credit, you don't think I'm that desperate, do you?"

"I'm sorry," he said again, spreading his hands in a hopeless gesture. "I love you, Finn, let me make it up to you."

As swiftly as it had overtaken her the anger dissipated. Everything that had gone through her mind as they stared at each other in the pub flashed through again. No, I'm not that desperate, she told herself, not for just any man, but Charlie — Charlie is special, Charlie is *mine*!

"Yes," she said into the tense silence.

The pub exploded into cheers, they'd been openly eavesdropping through the open door and the champagne corks flew. The landlord needed no specific signal from Delia, as Charlie dragged Finn back indoors.

"She said yes," he yelled over the noise and she laughed and nodded in confirmation. "She said *yes!*"

Then Julia was hugging them both, crying and laughing, and beckoning to Jamie to join in. He smiled at them but held back till the champagne was in sight then he commandeered a tray and four glasses and brought them over.

"Here," he said, putting it down so he could take his turn at the family hug. "A toast to the newest recruit to the Stuart dynasty. Welcome, darling Finn, you'll be an ornament to the crown of England when we come into our own!"

The four of them drank the toast and all the time Finn was electrically conscious of Charlie's taut body close by as he stood with his arm round her. A slight pressure of his hand on her waist made her turn to smile at him.

"Let's get out of here," he murmured, his eyes glinting with amusement and — yes, passion. Skilfully he extricated them from the celebrating masses and they slipped out, only Julia and Jamie aware that they had vanished.

The distance between the pub and Charlie's house was about a hundred metres and they reached the front door so quickly they could have won a gold medal for England. Upstairs and into the bedroom, clothes thrown on the floor, they fell into each other's arms and on to the bed.

"Oh God, Finn," Charlie moaned as he held her and kissed her hard. "I've been such a shit, I can't believe you've forgiven me."

"Who says I've forgiven you?" She struggled out of his grasp and grinned wickedly at him. "I only said I'd marry you, who mentioned forgiveness?" She stopped laughing and looked very seriously at him. "We can't have secrets, Charlie. Why didn't you tell me about Amanda? And about your mother? It must have been hell for you."

"I love you," he said and that was all the answer she had for the time being as he traced lazy circles with his tongue round her nipples, then, as she arched with pleasure, he abandoned all pretence of restraint and thrust into her again and again, as though banishing the years of anger and unhappiness, taking solace in her welcoming body.

Afterwards, as he slept, Finn was flooded with a vast tenderness and something that felt like awe, that this closeness, this recognition, all this was hers. I love everything about him, she thought, lover and child, arrogant and gentle, funny and sad. I didn't know this would be how it is. I didn't know I'd search so long for him. I never guessed it would be so worth waiting for.

"I wanted to tell you," he told her later as they cuddled close. "I'd made up my mind but then Amanda turned up and I completely lost it. I hadn't realised how much I still hated her till I saw her, then I wanted to kill her. I had to get away and sort my head out. Somehow it seemed important not to let you be touched by the whole stinking mess. What I had with you was so different, *is* so different, from how things were with her. I can't believe I was going to marry her."

"But you *did* love her?" Finn steeled herself to put the question, biting her lips not to follow it with did you love her more than me?

"I suppose so," he shook his head in bewilderment. "I must have done, mustn't I? I mean, I'm not the kind of guy who goes round proposing. I worked abroad a lot, remember, and the girls you met weren't the kind you marry. I met Amanda not long after I settled back in this country. I remember I was a bit surprised when she decided she wanted us to get married straight away,

216

I suppose . . . Oh, I don't know, I remember thinking there was no desperate hurry, but Amanda kept saying things like, how much Mum would like it, how she'd want to be reassured that I would be happily settled, that Pa would have both of us to lean on. My mother had just been given three months to live, you see, but even though I listened to Amanda I knew, really, that there was no way Mum would put any pressure on me — the pressure was all from Amanda. Mum actually told me she thought we ought to wait a while — till after she died, she meant, before rushing into anything, after all we'd only known each other a few months.

"I don't know, all I remember is being crazed with lust about Amanda and worried sick about Mum. What I didn't know till later was that Amanda had recently been dumped by her long-term boyfriend and got engaged to me on the rebound, hence the need, presumably, for a big splashy wedding, just to show. I suppose she was regretting it even as she finalised the arrangements. But she *did* know how ill Mum was, Pa wrote to me in Newcastle and told me what Amanda had said, but it's all a load of bull. I mean, what did she think Mum was doing in a hospice, for Pete's sake?"

"Let it go," Finn said gently. "Delia's put the curse of the Muncasters on her so she's doomed for ever more!" She leaned over and kissed him very lovingly. "I wish I'd known your mother, she sounds lovely. I hope she knows about us."

★ ★ ★

"So when do you think the wedding will be?" Ursula and Bobbie were ecstatic with spinsterly delight and their faces fell when Julia looked blank.

"No idea," she told them. "I doubt if they know themselves yet and I wouldn't dream of interfering, I'm not giving Charlie any scope for in-law jokes."

The Gang had adjourned to Daisy Cottage so that Delia could do what she called "some serious celebrating" — which appeared to consist of abandoning her customary gin in favour of very large measures of brandy, champagne and sugar lumps as she dished out champagne cocktails all round.

"Champagne's a pretty drink for a party," she informed Jamie as he raised his glass to her. "But when it comes to real celebrating you need a bit more oomph, in my opinion. Here's to the happy couple." And when they had toasted Finn and Charlie she raised her glass again. "And here's to dear old Margot, bless her. May she find a heaven where she can dance around naked all day and roger every husky young man she meets."

Subdued but smiling they drank to Margot and to Rosemary, then Delia called for refills.

"No need to be miserable about the old girl," she said, briskness failing to disguise how moved she was. "Best thing for her in the end, and for Rosemary. Drink up, chums, drink to our jaunt to the sun!"

Jonathan was looking longingly at the television and she nodded when he asked if he might watch the news, so he sat quietly while the others laughed and talked. Suddenly he shouted to them to be quiet.

"Listen!"

"— Island in the Caribbean, nineteen of the Japanese tourists taken ill in an outbreak of E-coli in the early hours of this morning are now on the critical list. Fifty-four other guests at the hotel, mostly Germans and Japanese, were allowed to leave hospital after treatment. The management of the hotel, which only opened in August, issued an assurance that the problem has been traced to one supplier, and that stringent hygiene measures are in place. A spokesman said that guests with reservations for next week should have no cause for alarm."

They listened in silence to the rest of the news bulletin then Delia pressed the button on the remote. There was a collective sigh as they all let out the breath they scarcely realised they had been holding.

"Ooh-er," said Sue, breaking the tension.

"That's torn it," Jonathan fretted and Marek nodded, his black brows drawn into a fierce frown.

Ursula was fussing and Bobbie's face was twitching with nerves, as Ursula turned wide blue eyes to Delia for guidance.

"You don't think, oh dear . . . You don't think we shall have to cancel our holiday, do you, Delia?"

"Whatever for?" Delia was bracing. "Food poisoning at the end of November isn't going to affect our holiday in the first week of July. Get a grip, Ursula, have another drink to wash the blues away. I've never suffered from food poisoning anyway, it's all a question of stamina, no moral fibre these Huns and Nips. Here, put this inside you, old girl." She pushed a refill into

Ursula's protesting hand and stood over the other woman while she drank it. "More to the point, you know, talking of our trip, what are you planning to do about Henrietta? Won't she kick up a stink if you take off for two weeks?"

Two lethal champagne cocktails on top of a couple of glasses of Delia's favourite Moët in the pub strengthened Ursula's nerve and she managed not to collapse into an abject heap.

"It's all taken care of," she said carefully, wondering why Delia couldn't keep still. Most inconsiderate of her, all that swaying made one begin to feel sick. "Henrietta will be taken care of. Since she had that second stroke she's been much eashier to handle." And sho she hash, Ursula thought guiltily. That'sh becaushe she'sh down in the air-raid shelter, that'sh why.

Finn woke early next morning and wondered for a moment why she felt so heavenly, then Charlie bent over and kissed her.

"About time you woke up," he teased. "I've been watching you by the light of the luminous hands on my alarm clock. I was just about to wake you."

"You and whose army?" she laughed at him, kissing his nose with enthusiasm.

"Don't need an army," he boasted and proceeded to show her. "*This* is how I planned to wake you up."

"Wow," she said some time later. "I have to agree, that would certainly have woken me up."

They lay wrapped in each other's arms until Finn wriggled round to look at him, her blue eyes serious.

"I was thinking about your father," she told him. "And about Julia. I couldn't bear it if you died, like your mother, or if you just took off, like Julia's husband. Promise me we'll always be together?"

His eyes laughed at her but he said nothing until he had kissed her soundly.

"I solemnly promise," he said affectionately. "I solemnly promise that we'll live happily ever after and die when we're in our nineties." At a protesting wriggle from her, he added, "We'll die in our nineties at the exact same moment, just after we've made love for the umpteen millionth time and our children and grandchildren will be absolutely mortified when the report of the inquest is published in *The Daily Planet* or whatever the hottest tabloid is then!"

CHAPTER
FOURTEEN

Next day the news from the West Indies was worse.

The day after that it was horrific.

"Sixteen people dead."

Delia and Julia were having an emergency meeting in the kitchen at Rosemary's house where Rosemary was making lists, sending letters to relatives and phoning in the notice of Margot's death to *The Telegraph* while her two friends kept her going with strong coffee and Danish pastries from the village shop.

"I know," Delia looked up as Julia read the casualty figures on Ceefax. "I thought I was a pretty tough old bird but I must admit that even I feel a bit queasy at the thought. All knocking on a bit, weren't they?"

"Uh-huh, sixties, seventies, that sort of age." Julia was frowning. "Makes you think, doesn't it? Getting bumped off en masse isn't what we had in mind when we dreamed up this scheme. I hope they'll have sorted out their hygiene by next summer."

"Safest place to be, if you ask me," suggested Rosemary, taking a break from her telephoning. "Oof! I'm bushed, any coffee left, Delia? Thanks." She took a long, grateful swig from the mug Delia held out to her.

"You know? They'll be paranoid about cleanliness after this, probably hose us all down before they let us in."

"Glad to see you're perking up," commented Delia, observing Rosemary's saddened but relaxed face, all the tension of the last few weeks — months, even — erased at last.

"How are you getting on with the arrangements for this 'green' funeral of Margot's?"

"It's surprisingly uncomplicated." Rosemary dropped into a chair and sat with her hands cupping her mug. "All you need is authorisation — and Hugh's a golfing buddy of the coroner, who's quite happily given his consent. As long as you don't pollute a watercourse and you register the burial place, the law's apparently pretty flexible."

She smiled her gratitude as Julia put a plate in front of her, bearing an apple Danish.

"Thanks, my favourite. As I was saying, some people even leave instructions that they want to be buried in their own garden, and that's quite legal as long as you don't snarl up the drains, etc. The cautionary note there is that it can have a really *bad* effect on your property value. Out on the edge of the field, where Margot wanted to be, poses no problem, so that's a relief. It's all set for Friday at noon, then back here for a bit of a wake."

"Very sensible," approved Delia. "We can use the same rota we had for my *conversazione* and drop the food in here during the morning, or the night before, then the main dishes can be left in a slow oven during the funeral. One of us can nip back to the house and

223

start hotting up garlic bread and we can all take turns as waiters and waitresses." A thought struck her and she flashed her predatory grin. "Unless you'd like us to act as professional mourners? Wailing and rending our garments? Ashes on our heads? Margot would have appreciated that."

"Indeed she would, what a charming picture." Rosemary's sarcasm simply rolled off Delia who just grinned even more. "Seriously though, that's such a kind thought about the food, it'll make life so much easier, thank you."

At lunch-time on Monday Charlie called round at the shop for Finn and patiently submitted to being congratulated by Hedgehog and Bernard, who had dropped in after a trip to the feed merchant.

"She's a lovely girl," Hedgehog told him, his shiny button eyes gleaming with emotion, ignoring Finn's twelve years' seniority. "You look after her, you hear?" He took hold of Charlie's sleeve in sudden anxiety. "You won't make her stop working here, will you? I can't do without her, y'know."

"No, of course I won't," soothed Charlie, only to be interrupted by his irate bride.

"Am I invisible or something?" Finn snapped indignantly. "What *is* this? *I* say where I'll work, not you, either of you — even if you *are* my boss," she added with a glare at Hedgehog.

"Atta girl," Bunny beamed approval. "How about Hedge and me as bridesmaids? Be a bit different, wouldn't it?"

She calmed down and grinned at him.

"Brilliant, Bunny! Both of you in tweed kilts, do you think?"

"As long as I've got somewhere to keep a bottle handy," he assured her. "I don't care what I wear."

"Oh wonderful." Charlie rolled his eyes and took Finn by the arm to drag her towards the door. "The wedding of my dreams, I can see it now, with Ursula and Delia as flower girls for good measure — grannies, drunks and dopeheads, just how I always pictured it."

Out in the town square he pulled her into the lee of the statue towering over them.

"Seriously, Finn," he brushed a raindrop off her nose and kissed her gently. "Are you sure about this? Getting engaged, getting married?" You haven't known me very long, are you sure this is what you want?"

"I've known you as long as you've known me," she countered, then, as she registered anxiety in his brown eyes, she sobered. "Yes," she told him eagerly. "I didn't know, till you asked me, that this was what I wanted, I just knew there was a gaping void when you weren't there, but this feels so right. Even when I was so angry, I knew I'd rather be furious *with* you than peaceful *without* you. It's taken me years to find out, but — everything falling into place, everything making sense — I can't explain it but — yes, it's exactly what I want."

On Wednesday night it stopped raining and by Friday morning it was actually possible to walk across Margot's field to her funeral without the need for wellington boots.

"I like the new vicar," Sue whispered to Julia as they stood at the grave-side listening to the brief address. "She's actually speaking like a normal person, sounds as though she's taken the trouble to find out what Margot was really like. She's not just rattling it off without thinking."

"That's a woman for you," Julia said. "Pregnant, too. Looks as if she's ready for maternity leave."

"I'm glad to have met Margot, even briefly," the vicar was saying. "Old age takes us all in so many different ways and sometimes the veneer of a lifetime of polite behaviour is stripped away, leaving us curmudgeonly, mean, fearful, some angry, some resigned. Some people are so fundamentally good that this quality shines through and others are blessed by an innate good-heartedness. From the stories I've been told Margot seems to have tackled old age and mental inability head-on, with a cheerful courage we could all emulate, though perhaps —" she gave a roguish smile. "Perhaps with a little less of the nudity!"

Back at the house Bobbie and Ursula, whose joint feline foster-motherhood seemed to be turning into a comfortable aunt-niece relationship, formed the advance guard, setting out casserole dishes and platters of goulash, shepherd's pie, garlic bread and salad, along with crisps and cheese, with apple pie and ice cream to follow.

"All right, Rosemary?" Julia paused in passing to give Rosemary a warm but precarious hug, with consider-able danger to the tray of glasses she was carrying in her other hand.

"I'm fine, thanks," Rosemary assured her and she looked it, Julia decided, heading towards the hall where Charlie and Finn had been cornered.

"A fine diamond," Delia pronounced, admiring Finn's engagement ring. "And when do you two propose to be married?" She looked Charlie up and down, apparently approving what she saw. "No qualms about *this* wedding, then? Not worried about being left in the lurch this time?"

"*Delia!*" Julia hurled herself into the breach. "You are the most impossible person I've ever met. Charlie, pay no attention to her, it's none of her business." As Charlie's only reaction was to laugh at the pair of them, she went on, emboldened. "It could probably be called *my* business, though, as big sister of the bride. *Have* you got round to thinking about dates and places yet?"

She stood waiting with avid curiosity, but Finn shook her head.

"You and Charlie's father will be the first to know," she said firmly, then she giggled. "I told you about Bunny wanting to be a bridesmaid, and dragging Hedge into it, didn't I?"

"Sounds good to me," Julia told her. "I should think *Hello* magazine will be panting to take photos, don't you? Seriously, though, we're rather poorly supplied with relatives, you know. Both our parents were only children and apart from Cousin Maeve in Killarney, and she smells, I can't think of anybody. Very poor breeding stock we are, I couldn't have children and your biological clock must be on its last gasp. Maybe you'd better reconsider, Charlie? I mean, you don't want to be the last heir of the Stuarts, do you?"

Charlie turned away from watching, with an appreciative grin, his father initiating the vicar — whose eyes were glazing — into the intricacies of the Stuart dynasty. "It needs thinking about," he said seriously. "I had no brothers or sisters, nor did Pa; my mother's only sister never married and she's a research scientist in the Antarctic, so apart from a few cousins somewhere down the line, we're pretty badly off too. I think we'd better call it off, Finn," he turned to her, towering over her in a manner deeply satisfying to his future sister-in-law. "I'd better find a girl who's the seventh daughter of a seventh daughter, then we can add some class to the breed. Hey," he grinned at Julia again. "I've just thought, I suppose Finn's a Catholic?"

"No," she shook her head decidedly. "When Finn and I visited Ireland to see an old aunt, I'd an argument with the priest at the aunt's church about the evils of divorce and bringing shame onto my good Catholic family. And him a whisky priest, too, and known to be fumble-fingered with the altar boys, so I gave up on religion and Finn never took to it at all."

They were interrupted by Rosemary who was tapping a spoon against her glass.

"I just wanted to thank you all for coming," she said, the nervous quaver in her voice vanishing in the sympathetic reaction her announcement evoked. "Margot would have been surprised and touched at the kindness you've all shown and I know she'd have been

228

in seventh heaven to see so many good-looking men in one room."

Gradually the rest of the company slipped away after speaking very kindly to Rosemary and the only visitors left were the members of the *Hope Springs* gang. Jonathan Barlow, after several false starts, managed to pluck up courage and talk to Finn.

"Orchids!" he said in an explosive whisper and when she looked puzzled, he took a deep breath and got the sentence out. "I grow orchids in my greenhouse, your sister might have said?" When she nodded politely he looked gratified. "I thought . . . at least, I wondered . . . Your wedding, I wondered if you'd like to have some for your bouquet? It would be my pleasure . . ."

"Oh!" Finn's glowing smile was answer enough and he blushed with awkward delight. "I *love* orchids. That's *so* kind, thank you."

Just at that moment the telephone rang and Rosemary Clavering apologised to Marek who was telling her, for the tenth time, about his bogus marriage, and went to answer it. Only Julia spotted that Rosemary's expression was one of extreme surprise.

"Listen, people." Rosemary called the group to order and told them to sit down. "That was the travel agent and you won't *believe* what they're suggesting." She had their attention now, so she explained. "The hotel chain are going ballistic about this food poisoning outbreak, naturally enough, and they're panicking because they've been inundated by people calling in to cancel their holidays. Apparently the phone lines have been jammed and the number of e-mails actually caused a crash. Anyway . . ." She paused tantalisingly. "Anyway, the agent says they're absolutely desperate to get tourists back so they can prove to the world that the hotel is up and running, so they're working down their lists of bookings and contacting people with offers they hope they can't refuse."

"So?" Delia was predictably impatient. "Spit it out, Rosemary. What offer have they come up with that we can't refuse?"

"They've offered us . . ." Rosemary looked extremely smug, then, as Delia threatened actual bodily harm, she carried on hastily. "They've offered that instead of our two weeks at the beginning of next July, we can have three weeks almost immediately, starting on Christmas Eve. *And,*" she shouted down the clamour her announcement provoked. "And, they say, it will only cost us a thousand pounds each, an enormous reduction. Christmas is *the* most expensive time of all."

"That's incredible." Julia spoke for them all. "Are we all game?" She smiled as they all shouted at once. "I thought so. We'll leave Bobbie and Delia to do the sums but surely that means we can spread the cost much more evenly and end up with a really decent surplus we could give to charity — Help the Aged, for preference — given our slogan — Comforts for the Elderly — it would be only fair."

Under cover of the hubbub Charlie smiled down at Finn.

"Do you remember actually agreeing that we'd go on this holiday with them?" he asked her. "No, me neither.

230

But I don't care, do you? We'll never get three weeks in the West Indies for a couple of grand any other way. How about we use this development and set the date for the wedding for two days before Christmas Eve? If you don't mind a honeymoon with a gang of — what? Eccentrics, is probably the kindest word for them?"

"Sounds good to me," she assured him, pulling his face down so she could kiss him again. "I've got to the stage where the prospect of a wedding *not* attended by pensioners and weirdos is unthinkable. What do we do about getting a licence?"

He glanced at his watch.

"We extricate the vicar from Bobbie's clutches and fix the time and date," he suggested. "She forgot her phone so Bobbie and Ursula caught her when she came back and last time I spotted her they were having an earnest discussion about whether animals have souls. I think Bobbie was winning."

"I'd be delighted," the vicar told them when they rescued her from the two cat lovers. "Twelve o'clock? An excellent choice for weddings, funerals or christenings; time to digest your breakfast and not get too hungry before lunch." She stopped joking for a moment and looked at them very kindly. "This is the point where I normally try to get couples to consider the implications of marriage," she said seriously. "But I've been talking to some of these good people today and they've all been vociferous in telling me of the grace and humanity you've both shown in helping out with their activities. It's my belief that a couple with

231

such kind hearts can be expected to work hard at their relationship and to make their vows meaningful."

She smiled at their astounded faces, shook hands heartily and left them to ponder her words.

"I'll be in touch about the arrangements," she reminded them and slid out, after a furtive glance round to make sure neither Ursula and Bobbie, nor Jamie Stuart, were in sight.

Meanwhile Delia was checking that her troops were ready for battle.

"How will those dates fit in with your term times, Sue?" she enquired and Sue set her shoulders resolutely and pursed her lips.

"I think it overlaps by about two days," she said then she grimaced and spread her hands in resignation. "Makes no difference, I'm still going. If it doesn't suit the powers that be, so what? I'm thirty-five with a whole world to see, I've been a doormat for too long, they can like it or lump it!"

"Well said," Delia nodded. "OK, what about passports? Everyone up to date? Anyone need to renew, because if so, we need to get a move on."

"I haven't got a passport," Ursula piped up and Jonathan Barlow nodded also, looking extremely anxious.

"Don't worry," Jamie assured them. "We can go into town now and pick up the forms and get your photographs done, then one or other of us can sign them for you and we'll send them off express. If you like I'll give the Passport Office a ring and see what the position is, bearing in mind the Christmas postal situation."

"Excellent," Delia made a note and frowned at Ursula. "What about Henrietta? She can't be left for three weeks, can she? Do you need any help with the arrangements?"

"No thank you," Ursula spoke with dignity. "A friend of the family will keep an eye on things for me." Unseen by anyone else the angel, who had been hanging around the funeral in, as he said, a professional capacity, winked approvingly at her. "*Well*," he had suggested on his last visit. "*That's all you need say, after all, I am a friend of the family, aren't I?*"

With a doubtful glance Delia made another note, then turned to Jonathan again.

"How will you manage with Pauline? Won't she kick up an awful stink?"

"She won't cause a problem," he asserted stoutly and refused to elaborate.

Ursula had a sudden thought and cast a sidelong look at him, then at the angel, who shook his head, golden finger to gleaming lips. "*Don't be silly,*" he whispered in her ear. "*His wife is alive and well and twice as repulsive as normal. His plans don't include burying her in his allotment, though I heartily approve of what he is intending to do.*"

Within a few days events were gathering pace. The wedding day and time were set and Finn was starting to think about what she would wear. Her initial plans for something simple were overtaken by the desire of the whole gang for a proper white wedding to start their holiday of a lifetime with a bang. On its own this would not have influenced her but first Julia and then Charlie started to sigh and say how much they'd love to see her in full regalia. When she argued that, at forty-five, she would look ridiculous, Charlie gave her a spaniel-eyed sigh and Julia laughed at her so she gave in and started haunting the bridal shops in all the neighbouring towns, looking for something suitable for her "mature years" as Julia termed it.

Rosemary was surprised to receive a visit from Hedgehog and Bernard, both looking unusually ingratiating.

"Finn told us about the holiday," they chorused. "Is there any chance we could tag along? Would you mind?"

"But didn't Finn say you were booked for some religious retreat for Christmas?" Julia said, having been summoned across the Green for support.

"It's been postponed," Bernard mourned. "The leader's got to go into hospital for a hernia operation, so it's all up in the air."

"Besides," Hedgehog expanded. "We checked their website and decided it's not for us. Turns out they're some militant group, Gay Farmers for Jesus, and that's no good for us. Bunny's already as far out of the closet as he's coming and I was hoping some bird might be full of Christian charity towards a sinner! Go on," he pleaded. "Find out, there's a love, and if it's all right with the tour people and with your gang, we'd love to come."

"I've no objection," Jamie said at the emergency meeting that night. "The more the merrier, those two will enhance the party, I'd say."

The others agreed, though it was decided, by unanimous vote, that Hedgehog and Bunny need not be enlightened about the nature of the fund-raising.

"I think they've got a pretty good idea," Charlie murmured to Finn as they stood at the back of the meeting in the pub. "Wouldn't bother either of them, if they did know, Hedge's mind is as broad as a dining table."

"You're in, then," Julia and Rosemary told the new recruits. "Mind you," Julia warned. "They're a bit puritanical, you know? Sniffy about gay couples and that's what they'll assume you are, so don't be surprised to find yourselves allocated Bobbie or Ursula as official room-mates. It's only for the name of the thing, we'll sort ourselves out when we get there."

At this point Finn and Charlie moved forward.

"Good dinner?" enquired Jamie, shifting up on an oak settle to make room for him.

"So-so," Charlie told him. "Mind you, it was great to be on our own for a bit, this communal social life gets a bit wearing sometimes."

"Ah well," said his father tolerantly. "You're young-ish — yet. Once we get to the Caribbean you needn't speak to any of us, if you don't want to."

"Come to any decisions?" Julia asked Finn who was sitting beside her on the opposite settle. "About what sort of 'do' you want?"

"Sort of," sighed Finn. "All we want is a quiet wedding in church and a nice lunch somewhere afterwards — with you lot, believe it or not. I've lost touch with my old friends in this country and I definitely don't want to invite anyone from Brussels. Charlie's pretty much the same, I don't think he wants anything that might remind him of last time." She watched Charlie talking to Jamie. "He says that since he moved here he's been too busy to make friends apart from his business partner and clients. And I've looked at dresses and I hate them all. Why can't you sew, Julia? It'd make life so much easier if you could just whip me up a little number."

As Julia opened her mouth, Rosemary, blushing slightly, interrupted.

"But *I* can sew," she informed Finn. "If you tell me what you want, I'll come with you to choose material and I'll make your dress. If you'd like me to, I mean."

"Brilliant," Finn was alight with gratitude.

"Of course," Julia spoke at the same time. "I completely forgot you could sew, Rosemary. She does marvellous work," she told Finn. "I'll make the cake, though," she added. "That's something I can manage pretty well. Great, that's two things out of the way, what else? Where to have the reception?"

"Er ..." Hugh Taylor was clearing his throat importantly. "Might I offer my drawing room? It's quite a large room and it opens up, first into the dining room and then into the conservatory. It makes it very pleasant and spacious for entertaining."

"Oh yes," Rosemary gazed at him in admiration. "It's such a lovely room, Finn, it would be perfect. How clever you are, Hugh!"

"And I've already offered orchids," Jonathan was obviously carried along by the wave of enthusiasm. "There will be plenty, for your bouquet and button-holes, and I've plenty of late chrysanths coming along that would be nice in the church."

Finn looked helplessly at Charlie who shrugged and mouthed, "Up to you" so she thanked Jonathan nicely too and turned to find Bobbie almost jumping up and down on the spot, lifted right out of her customary timidity.

"Oh, how lovely," she squeaked. "I do love a wedding! Please, Finn, may I do the flowers? I know how to make bouquets and do flower arranging, my mother used to belong to a flower club. It would be such fun!"

"And I could do some cooking for the reception," Ursula chimed in excitedly. "We must make a list, like we did before."

"I'll provide the champagne," Delia put in. "I've got my man at Threshers under my thumb, won't be a problem. What else do we need? Charlie? What about a best man? Your partner in the business?"

"He's away till Christmas Eve," Charlie shrugged again then started to laugh. "It'd better be you, Pa, we might as well keep it in the family, mightn't we? Who will give you away, Finn?"

Even as Finn caught Julia's eye she was aware of Marek standing slightly aside, proud and forlorn as the others all made offers that he was unable to match.

"Marek," she said, moving over to take his hand. "Will you do me the honour?"

"Oh, my dear young lady." He capitulated at once, unable to conceal his emotion. "The honour will be all mine."

"I'll help out with the cooking and the flowers," Sue announced hastily. "Just in case Delia decides I ought to play the organ or sing, or something. I must say," she told Finn with a smile. "Not many brides would let us take over their big day. Are you sure about this?"

"The only thing I'm sure of is that I love Charlie," Finn told her frankly with a smile towards him that made the other women sigh for their own lost loves. "As far as I'm concerned you're welcome to arrange everything just as you like."

The twenty-second of December turned out to be one of those perfect winter days, beginning with a silver frost that spangled the bushes outside Finn's window and continuing into a panorama of gold and blue and green, in pale winter sunshine, chambray sky and the verdant prettiness that made Bychurch a byword.

"Just us," Finn looked across at Julia who was forcing herself to eat a leisurely breakfast. "Like it's always been."

"Soppy thing," Julia tried not to look as moved as she felt but her eyes betrayed her and Finn jumped up to give her a consoling hug.

"You *are* happy about Charlie and me, aren't you, Julia?" she asked, nuzzling her head against her elder sister's shoulder just as she had done as a small child.

"Of course I am." Julia thought she would break down completely if this went on. "Come on, Finn, what mother wouldn't want her daughter — and you know that no real daughter could have been dearer to me — to be marrying the heir to the throne of England? Specially as he's such a darling." She patted Finn's shoulder and got up to pour another cup of tea and to wipe away the sentimental tears at the same time. "Seriously, Finn, I think he's just right for you; strong and kind, thoughtful and funny, and dead sexy with it! And don't worry about me," she added. "After all, you'll be nearer, living just across the green, than you've been for nearly ten years on the Continent. I do think you ought to set about making some other friends, though. As a temporary measure the Gang is fine, but we might be considered a rather eccentric social circle, mightn't we?"

"Maybe," Finn wandered to the sitting room window to look out over the village green. "But they've all been so kind, you'd think I was family. Look at Bobbie, she's decorated the church and made all those flower arrangements for the 'do' afterwards, not to mention taking over and making up my bouquet. And then Hugh, I feel a bit guilty after the way you and I have laughed at him; letting us use his fantastic house like this."

"You *are* family to them," Julia told her. "Bobbie has no near relatives, apart from those cats of hers now, and

239

she said she's never had a hand in a wedding before. Same with Ursula, though I do worry about *her*, she insists that Henrietta isn't making any fuss about her going on holiday for three weeks, but she refuses to tell us what arrangements she's made. And the others — Delia's in her element, marshalling her troops, providing the drink and so on. Jonathan too, his greenhouse and the allotment have always been his escape from that wife of his and he's thrilled to be able to bring something positive out of it with your flowers."

"As for Marek . . ." Finn began to laugh. "He's been on the phone half-a-dozen times a day, worrying about what the "father" of the bride has to do. I think he's disappointed that it's actually so little." She turned away from the window. "I wish I knew what Hedgehog and Bernard were planning to wear, that's the one real worry I have, that they might dress up in something outrageous, specially if Bunny's drunk and Hedge is stoned."

"What if they do?" Julia spread her hands. "Will you care? Charlie won't, that's for sure, nor anyone else. You can always refuse to let them be in the photographs if they turn up in bridesmaid's dresses, though I think it might provide that certain something."

Besides providing his house and drawing room for the reception, Hugh Taylor was also transport chief, his Mercedes would take Charlie and Finn back to the house. At eleven-thirty he arrived at Forge Cottage in his auxiliary role as official photographer, sporting his Leica. He found Marek marching up and down muttering and Bobbie alternately fussing about the flowers and mopping her eyes from which sentimental tears flowed at any given moment.

"Oh, Hugh, she looks a picture!" She pounced on Julia who looked in to nod a welcome to Hugh. "Come and let's look at *you*, Julia. Oh, how *lovely*! That green velvet suits you so well, and I love the hat, you look so Christmassy."

Julia preened in the mirror, admiring the emerald velvet suit with its matching Edwardian-style hat which was trimmed with a spray of Christmas roses, leaves and berries.

"I know it's a bit over the top," she admitted. "But hey! I never was a shrinking violet, so why not go for the festive look?" She heard movement upstairs and her face softened with loving pride as Finn carefully negotiated the dog-leg staircase.

"Oh, darling," she exclaimed. "You're *so* beautiful!"

Hugh took some photographs until Finn looked nervously at herself in the long mirror in the hall. Terrified of looking like mutton dressed as lamb she had approved Rosemary's suggestion of the simplest possible dress; lowish, round neck, long, narrow sleeves, long, narrow skirt, fitted to show off her waist, the whole in soft, ivory velvet.

"These are the pearls Jamie gave me," she touched the single string round her throat. "They belonged to Charlie's mother, wasn't it sweet of him?" She cast another, anxious, look at her reflection. "Are you sure it looks all right? Not too girly?"

"It's just right," her audience chorused and Bobbie gave her an appraising look. "No," she pronounced.

"Having gone for a wintery-Christmas effect I don't think you could better it. Your hair looks just right, up like that, with the wreath of leaves and berries and those little white orchids of Jonathan's, and so does your bouquet, though I say it myself. You look just like the spirit of Christmas — warm and generous and loving and beautiful!"

On this eloquent note Bobbie surpassed herself and was overcome by emotion again, so Julia took charge.

"Time for the off," she said, manhandling the sniffling Bobbie towards the door where Hugh was waiting. "Be happy, dearest, *darling* Finn."

Finn and Marek walked the short distance across the green to the fourteenth-century church, cheered on, it seemed, by half the village who had turned out to greet her. The other half of the village were inside the church, as choir, organist, verger and supporting congregation.

"I want all the proper things," Finn had said when she realised she would have to give in and have the wedding they all yearned for. "I want *Here Comes the Bride* and the *Wedding March*, as well as the King James Bible and the proper prayer book," so she and Marek processed up the aisle to the familiar strains.

A collective "Aaah!" met her and she smiled and looked towards the altar to see Charlie and his father splendidly arrayed in full Highland dress, Royal Stuart tartan, black velvet jackets, frothing lace, the works. They looked sensational and as she met Charlie's eyes she saw that he knew it.

"You look lovely," he whispered and grinned as she whispered right back, "So do you!"

242

The vicar smiled benignly at them and began the service, apparently quite calmly, but Julia was concerned.

"Don't make a fuss, Julia," Finn had said crossly the night, before. "She says she'll be fine, she's got another month to go."

Julia had her doubts. "She might be *only* eight months pregnant but old professional instincts died hard, and even though her last midwifery stint was a while back, Julia had a feeling that the vicar was going to cause trouble.

Her feeling was only too justified. There was the usual sigh of relief when nobody leaped up with a "just cause or impediment" and the vicar had turned to the bride and groom.

"Wilt thou, Charles Edward, *Oh my God!*"

Heads jerked up to see the vicar clutching her bulging belly and gazing in dismay at the trickle of water seeping down the steps. After a few moments she shook her head and held up her hand.

"Sorry about that, folks, I'm fine just now, but we'd better get this show on the road. Ready, Charlie?"

The wedding proceeded at an accelerated pace. It was obvious that the vicar was far from fine and the vows began to be punctuated by groans of pain.

"Who giveth this woman — *aargh, oh Jesus!* — to be married to this man?"

Marek hastily shoved his temporary charge towards her bridegroom and retired in confusion to the pew beside Julia.

And so it went on, the vicar steadfastly refusing to give in, though her words, as well as her moans, were coming faster and faster until the final pronouncement was made in a muted scream.

"I pronounce that they be Man and Wife together, In the Name of the Father, and of the Son, and of the Holy Ghost. *Aarghh!* Amen!"

"Is that it?" Julia demanded, surging forward. "All the legal stuff done?"

The vicar nodded, panted for a few seconds, then managed to gasp out: "Register, got to be signed 'n'witnessed. All ready, but must be done."

Julia waited for the next contraction then summoned Jamie to the rescue.

"Let's get her into the vestry," she commanded. "Somebody call an ambulance and someone else get hold of her husband, he's an accountant in Southampton, isn't he?"

"Can't walk!" wailed the labouring vicar.

"You don't have to." Charlie came to help carry her to the relative privacy of the vestry where she scribbled her name in the register during the next brief pause between contractions.

"That's it," Julia scrawled her own name, after Jamie's, the other witness, and organised her makeshift labour ward. "Jamie, tell the organist to strike up, and get Finn and Charlie safely out of here. Delia, ask if there's anyone in the congregation who knows about childbirth, and the rest of you'd better make tracks. This won't take long from the look of it."

244

Finn and Charlie were caught between bewilderment and hysterical laughter as Julia assured them that everything was perfectly straightforward and she'd catch up with them at Hugh's house. As they set off back down the aisle the notes of the *Wedding March* were hard put to conceal the blood-curdling screams now coming from the vestry but after exchanging another anxious look, and avoiding the ominous damp patch on the carpet, they made it to the church door, just as the screams ceased and were succeeded by the welcome wailing of a very new baby.

As they emerged into the pale winter sunshine the ambulance arrived and the crew rushed in to the church, the driver pausing for a moment.

"Lemme kiss the bride," he winked. "Got to be just as lucky as a sweep, hasn't it? And cleaner."

He planted a smacking kiss on Finn's blushing cheek, winked again at Charlie and dashed indoors after his colleague.

"Well!" Charlie took a deep breath and clutched his new bride in his arms. "Come here, Mrs Stuart. Let me tell you, after that performance I'm not so sure about continuing the Stuart dynasty — bloody hell, if it was half as painful as it sounded I don't think I can let you go through it."

"Mmm?" Finn sounded non-committal but inwardly she was counting. Oops! During the dreadful week when Charlie had decamped to Newcastle to sort himself out she had forgotten, in her deep depression, all about taking the pill and although she had resumed after he came back, she had a sneaky feeling it was too late; ten, twelve, no fifteen days overdue, she thought guiltily. It might, of course, be the beginning of an early menopause, but somehow she didn't think so.

Hugh posed them in the doorway and started taking photographs, interrupting the proceedings only when the ambulance crew appeared with a dishevelled vicar in a wheelchair, clasping a very angry baby girl in her arms.

Waddling alongside Julia was the Gang's bugbear, Mrs Parsons, looking pleased with herself.

"She was actually quite helpful," Julia confided to Rosemary who raised her eyebrows. The temporary assistant midwife straightened her hat and stared at the two women.

"See you got yourselves a couple of men," she remarked affably as she turned to go. "Told you so, didn't I?"

Julia shrugged as she watched her go, saw her patient into the ambulance and rejoined the wedding party.

"You're looking remarkably clean and tidy," Finn greeted her with an appraising look up and down. "I thought you'd be a complete mess after all that."

"Borrowed a surplice off the back of the door," Julia answered laconically. "I've shoved it in a cupboard, heaven knows what the locum vicar will think." She grinned at her sister's scandalised expression and turned to Hugh. "All finished, Hugh? Thank God for that, let's get back to the reception, I think we all deserve a drink."

246

CHAPTER
FIFTEEN

Back at Hugh's house Charlie and Finn held court while the members of the *Hope Springs* gang revived their flagging spirits with Delia's champagne and the buffet spread they had contributed between them, in spite of Julia's protests.

"Finn and I weren't going to do it all by ourselves," she had objected when Sue and Delia showed her their lists. "We were just going to get Waitrose or M & S to do some of their party platters, it wouldn't be any trouble. I can't ask the Gang to provide my sister's wedding reception."

"Did anyone ask you?" Sue inquired severely. "Well, then. Seriously, Julia, we all had a mini-meeting and decided we wanted to help out. Finn and Charlie, God help them, are part of the group and they've contributed considerably to the excitements lately — besides, we *were* originally a barter organisation."

"Feeling better?" Charlie cuddled his bride in one arm and finished his second glass of wine.

"Me? I was fine, it was you that came over all queasy." Finn leaned her head against his shoulder, then drew back to take a better look at him. "You look sensational in full Highland regalia, Charlie; why didn't you tell me? I nearly fainted with the glamour of it all."

"Wanted to surprise you," he said complacently, then he gave the giggle she found so adorable. "Have you actually taken on board what Hedgehog and Bunny are wearing?"

Finn straightened up and took a look round the room. Her employer and his brother-in-law were standing in the big bay window, in animated conversation with Delia and Rosemary. Hedgehog was immaculate in full morning dress but like Charlie and his father Bunny had elected to wear Highland dress. Unlike the bridegroom and his paternal best man, he had chosen pink tweed for his kilt.

"Well, Finn," Bunny told her, deadpan, when she accosted him. "It was your idea, after all. You were the one who suggested a tweed kilt, weren't you?" As she groaned and hit her head in self-recrimination, he gave her an injured stare. "I thought you'd appreciate it. I spotted the material in Debenham's and got my Mum to make it up for me. Hedge wouldn't co-operate so he found his outfit in a charity shop for thirty quid."

"I give in," she told him, beginning to laugh as Charlie came over to them. "You're quite right, it was my fault, and you look great. I'm just grateful you didn't go the whole hog and have a posy on your sporran."

"Don't think I didn't want to," Bunny warned her. "I'm the creative kind, you know, but Hedge thought you wouldn't like it and he's too frightened of you to upset you."

"Quite right too," Finn told him stoutly. "Let's take a look at how everyone else is kitted out. Wow, Delia, you look a million dollars."

"Thank you, my dear." Delia was wearing another of her Jackie Onassis outfits, an aquamarine wool coat and dress, with matching pillbox over the customary glossy black helmet of hair. "We all wanted to put on a good show."

She spoke nothing less than the truth. From Marek's antique navy suit to Ursula's fluffy mohair beret and drooping beige knitted suit, they had turned out in their best. Bobbie, in navy blue — no change there — had splashed out on a pink hat from the hire shop in town. As she bustled about checking the flowers and helping to serve food, her salmon-coloured feathers drooped and clashed with her unusually rosy cheeks but Finn could see that she was supremely happy.

Somebody else who looked blissful was Rosemary Clavering, wearing lavender. She and Hugh appeared to be joined at the hip and the anxious, restless look she had worn when Finn first met her had quite vanished, while Hugh was wearing a proud, proprietorial air as they processed around the room together.

"All packed?" Sue Merrill found herself beside Julia. "I can't wait, can you? It'll be so wonderful to be away from this awful weather — it's nice today, I admit, but you can't trust it to last."

"I haven't had a moment to ask you, Sue," Julia checked that they were alone. "What happened about that young man's wife?"

She hardly needed Sue to tell her, the sadness in her face was enough.

"She died two days later," Sue said heavily. "I sent a card, and a donation to Cancer Relief but I've kept out of the way, there's no place for me there." She shrugged and suddenly smiled at Julia. "In the meantime I've instructed my solicitor to start divorce proceedings, and I've booted my husband out of the house."

"Goodness!" Julia was impressed. "That's pretty good going, you haven't had long. How did he take it?"

"He was most affronted," Sue grinned, taking a sausage roll from the tray Ursula was proffering. "Apparently it wasn't part of his script for *me* to be the one who acted first. He told me, quite seriously, that *he'd* planned to divorce *me*, next year."

"On what grounds?" Julia was fascinated.

"He didn't specify." Sue was looking more at ease than Julia had ever seen her, and more attractive, in a cream outfit from Wallis, with her hair cut short and styled. "I stood over him while he moved his stuff out, then I changed the locks and reset the codes on the burglar alarm. If he tries to break in while I'm away he'll get more than he bargains for."

Just before Finn and Charlie slipped away to Charlie's house for the next two nights Delia waylaid them.

"I know what you're thinking," she said. "You needn't worry, I'm not suggesting you join our elderly orgy of celebration, you get off and have your own. But before you do go, I wondered about a wedding present."

250

"For goodness sake, Delia," Finn exclaimed in surprise. "You've already done so much, what with all the drink and so on."

"My pleasure," Delia interrupted her with a lordly wave of the hand. "No, this is more practical stuff. I've had the doubtful pleasure of visiting Charlie's house and no doubt he had his own reasons for living in that welter of flock wallpaper, but I don't see why he should expect you to."

"Oh, come *on*, Delia!" Charlie protested. "Of course we'll redecorate, but give us time; we've hardly had time to turn round since we got engaged."

"My point exactly," she told him smugly. "Now, my nice, competent decorator tells me he'll be at a loose end for a few days in the New Year. Suppose I get him to go through the house, stripping off the ghastly wallpapers and painting the whole white — or cream — or even pink, whatever you choose?"

"It wouldn't be pink," Finn was close to tears. "You really are the kindest, most sentimental creature, under that hard front. Charlie? How can we refuse such a kind offer?"

"We can't," Charlie replied frankly. "I second my wife's remarks, Delia. You're a soppy old dragon and I love you!" He clasped the startled Delia in his arms and planted a smacking kiss on her delicately tinted cheek. "But definitely not pink, white's fine with me, thank you."

For the next two days Finn and Charlie stayed holed up in his house, alternating bouts of lovemaking with fits of tidying up in anticipation of Delia's tame painter and decorator.

"I never believed it could be like this," Finn lay in Charlie's arms the night before they were to depart on their honeymoon. "It just gets better, every time."

"Practice," Charlie murmured sleepily. "Gimme ten minutes and we'll practise some more." His voice drowsed away and when she shifted slightly she saw he was already asleep again.

"I love you," she told her sleeping beauty. "Always and forever, world without end."

From the moment when, suddenly shy, she had slipped out of her wedding dress, there had been this sense of a difference, a new dimension, to their lovemaking.

"You're unbelievably beautiful," Charlie whispered huskily as he traced a line from her lips to her breast. "I wish I could write poetry, not just software, I just can't find the words to tell you." He bent to kiss her, with a strange, delicate formality and she felt tears prickling at the back of her eyelids.

For a moment they stayed like that, as if unwilling to shatter the feeling, then Charlie grinned at her with the familiar mischief dancing in his dark brown eyes and the long dimple in his right cheek even deeper than usual.

"Enough about software," he bragged with mock-macho heroics. "What we have here is hardware, and plenty of it!"

"God! You're such a romantic smoothie," she giggled, then there was no time for laughing as they drowned in their mutual passion.

252

At six o'clock on Christmas Eve morning Ursula Buchanan was putting the finishing touches to her packing, a couple of flowered cotton dresses, two viscose skirts with elasticated waists and sad, drooping hemlines, some limp blouses, sensible cotton underwear and — most important of all — her swimming costume.

The angel sat on her bed watching the proceedings.

"*Well?*" he asked, directing a stern glance at her.

"I don't know what you mean," she tossed her head and refused to meet his all-seeing, all-knowing golden eye.

"*Yes you do,*" he told her, with heavily-laboured patience. "*Do I have to spell it out? All right then, in a word — Henrietta!*"

"What about her?" Ursula managed to maintain her defiant stance. "I've told the others I've arranged for a sitter while I'm away, what more do you want?"

"*For a start,*" he said, looking a little less minatory, "*I want to know why you rang her solicitor yesterday?*"

"I thought you knew everything." The angel met her accusing glance with a bland smile. "Oh, very well. If you must know, and I'm sure you already do, I pretended Henrietta was concerned about her will and wanted to know if she'd made an inventory of the house contents."

"*And?*"

"She hadn't," Ursula checked the suitcase once more, then fastened it and lugged it down to the hall. "I suppose you want me to spell it out, do you? Very well,

I was concerned that if anything happened to me the lawyers might be able to trace the sale of some of the china back to the others in the Gang." She frowned at him. "And you needn't look at me like that, I knew all along that I was in the wrong and I don't care, but I didn't want it to back-fire."

"*And the letter you've left in the bureau?*" The angel forbore to comment. "*What's that all about?*"

"You do like to have the t's crossed and the i's dotted, don't you? We've all sorted out our affairs, just in case — Janathan and Marek and me. I've written down what happened, about Henrietta dying like that, and how I didn't want to lose my home. So if anything *does* happen to me, they won't waste time trying to find her."

At the other end of the village Jonathan Barlow was also writing a note.

"*I shall be away for three weeks,*" he wrote, pausing to chew anxiously on the end of his biro. "*I've left you enough money for food and other expenses in the tin on the kitchen shelf. Don't try to draw anything from the joint account because I've transferred all the money from it and rearranged our finances. In future my pension will be paid into my personal account. I'll pay all expenses from it and I'll allow you pocket money if you behave in a proper wifely manner. Don't try to find me, it won't help. You've got three weeks to practise and I'll see how you cope. If you don't change your ways I shall have to take more drastic action.*'

Trembling with nervous excitement at his own daring Jonathan signed the note, sealed it, and left it on the kitchen table, then he checked his pocket for his wallet and passport and crept out into the December chill.

Rosemary Clavering looked wistfully out of her kitchen window towards the huge old oak tree in the eastern corner of the field behind her house.

"I hope Margot can see me now," she told Hugh, who had spent the night with her. "She did love me, in her own eccentric way, and I know she'd be glad to see me so happy now."

Hugh's manly responses about love and duty were drowned by the sound of the minibus drawing up outside and the clamour of excited voices urging them to hurry.

"Come along, come along!" cried Delia. "We've no time to lose, I'm not missing the plane while you check if you've turned off the gas, Rosemary."

"No chance," her victim retorted. "Are we the last ones?"

To Finn's relief nobody burst into song on the journey to Heathrow. She had been afraid that the Gang's exuberant high spirits might lead them to excesses such as *Ten Green Bottles*, but no, although high as kites on excitement, they were, as she reminded herself, civilised people.

Much the same thought had struck Julia, as she turned to speak to Rosemary, sitting behind her.

"Help! Didn't we say right from the start, that we weren't going in for old folks' outings? And look at us now."

"Come on, Julia," Charlie chimed in. "You're hardly run-of-the-mill old folks, are you? But seriously, I do hope you're all going to behave when we're away, and not embarrass Finn and me. I don't want to have to spring anyone else from the police station, eh, Bobbie?"

"What on earth are you talking about?" Julia was intrigued and at the same time Bobbie turned on Charlie reproachfully.

"Oh, Charlie! You promised!"

Charlie was overcome with remorse and apologised handsomely to Bobbie, who nobly forgave him when he smiled at her. The others were not to be silenced, however, and Finn found herself elected to explain.

"It was a couple of days before the wedding," she told them. "Hedgehog and I were hungry so I nipped out to the coffee shop in the Square to buy a couple of Cornish pasties for lunch. When I got there I saw Bobbie and Ursula being arrested!"

"But what for?"

Finn glanced at Bobbie who was blushing deeply.

"Shall I go on?" she asked and continued when Bobbie nodded bashfully. "They were being had up for drug pushing," she announced dramatically.

When the clamour of disbelief died down Bobbie rallied and took her turn at the story.

"It was such a silly mistake," she told them. "You know Ursula and I have been helping out at the Cat Rescue lady's? Well, we've decided that after Christmas we'll go on with our fund-raising, as it's been such fun, only this time we'll raise money for the Cat Shelter. The day Finn's talking about, Ursula and I had been to Andover by bus. I met the mother of one of my former Brownies a few days earlier — she and her husband moved a year or so ago. I don't know how we got on to the subject of cats — I suppose I told her about our darling pussies, and she said what a pity she hadn't known as she'd got a lot of catmint she picked and dried in the summer. If she'd known she would have brought it into town for me."

"Yes," Ursula joined in eagerly. "Bobbie told me and we thought it would be such a good idea to make up little sachets to sell if we have a stall some day, so Bobbie rang up and we arranged to go over to collect the catmint. Such a nice little outing, and such a nice lady."

"Well," Bobbie took over the conversation again as Ursula paused for breath. "We were enjoying our day out so I said, why not have a cup of tea and a toasted teacake in town, before we went home. So we did, and while we were having our tea, we opened up the bag of catmint and tried to work out how many little sachets we could make up from it."

She gazed at her listeners with round-eyed awe.

"And after a few minutes a young man who was sitting at the next table got up and came over to us. We had no idea who he was and I must admit I felt very nervous, he was rather — I suppose rough would be the word. You know, a shaved head and an earring! But he was quite scrawny and young. He just stood there for a moment looking at the bag I had on my lap, then he asked how much we reckoned to make with it."

Julia began to snigger quietly and Finn, who was tucked in between her and Charlie, nudged her to be quiet. Bobbie went on with her gripping tale.

"I didn't quite know how to answer, he didn't seem the type to be interested in animal welfare, but then I thought how uncharitable that was; after all, the most surprising people can be cat lovers. So I said I thought it would make up into about ten generous sachets. He sort of grunted and then he said, how much would I be expecting to charge per sachet?"

"And Bobbie said," Ursula butted in again. "Bobbie said about one-fifty, which I thought was a reasonable price, and the man looked really surprised then just nodded and reached in his pocket."

"What did he do?" Sue and Rosemary were hanging over the seat to hear the story.

"He said, would I sell the lot to him?" Bobbie told them. "He was rather pathetic, actually. He said, 'I really need it, man, but I ain't got much cash and you're asking way too much'."

"And *I* said," Ursula put in. "I said, do you have a lot of cats, then? And he looked a bit startled and just mumbled again."

Bobbie nodded. "So I thought, why not? My friend had said she'd got plenty more catmint if we needed it, so I said of course he could and he could pay what he had, so I shut the bag and handed it over to him. That's when I got the shock of my life!" She rocked backwards and forwards in her seat as she recalled the moment.

258

"He handed over a wad of notes and just took off with it."

"That's when the plain-clothes CID officer, who was on a break in the café, took a hand," Finn was dying to get in on the act. "And that's when I came on the scene. He was just reading Bobbie and Ursula their rights when I walked in and a police car drew up outside. He wouldn't listen to me and insisted on bundling them into the Panda car and carting them off to the nick."

"So Finn called me on her mobile," Charlie joined in. "And I rushed round to the cop-shop and met her on the doorstep."

"Yes," Finn went on. "Luckily I spotted that Bobbie had dropped the loot in the confusion so I picked it up and shoved it in the glove compartment of Charlie's car while we went in to spring the criminals out of jail."

"You can laugh now," Bobbie said with dignity. "But it wasn't funny at the time. Ursula and I were terrified and we had no idea what we were supposed to have done wrong."

"But how did you convince them you were innocent?" Julia wanted to know.

"Luckily I still had traces of catmint in my shopping bag," Bobbie said. "And I gave them my friend's phone number so they could check. I'm hoping it'll be a nine-day wonder amongst my ex-guiding cronies and that they'll have forgotten about it when we get back."

"Besides," Finn was bubbling with laughter. "They picked up the skinhead and checked out the stuff. You should have seen his face when they told him!" She shook her head in amusement at the memory. "Meanwhile, in the interview room they asked Bobbie where the money was, she couldn't find it so she said she didn't know, she must have dropped it in all the confusion."

"But I don't understand," put in Jonathan, who was looking confused. "Why did the man give you so much money? When you'd told him you only expected to get fifteen pounds?"

"Why, don't you see, Jonathan?" Ursula was almost stammering with excitement. "He thought we meant a hundred and fifty pounds, not one pound fifty, no wonder he thought it was expensive. When the police realised we were telling the truth, they laughed and laughed and then they let us go and that's when Finn gave us back the money — there was nearly sixty pounds! We didn't know quite what to do, but Charlie thought we ought to keep it, because the police would hardly allow us to give it back to the young man. Charlie advised us to sit on it for a bit, then to feed it gradually into our fund-raising for the cats."

"You can say it's from an unknown benefactor," grinned Charlie appreciatively.

The flight was uneventful, but for Bobbie, Ursula and Jonathan, who had never flown before, it was enthralling from start to finish. Even the weary waiting in the airport lounge took on the glamour of the unknown. Marek was very conscious of his superiority, having flown in a transport plane during the war, and to Australia, so he had to conceal his own thrill at being served with food and drink on the plane. Even the rather mature stewardesses with their grim smiles were entrancing to him and he blossomed into a stilted flirtation with one.

Finn and Charlie spent the journey still wrapped in their happy dream and they joined in very little with the cheerful banter from the rest of the group. At one point, however, Finn roused herself to speak to Jamie.

"Tell me," she asked him. "Do all the Stuart men have to have the same names? I mean, will we have to have a James or a Charles? What was Charlie's grandfather called, I don't think I've ever heard?"

"It's not written in stone," he assured her. "It's just a family tradition and no, there isn't a distinct pattern. Other Stuart names are Henry and Maurice, or Anne and Henrietta, Elizabeth too. My father? He was christened Rupert, after Prince Rupert of the Rhine, Charles the Second's brilliant soldier cousin. Why do you ask?"

"No reason," she said. Rupert, she thought, that's nice, or maybe Elizabeth. Not Henrietta, I wouldn't want to be reminded of Ursula's Ugly Sister.

As the plane circled in to land on the island the group's flagging spirits began to revive. "We are getting on, after all, some of us at least," Delia murmured to Julia. "We tend to forget that, don't we? We ought to be in bed after a day like this, and that includes our honeymooners too."

After a bone-shaking half-hour drive in two ramshackle minibuses to the north of the island they tumbled out and looked around them as they staggered stiffly towards reception.

"You ought to enjoy this place," Julia remarked to Delia as they surveyed the pink-washed walls of the original plantation house. "Might have been made for you."

The harassed young man at the reception desk scanned the lists in front of him.

"There seems to have been a little mix up," he told them disarmingly. "We have only three double rooms for you and then there are three twins and two singles. Will that be in order? I can only apologise."

"That'll do nicely," Delia told him graciously. "We'll sort ourselves out, don't you worry." She followed his eyes as he gazed uncertainly at the motley assortment of tourists in front of him. Finn and Charlie, well, no doubts about them, nor Jamie and Julia. Rosemary and Hugh. He was staring in fascinated surprise as Hedgehog stood with his arm clamped possessively round Bobbie's thin shoulder, while Bernard draped himself around a shrinking Ursula whom he insisted on referring to as "sweetie pumpkin" and planting loud, juicy kisses on her blushing, fluffy cheek.

The receptionist withdrew his appalled gaze and looked pleadingly at Delia, who just grinned and nodded.

"I'll have one single and Mr Barlow will have the other," she told him, nodding towards Sue and Marek who stared at her in shell-shocked horror. "As you can see, all our lovebirds have sorted themselves into pairs."

This encounter gave Delia a new lease of life and she ignored the vociferous recriminations of her troops as they were shown to their rooms. When the house-boys had left she turned on them.

"What a load of old women," she told them frankly. "What a fuss! Here we are, sort yourselves out, I'm having a single room and I suggest you do too, Sue — unless you and Marek have other ideas? No, well go and stake your claim. No, Jonathan, it was a joke, you're sharing a twin room with Marek, don't worry. See you all at dinner." She nodded to Charlie and Finn. "That doesn't include you two, by the way. We won't be upset if you don't speak to any of us for the next three weeks."

Late that evening Hugh and Rosemary sat on the beach looking out at the silver sea.

"Rosemary," Hugh coughed as he broached a delicate subject. "You know how much I loved Joan?" She nodded, surprised, and he continued. "She was a wonderful wife and we had a very happy marriage, but when she knew how little time she had left she made me promise that if I met someone I could care for, I must take the chance. She said —" he shook his head in wonder. "She said I wasn't the kind of man who should be single, I'd been too well looked after and I'd need someone else to look after in turn. She was right."

He looked into Rosemary's wondering grey eyes.

"Marry me, Rosemary? I know we're not young but I do care for you. Joan was right, I'm not the bachelor kind. Make me the happiest of men, please."

Julia would have laughed at his formality but Rosemary was enchanted by it.

"Oh, Hugh," she sighed, leaning her head on his shoulder. "Oh yes *please*."

"I had a word with both the girls when we met up with them before we came away," he told her, glowing with satisfaction. "I told them what was in the wind and they both wished me well. They liked you so much, in fact they both said, quite independently, how much like their mother you are. So how about it, Rosemary? Shall we get married here, on this island? You only have to give seven days' notice."

Elsewhere under the tropical dusky sky Jamie and Julia were paddling in the waves which lapped at their toes.

"Julia," Jamie cleared his throat. "I wanted to ask you something, something important."

"Oh no, Jamie," she looked at him, her green eyes anxious and loving. "Don't, not if you're going to say what I think you are."

"What do you mean?" he sounded nettled. "I was going to propose to you, my dear."

"That's what I thought," she said mournfully. "And I don't want you to. It isn't that I don't love you, Jamie, I do, with all my heart. But I've been married and it wasn't a success, so I don't want to repeat it; and you were married so happily to Janet. Let's just go on as we are, as loving friends, with me in my little house and you in your little flat just down the road. We can have such fun visiting each other, it'll keep the excitement going; and when I'm tired and cross, or if you want to

264

mug up on your ancestors, we can agree to have some time apart."

Christmas morning dawned brilliantly, blue and sparkling, and the disparate members of the Gang straggled in to a late breakfast. Charlie and Finn bounded in looking insufferably smug after an early swim in the bay.

"*And* we jogged along the beach for a stretch," Finn boasted.

"How nauseating," Julia was unimpressed. "And what are you two doing up and about like this? Honeymoon couples are supposed to spend all day in bed."

"You are *so* old-fashioned, Ju." Finn rolled her eyes. "It was only like that in the Stone Age when you were young because people hadn't had sex before marriage."

"Sez who?" Julia was all set to argue but was distracted by the sight of Bobbie and Ursula trotting into the open-sided tent that served as the hotel dining room. Neither of the women could ever have been mistaken for anything other than an Englishwoman abroad. Bobbie, as always dressing to suit someone twenty years older, wore a sensible royal blue button-through dress that had to be a relic of her Brown Owling days, accessorized by a floppy white sunhat. Ursula, despite the beginnings of a cold, had arrayed herself, with unbelieving delight, in a rose-patterned skirt and short-sleeved white lawn blouse. She, too, wore a hat, in her case a garden straw that had belonged to her mother in the fifties, and in her hand she carried her grandmother's parasol.

"It was in the umbrella stand in the hall," she explained. "Wasn't that lucky?"

In spite of the urging of the others Finn and Charlie decided to eat with the Gang.

"I'm not saying we'll do it every day," Finn told her sister. "But it's nice to catch up now and then, and it *is* Christmas. Aren't they enjoying themselves?"

They truly were.

Marek and Jonathan had also taken a stroll along the beach earlier that morning and were full of their plans for a joint venture when they reached home.

"We thought perhaps we could make a little pocket money," Jonathan explained. "Doing rather what we've been doing as a group, but charging for it; you know, odd jobs, repairs, a spot of gardening? Marek's going to be in charge of the business side and I'll provide the allotment and the garden tools." When the others applauded this enterprise, he looked slightly anxious and continued, "naturally we won't be charging amongst ourselves. We will be carrying on, won't we?"

The rest of the group looked at him and at each other. They had achieved their objective magnificently, as well as handing over a handsome donation to Help the Aged, to salve their consciences. But what of the Gang?

"Of course we'll carry on!" Julia cried. "Don't forget we were a social group long before we took up fund-raising; we can't just let it drop, why should we?"

"Thank goodness for that," Sue put in. "If it hadn't been for the group I'd never have had the nerve to put a stop to my husband's antics and although it's meant ending my marriage I can't tell you how much better I feel now I'm in control. I still need the back-up and the friendship — and the fun. We can't possibly stop."

"Well said," Delia spoke heartily with little trace of her usual flippancy. "Speaking for myself, your friendship," she gestured to the circle of friends. "Your friendship has meant a new lease of life for me. I moved away from London to escape the memory of a tedious and unfulfilled marriage — I never had the courage to do what you're doing, Sue, and others like you — and though I was left extremely comfortably off, I had no idea what to do with the rest of my life. Now I do know. I'd like — if you'll go along with me, my dear friends — to continue our fund-raising efforts now and then. For the elderly, mostly, but I don't see why we shouldn't throw some support in the way of Bobbie and Ursula's cat-lady."

"Oh, what fun!" Bobbie was jigging up and down with glee. "I heartily endorse every word that Sue and Delia have said! I was sad and aimless when we all met and now I've a set of dear, dear, friends, all of you, and a purpose in life too. I might even be brave enough to look for a part-time job as I feel so much fitter now."

"This is all getting a bit too emotional," Delia thrust her moment of sentiment behind her and resumed her usual persona. "What does everyone plan to do today? I hear lunch will be a light one, followed by a slap-up Christmas dinner tonight? I, for one, intend to take a book down to one of those sunloungers and summon a squad of those glorious young men to bring me regular injections of rum!"

"Changing your tipple to suit your surroundings?" Julia grinned affectionately at her. "Sounds pretty good to me."

"We've got some business to attend to," announced Hugh, looking important. "Rosemary and I are going to book a wedding."

"Oh, Julia." Rosemary was hugged and kissed all round and ended up beside her oldest friend from the village. "It's like a fairy tale, I can't believe it! You'll be my matron-of-honour, won't you? This would never have happened if you and I hadn't become friends." She mopped her eyes and looked hopefully at Julia. "Any chance of you and Jamie doing the same?"

"No fear," Julia assured her. "I don't say we haven't discussed it but on balance we think it'll be more fun to live in sin."

The first week flew past. On New Year's Day, some time after the so-called light lunch the hotel provided, Charlie and Finn emerged from their room to go for a wander round the hotel gardens.

"Oh look, how sweet." Finn pointed to Bobbie who was sitting on a stone bench surrounded by scrawny cats, her expression one of complete bliss.

"She'll get fleas," Charlie warned, then added, with a shrug: "Don't suppose she cares, though. Who's that? Look at Jonathan and Marek, they've buttonholed one of the gardeners. What do you bet Jonathan goes into tropical plant growing when they get home? And Marek could make wooden planters, he's good at that sort of thing. Remind me to suggest it as part of their money-making scheme."

Finn was counting heads. Rosemary and Hugh were also heading out towards the gardens and already the drone of Hugh's voice could be heard as he pointed out choice plants to his betrothed. Julia and Jamie were at the head of the beach, lounging under large sunshades, companionably sipping their rum punches. Delia was laid out under an umbrella of her own, a thin black linen kaftan draped around her bony frame, while Sue and Bernard were strategically placed near the bar so that they could both ogle the near-perfect brown bodies of the waiters and beach boys, all of whom had to pass their table, unaware that they were being awarded points out of ten. At the same time Hedgehog was happily chatting up the girl from the beauty parlour.

Only Ursula was apart from the sybaritic scene. She had been suffering from a heavy cold but now, for the first time, she was down at the water's edge, clad in a modest bathing costume and earnestly listening to the kind young man who was instructing her about snorkelling.

"I'm really sorry, Miss," he had told her at first, brown eyes melting with regret. "I can't teach you to dive, really I can't. There's an age limit, you see, and my boss, he'd go mad at me."

269

"Oh please, don't worry," Ursula tried not to look disappointed. "It's not important, you mustn't get into trouble."

"You could try snorkelling?" The boy offered it as a sop. "That's better for you, Miss, you could do that, easy."

"Really? You really think I could manage that?" she asked in delight.

After a few trial dips the boy helped Ursula to adjust her mask, handed her the snorkel and waved expansively at the lapis lazuli sea.

"There you are, Miss, it's all yours."

She smiled and nodded, then waded out another yard or so, breathing hard and concentrating on what he had told her. Her long-sighted eyes spotted Finn and Charlie back on the beach. They had paused to watch her solo performance. Finn gave her an encouraging wave in response and she bent tentatively down and into the water.

At once the awkwardness vanished as the sea took her and cradled her creaking, arthritic body. Floating motionless, apart from the rhythm of the waves, she was entranced to see a flight of tiny golden fish flash no more than six inches past her nose. Awed, she gazed eyeball to eyeball with another, larger fish, which then swam off with a flick of its tail.

"I'm scuba dancing!" she called out in triumph to Charlie and Finn, who waved again, smiling at her with deep affection as she plunged exuberantly back into the water, eager not to lose a moment of this unimaginable bliss.

270

Oh, it was magical, and despite the pain in her chest she felt so light, so liberated, beyond anything in her dreams, and suddenly she *was* dancing, whirling and twirling, dipping and swooping, to a tune only she could hear. Far away Finn had a sudden foreboding and she clutched at Charlie's hand. He followed her pointing finger and they started to run down the beach, but Ursula was not aware of them.

Partnering her as she waltzed in her enchanted ballet, weaving patterns down into the depths of the sapphire and turquoise of the Caribbean, up into the azure and amethyst of the tropical sky, was the angel.

"Oh, it's *you*," she exclaimed with delight, laughing as they performed a graceful arabesque against the glitter of the sun. "Look at me, angel, I'm scuba dancing!"

"Yes," agreed the angel, and all trace of his normal cynicism vanished as he smiled at her with a glow of love in his unfathomable golden eyes. *"Yes, I reckon you're right, Ursula! You're really scuba dancing at last!"*

Also available in ISIS Large Print:

Voyage of Innocence

Elizabeth Edmondson

In 1932, three young women go up to Oxford: Verity, a clergyman's daughter, her aristocratic cousin, Lady Claudia, and Lally, a senator's daughter from Chicago.

Verity and Claudia plunge into university life with passion and energy, forming new friendships and questioning the orthodoxies of their background. Swept into the political fervour of the time, Verity falls under the influence of the intense Etonian communist, Alfred Gore, whilst Claudia is drawn to the urbane, pro-German economist, John Petrus. Lally simply watches on, keeping her own counsel and earning respect and affection from the whole circle.

Verity's convictions lead to agonizing decisions, which affect her own future and also that of her family and friends. In the fearful days of 1938, almost destroyed by her choices and disillusioned with her beliefs, she embarks on a journey to India.

ISBN 0-7531-7638-6 (hb)
ISBN 0-7531-7639-4 (pb)

Not Married, Not Bothered

Carol Clewlow

Riley Gordon would not go as far as her best friend Magda, who decides to make the ultimate statement to mark her satisfaction with the single life. Her idea becomes Riley's call to arms, her challenge to celebrate singleness.

For the life of Riley, as far as she herself is concerned, is a good one. With strong views on marriage, on lifestyles, on age, on families, but most of all on freedom, Riley firmly believes she's got things sorted. Friends and family, however, all as keen to give their opinions as Riley is, would beg to differ. So would her ex-lovers, one in particular . . .

ISBN 0-7531-7604-1 (hb)
ISBN 0-7531-7605-X (pb)

Daydream Girl

Bella Pollen

Sometimes life can be like a bad movie. You sit through it, hoping it will get better, suspecting that it won't and wondering at what point you can reasonably walk out . . .

Kit Audrey Butler is the manager of the Orange, a dilapidated independent cinema. Estranged from her father, undermined by her boyfriend and, with her third screenplay recently rejected, Kit finds herself badly adrift. Her favourite therapy, renting the appropriate video and scrutinizing the footage for clues on how to behave, no longer provides her with all the answers. But when new ownership threatens the Orange, Kit is forced to confront reality and discovers that help and heroes come in the unlikeliest forms . . .

ISBN 0-7531-7511-8 (hb)
ISBN 0-7531-7512-6 (pb)

True Colours

Sue Haasler

Last Reach Point lighthouse has been home to the Jackson family for years, but when half of its garden crashes into the sea, Beth Jackson knows that it's time to find a new place for her family to live.

Out of the blue, Beth receives an unusual offer of help from her smooth-talking local MP. Gareth Dakers gives Beth, her teenage son and her father the chance to stay in his London flat while they sort themselves out.

Faced with the traffic, pollution and the crowds of the city, Beth longs to turn straight back, but her father, Bill, and her son Danny seem to be eager to start a new life there.

Squaring up to life in the big city, Beth does her best to shake off her doubts. However, it's not long before she begins to realise that there's more to Dakers' generous offer than meets the eye . . .

ISBN 0-7531-7475-8 (hb)
ISBN 0-7531-7476-6 (pb)